THE LIGHT REMAINS

A BLACK BEACONS MURDER MYSTERY

DCI EVAN WARLOW CRIME THRILLER # 11

RHYS DYLAN

WYRMWOOD
BOOKS

COPYRIGHT

Print ISBN 978-1-915185-21-1
eBook ISBN 978-1-915185-20-4

Published by Wyrmwood Books.
An imprint of Wyrmwood Media.

EXCLUSIVE OFFER

Please look out for the link near the end of the book for your chance to sign up to the no-spam guaranteed VIP Reader's Club and receive a FREE DCI Warlow novella as well as news of upcoming releases.

Or you can go direct to my website: https://rhysdylan.com and sign up now.
Remember, you can unsubscribe at any time and I promise I won't send you any spam. Ever.

OTHER DCI WARLOW NOVELS

THE ENGINE HOUSE
CAUTION DEATH AT WORK
ICE COLD MALICE
SUFFER THE DEAD
GRAVELY CONCERNED
A MARK OF IMPERFECTION
BURNT ECHO
A BODY OF WATER

LINES OF INQUIRY
NO ONE NEAR

CHAPTER ONE

Pain.

Pain, terror, and something else his muddled brain couldn't articulate. He fought to grasp it through the throbbing ache in his head and the crawling sensation of blood, warm and thick, sliding down his face and neck. But then it came to him in a searing millisecond of clarity.

Humiliation.

They'd managed that the minute he'd been dragged out of bed and stripped naked. But he'd buried it in fear. He'd heard the laughter, the derision, the disgust in the voice. Or was it voices? Younger than his, of course. But then, whose voice wasn't now?

Yet, besides the sickening realisation that he was in very deep trouble, came the knowledge that his sister had been right. As soon as she found out, he'd suffer the ignominy of her eye-rolling 'I told you so.'

But that would depend on him surviving this.

His sister, a good decade younger, wanted him to move. Or down-size at the very least. Perhaps even find sheltered accommodation. Somewhere he'd feel safe. But in truth, it was she who wanted to feel safe. To be rid of the worry of having her older brother – six months shy of his 77th birthday, and how the hell did that happen? – living in a huge house, too big to manage. Shelling out for someone to look after his too-large garden. Spending too much money on keeping the place too warm.

But it was *his* house and *his* garden. The place he and Sian, his wife, God rest her soul, had made into a home. And yes, they were right; he ought to give it up. But while he still could, he'd wanted to stay put.

Ronnie Probert wanted only to be comfortable.

He winced. Partly pain. Partly from hearing that word in his head and realising, in this situation, how laughable it sounded.

He wasn't comfortable. He was as far from comfortable as he could possibly be.

They wore masks, and he'd struggle to say how many there were. Sometimes he thought only one, sometimes it felt like half a dozen. Clones because there was only one face. The same face. His brain tried to put it all together and failed.

There were certainties, though. Like the claw hammer. And the crowbar.

They'd hit him with a crowbar first. Right after he'd been shaken rudely awake from a dream of being in school. Running around when no one could catch him. Being a kid again.

The sub-conscious. What an ironic bloody cove it was.

They'd woken him up with. 'Oi, wake up, you old bastard.'

He'd opened his eyes to see him leering down. An interloper in his home, in his bedroom. An old man like Ronnie, staring at him without expression.

It took him several moments to realise something had to be off with this man. Something to do with the shape of the body beneath, the angular, younger shoulders under the bald head and the big, exaggerated nose.

Ronnie didn't put it together, not at first. But the voice hadn't sounded right. Muffled and hasty.

He'd twigged the mask then. The kind of latex thing you wore as a hood.

He'd groaned, confusion fed by his semiconscious brain, said something incoherent, before the stinging clunk of the metal bar hitting the side of his head and the ringing noise in his ears as the pain came.

More blows followed. He heard the crunch of his nose breaking before he felt the pain of it and tasted blood in his mouth.

He'd been dragged out of bed, stripped, all the while the masked raider screaming demands.

'Where's the money? Where's the fucking money?' The mask failed to filter the hateful disdain that drove the voice.

Ronnie said he didn't have any money.

'Don't. Fucking. Lie.'

He covered his face, pulled up his knees. It all happened so fast. Hard to be certain if there was one burglar or many in the house. But it was just the one face he saw. The same face. The mask.

He saw the claw hammer come down on his wrist. A quick and accurate blow. He'd passed out with the pain and come to when cold water hit his naked body, gasping in air and sensing another wave of deep agony from his arm as he brought it up. A wave that threatened to bring up his supper with it.

He'd stuttered out the words. About his wallet and the four hundred he'd withdrawn to pay the gardener and the odd-job man. He kept that in the bureau in a see-through envelope. But they kept shouting for the "real cash".

He didn't have any actual cash. Not in the house. His

advisors insisted on him tidying it away in ISAs and National Savings every month. None of it was accessible.

He heard noises as the place was ransacked. In his head, he imagined drawers ripped out, vases smashed, the figurines Sian had so lovingly collected on their many trips abroad thrown down and crushed.

He felt helpless, knowing he couldn't fight back. Frustrated by the knowledge that once, when he was much younger, the bastard, or those bastards, if there was truly more than one, wouldn't have stood a chance against him. He recognised it as hubris. But still, the frustration ate at him.

He'd lain there in pain, unable to move his arm, fighting the nausea threatening to poleaxe him, trembling and shivering.

The old man thief came back and glared down at Ronnie lying there, feebly trying to protect himself. The latex face expressionless, yet the malevolent eyes somehow moved with the muscles beneath to transmit the blazing aggression and threat. It was at that point Ronnie realised that this man hated him.

'Where's the money?'

The hammer came down on Ronnie's shin, and he howled with pain. A howl blocked by a gag rammed quickly into his mouth. Something dusty and bitter. All he did after that was whimper and shake his head and swallow blood.

The thief hit him again. More than once. After five blows, he passed out, wishing only that he'd had the strength to pull a sheet over himself so that when they found him, he wouldn't be naked. A tiny voice in his head that tried to bring a sliver of relief to his tortured mind. His last thoughts before unconsciousness came were conciliatory. Was there any solace to be found in an end like this? No more hospital appointments. No more bloody pills, morning and evening. No more wondering if his prostate was the size of a grapefruit.

There was that.

But there would be no more hectoring chats with his sister. No more walks in his beloved garden when spring brought the buds out.

No more.

Impossible to find a sliver of comfort in being robbed, having your house invaded, and beaten unconscious.

No dignity at all in a death like this.

———

BRANWEN MORSE WORKED from home three days a week, only travelling to the office in Swansea on Thursday and Friday. That was the back-to-work deal they'd required after Lockdown. Branwen didn't mind because that meant she could be at home for the kids after school more often than not, leaving Kevin's mother to manage Thursday and Friday afternoon pickups.

In fact, Jenny Morse, Branwen's mother, would have been more than happy to pick the kids up the other days as well. They were so lucky with Kev's mum. They'd sat down and worked out how much money they might save having a grandparent within five miles of where they lived. It had been a factor in the house purchase. A no-brainer. Her parents were over in Cardiganshire, and Branwen's sister had stayed local, so her children had first dibs there. But in school holidays, Branwen's mum would insist on the Morses coming over, too.

Yes, they were so lucky.

The kids, Josh, seven, and Rita, eight, were back in school now that Christmas had come and gone. And that meant Branwen could do her morning jog as soon as she'd dropped them off.

As an electrician, their father, Kevin, had long gone by the time the kids set off for school. Out of the door at seven-thirty, earlier if the job was further away. That meant Branwen had thirty minutes of her own time to get a run in, get home, shower, and be at her desk fully caffeinated up by nine.

She needed this routine. Make it feel like she'd been on a commute and was going to work. Given the number of distractions at home, some kind of psychological separation involving getting out of the house made coming back to work in it... better. Her route took her up the hill on the B4309 from her modest house in Five Roads to meet the cycle path where the road crossed over it. She switched back on this to Horeb Chapel and the quiet road to home in a two-and-a-half-mile circuit.

The cycle path itself, along a disused railway line, ran for ten miles from Tumble to Swiss Valley, but she accessed only one-tenth of it on her circuit, running south for a mile as one side of the triangle. And this circuit suited her three times a week. Combined with a long walk with Kev, the kids, and the dog on the weekend, and a dance class on Thursday nights, the whole shebang kept her in trim. Or so she liked to think.

Kev had offered no objections, anyway. In fact, to the contrary.

'Whatever it is you're doing, keep doing it,' was what he'd said just this weekend when he'd caught her coming out of the shower. His eyes getting bigger the more she rubbed her hair dry.

Branwen smiled at the recollection they'd both had to shower again twenty minutes later.

She wore gloves this morning, a thermal hat over her earbuds, and had one of her favourite podcasts up and running. The kind of thing Kevin rolled his eyes up at. *Sentimental Garbage*, or *The Guilty Feminist*, *Desert Island discs*, or sometimes, just her playlist. It all depended. Today was *My Dad Wrote a Porno,* which she was only on season three of.

Branwen sometimes wondered if she looked totally barmy to passing motorists whenever she giggled out loud at something she'd just heard that no one else could.

Josh and Rita were recovering from colds, and the last couple of nights were the first of the new year when neither of them had woken up coughing. She'd slept well too, and Branwen felt good on this crisp, clear winter's morning with the breath billowing out of her mouth as she ran up the hill from Horeb on the base of her triangular circuit back towards home.

One more house and then fields on either side for two hundred yards before she reached the eastern limit of Five Roads and the houses there.

Yet, she slowed at this last house in Horeb because Ronnie Probert lived there. Everyone knew that. A lovely man who'd earned an OBE for his services to sport, as a player and then for his charity work. His international career had been cut short by injury, so the rumour went, but in that short time, he'd captained his country and been a British Lion. He'd done a load of work for charity too until his wife died.

Nothing short of Welsh royalty was Ronnie. And still, people drove along this road because he lived here, pointing at his house and whispering to one another that Ronnie Probert lived there. In the summer, Branwen sometimes saw him out early as she ran, weeding or cutting the lawns with a big bush hat on his head.

He'd wave to her with a smile.

And so, on this clear, crisp morning, she slowed a little as she jogged past. Not that she expected to see him in the garden in late January, but you never knew.

The front lawn stretched thirty yards in from the roadside to the front door. The house stood in its own grounds: red roof, cream walls, one gable end facing the road, standing apart from the rest of the ribbon development a good thirty yards from the nearest property in Horeb, two hundred yards from Five Roads.

Branwen didn't like to stare, but Ronnie's house was always one she'd fancied. The kind you hoped to end up in one day. Private but near enough to other people, within walking distance of a pub in Horeb and another in Five Roads. And Ronnie liked a pint. He always had a word for you if you met him in one of the two. Always a nod of acknowledgement.

A real gentleman.

When she saw movement from an upstairs window, at first, she thought it might be a trick of the light. Still, the movement caught her eye and registered enough to make her come to a stop and retrace her steps to make sure.

No, nothing.

Or was there something fluttering? A rag or a piece of paper?

Branwen stopped the podcast and took a step up the little drive running next to the front lawn. Damn. The sun turned the windows into mirrors this time of year. She shielded her eyes.

No movement for several long seconds. She shrugged, but as she turned away, something flickered again. Yes, there it was. And not paper or material. This was a hand above the windowsill. Pale and marked with dark patches.

Branwen looked on, bewildered.

The hand waved again feebly and fell against the glass before sliding down.

As it did, something glistened like a slug's trail behind it. Something thick and ochre.

Branwen's hand flew to her mouth. She ran to the front door. Knocked.

No answer.

She knocked again. Then knelt and lifted the letter flap.

'Ronnie? Ronnie?'

The reply, from somewhere in the house, did not sound human. Or at least not a sound she'd ever heard coming from a person before.

The sound of a wounded animal in pain.

Branwen turned, stepped back, and looked up at the bedroom window again.

A hand, trembling and weak, fluttered there like an injured bird.

She took out her phone and dialled 999.

CHAPTER TWO

FOUR AND A BIT days later and nine thousand miles away, at the John's Street café near Cottesloe Beach in Western Australia, the Warlows were having Saturday brunch. Luckily, they'd booked because the place was busy. A mid-summer weekend with the temperature at twenty-six with sunny intervals. In all honesty, it was more blisteringly clear with the odd cloudy interval, given that Perth had the rep of being one of the sunniest cities in Australia. And that was saying something.

Tom Warlow, Alun Warlow, and Reba, Alun's wife, had gone for the truffle mushroom with added halloumi and sweet potato chips served on a plate with all the trimmings. Warlow and Jodie, Tom's partner, had opted for the smashed avo on sourdough toast, but with cherry tomatoes, basil, feta, dukkah, ciabatta, and a poached egg. So, on principle, and because it was stuck on as an easy-add item, Warlow opted for bacon on the side.

That's what he loved about Australians. They were not precious about anything.

Warlow had insisted they go out on this their last Saturday before his long flight home mid-week. Tom and

Jodie were jetting off in the early hours on Singapore Airlines with a two-hour stopover in Changi. Warlow was on Qantas, and an early evening direct flight that would take almost seventeen hours non-stop. He'd need to tag another four hours plus before he could get home to Nevern, in Pembrokeshire. Still, that was a few days away, and for now, they were all here and all healthy.

The food came. They ate. Alun fed his son, Leo, some fruit loaf with cinnamon maple butter, which, apparently, was his favourite thing. Though, from the amount Al ate in the process, it looked likely to be in his top ten, too.

Warlow was not big on speeches and, as a family, they were not a demonstrative lot. He'd grown up at a time and in a community where you hugged someone if you were going to take them to the pictures – not as a casual greeting.

Seeing TV dramas from across the pond, where every two minutes someone was telling someone else they loved them, made his skin crawl. And yes, he'd got the memo about repressed feelings, but hearing it a dozen times a day rendered it bloody meaningless in his opinion.

Jeez Denise, his deceased and ex-wife, had weaponised the term, anyway. As if reiterating it, either directly, or through him to their sons, had somehow excused her alcoholism and the Jekyll and Hyde behaviour it threw up.

'You make sure the boys know I love them, Evan. You'll tell them that, won't you?'

There'd been periods when Alun, especially, had distanced himself from his mother. Warlow had suffered collateral damage as a result.

Ironically, when he took leave of the family home and left both it and her in the process, once the boys had gone, Warlow's connection with their sons had improved.

This holiday had cemented this new phase in their relationship. The unspoken truth of it being that the passing of Denise had removed her spectre. A shadow that somehow, while she'd been alive, tainted every link-up and conversation he seemed to have, especially with the Antipodean branch of Warlows.

And so, under the shade of a couple of umbrellas on the café's patio, Warlow waited until Alun returned with Leo. They'd gone for a quick walk across the street to examine a red car, which was one of Leo's current toddler fetishes. Now back at the table, Warlow filled everyone's glass with fresh water and cleared his throat.

'Right. I'm not one for mawkish displays, but when the occasion demands it—'

'Don't tell us. This was a Dyfed Powys covert operation, and we're all under arrest.' Tom delivered the line with a lopsided smile. The family joker, as always.

Warlow quirked an eyebrow. 'No, your alibis check out. I'm satisfied on that score.'

Tom geared up for a rejoinder, but Jodie turned his face gently towards her with an open palm on his cheek and said, 'Shush.'

'I only wanted to say,' Warlow went on, grateful for Jodie's intervention, 'how much I've enjoyed this time with the seven of us together.' He looked at each of them in turn. His boys. Tom with that constantly amused expression of his, always ready with a droll remark. Alun, distracting his own eldest child in his lap with an iPhone, looking bemused and alarmed at this unexpected show of gratitude. The women tanned and pretty, the both of them in different ways. Jodie smiling. Reba, with Eva, the newest Warlow, at her breast, regarding him expectantly.

'I know we've all been through a lot, as a family, and as individuals.' He nodded at Reba and let his gaze fall to the miracle that was his tiny, weeks-old granddaughter. 'Us Warlows have a knack for never making things easy for ourselves. But you two,' he looked from Reba to Alun, 'are fantastic hosts. Thanks for putting us up and up with us, and for all the hospitality. I suspect there's no need for me to say this, but I feel I ought to. Denise, the real one, not the…' He searched for the right words here. Lots sprang to mind: belligerent, bellicose, bitch. But he buried them all and picked out the kindest. '… lost shell of a person she became that no one recognised at the end, would've given anything to have been here with all of you. So, let's raise a non-alcoholic glass to three generations of the Warlow clan, and toast absent friends.'

Everyone raised their water glasses. Everyone except Alun, who kept his head down before lifting a pair of moist and troubled eyes to regard his father.

For a moment, Warlow panicked, wondering if he'd said too much, made a catastrophic error of judgement. It would not have been the first time. But then a stuttered inhalation broke in Alun. He elevated his glass and uttered a quiet, 'Well said, Dad.'

A chorus followed. 'To absent friends.'

Leo, distracted by the noise and clink of glass, turned to consider his dad, sensing an unusual emotion. He signalled a pudgy finger towards Alun's face. 'Daddy leaking.'

He wiped away the tear that had run from the inner angle of one eye towards his father's lip.

'Anyone fancy a sticky bun?' Tom asked, pricking the emotional balloon.

'Ooh, go on, then,' Reba said. 'I'm still eating for two, me. Once we start formula, that's when the diet begins, and someone else can help with the night feeds.' Though she didn't look at Alun, he nodded sagely in reply. But Reba's bluff words belied the emotion that bubbled under the surface. It was her turn to look around the table. And when she spoke next, it was with a cracked voice. 'It's been amazing having you all here. About time if you ask me.

And, since you all know where we are now, we will expect return visits regularly.'

Jodie smiled, put a reassuring hand on Reba's, and spoke. 'Don't you worry. You've started something now. This winter sun is like a shot in the arm.'

Alun blew his nose. 'No need to rush back, mind,' he said, into the tissue. 'I mean, we're all busy people, right?'

'And there he is,' Tom said with a throaty chuckle. 'The curmudgeon has returned.'

Reba hit Alun on the arm. He turned to her with mock indignation. 'This week has cost me a fortune in bloody barbecue briquettes I'll have you know.'

Leo got up from his father's knee and wandered across to Warlow's chair.

'Sea, sea.'

'You are right,' Warlow said. 'The sand on that beach is not making itself into a castle, is it?'

Warlow stood and took Leo's tiny hand in his. 'I'll walk him down to the sea and back. You lot finish your brunch.'

'You sure, Dad?' Alun asked.

Warlow ran his index finger across an imaginary badge on his chest. 'Can't you read? It's in the job description. See? *Tadcu.*'

Leo was already pulling him out of the restaurant and onto the pavement.

'Hat,' Warlow ordered.

Leo dashed back between the tables and took the floppy blue hat his mother proffered before jamming it onto his head, much to the hilarity of the viewing diners. Then, suitably attired, grandson and grandfather headed for the beach.

———

Reba and Alun took Eva home to Miloso Street in Subiaco, an inner suburb within the larger urban spread of Perth, while Warlow and Leo, joined by Tom and Jodie, stayed on the beach for another half an hour. They drove back mid-afternoon along the clear, wide roads in Tom's rental, Leo strapped into the hired car seat.

'Impressions?' posed Warlow as they entered the city limits of Subiaco.

'Of what?' Tom asked.

'The whole "Down Under" lifestyle.'

'Just amazing,' Jodie said.

Warlow eyed her. 'You ever thought of upping sticks?'

It was Tom who answered. 'Jodie'd get a job tomorrow. They're crying out for nurses. For me, even when I get my consultant ticket, not so easy. They're funny out here about reciprocity.'

'Really?'

Tom nodded. 'Lots of hoops to jump through. More exams. Think I'll stick to rainy old London for now. But who knows where we'll end up?'

He pondered this. 'Fancy coming back to Wales?'

A quick and loaded glance was exchanged between the couple. It didn't take a genius to work out that this was a discussion they'd kicked around already.

'So, all options open, then?' Warlow observed when neither answered.

'You have to go where the jobs are,' Jodie said.

'But from what I understand, there's a lack of everything.' Warlow leaned down to pick up a stuffed toy that Leo had dropped.

'There is. And Tom could walk into any non-teaching hospital. Depends what we want out of life, I suppose.'

Warlow peered out the window of the car. 'There is that. But it's way too hot and sunny for philosophy. That sort of talk needs dimmed lighting and a good wine.'

'You're right, Dad. I could do with a beer.'

'Just as well I put extra in the fridge before we left, then. Just to keep Alun sweet.'

Tom laughed. 'He's such a misery guts.'

'Fuss-arse is the term we use in the force.'

Jodie giggled. 'Is that a technical term?'

'In my team, it most definitely is.'

CHAPTER THREE

THEY HAD THE BEERS, helped bathe Leo and, while Jodie and Tom checked their packing and Reba and Alun sorted Leo's bedtime ritual, Warlow sat in a chair on the patio as the day cooled, holding his granddaughter in his arms.

He'd dared to dream of this moment after banishing the nightmare of what might have happened had Reba's uterus ruptured anywhere other than the hospital she'd been in when it occurred. A hospital that took less than ten minutes to deliver this little package into the world.

They had a lot to be grateful for.

Eva held on to his finger as he hummed to her gently the melody of *Suo Gân*. A traditional lullaby he'd forgotten all the words to bar the first verse. A song made famous by Christian Bale saluting kamikaze pilots in Spielberg's *Empire of the Sun*. But Warlow's mother had sung it to him in its original form, in her native Welsh, long before the film brought it to the attention of the world.

He hummed it now, unheard by anyone other than the two of them, grandfather and granddaughter. And yes, he wished that Denise could have been there. The old Denise.

If only his beloved black lab, Cadi, had been there to share the moment with him, it would have been perfect.

Guilt plucked at an emotional guide wire. Cadi over Denise? But the wounds his ex-wife had inflicted on him as a husband, and on the family, ran deep. Still, he was not one to think too ill of the departed. He'd found it healthier to steer his mind only towards the good things. And could there be anything better than this moment he was sharing with the latest Warlow? He had no room for regret. Not at that moment.

Later, with Eva asleep, they had a final barbecue. Tom and Jodie's plane was leaving at 1:30am, which meant being at the airport at 11pm at the latest. They would be back in London the following day.

It was as they brought the cases down for loading into the car that Tom held his phone out for Warlow. 'Did you see this, Dad? I've deliberately not looked at anything from home on pain of death from Jodie. But I glanced at this since we're on the way now.'

Warlow slipped his glasses on and read an article from Wales Online. The headline screamed out at him.

76-year-old ex-Wales rugby legend still critical after being robbed and battered in his own home.

'You know Ronnie, don't you, Dad?' Tom asked.

'Yes. A genuine legend in his own lifetime. We did some work together for a charity when I played a bit. Sounds more than it was. He was the star. I sold raffle tickets. I wouldn't say we were best buddies, but he is a good bloke. I haven't seen him for nigh on five years. He didn't deserve this. No one does.'

The photo was awful. Ronnie Probert lay in a hospital bed, his face unrecognisable. Both eyes bruised mounds swollen shut by haematomas, blood congealing on a cracked and swollen lip. Warlow counted at least thirty stitches on the side of a football-sized face, and around his neck, under the oxygen mask, Ronnie wore a brace. Impossible to tell from the photograph if he was conscious or not.

'I might text one of the CID boys. Get the story on this.'

'Sorry, Dad,' Tom said. 'You're supposed to be on holiday.'

'I still am. I mean, there's not much I can do from here, is there? When did this happen?'

'Five days ago, it says.'

Warlow handed the phone back, shaking his head. 'I'll text his sister. Offer my five penneth of condolences. Not that it'll do any good.'

But then it was time to say goodbye to Tom and Jodie, and everyone found it difficult. Tears were shed by Reba and Jodie. It had been a wonderful break, and no one was happy to see the end of this Australian adventure. But life, like the planet it was on, never stood still.

Four days later, Warlow stood in the same hallway, saying his own goodbyes, packed suitcases ready to go, holding his granddaughter Eva for the last time and hugging his daughter-in-law before his son took him to the airport.

He waved as they pulled away and then turned to face the front.

'Fancy coming back?' Alun said, as they set off.

'Try and stop me,' Warlow said. They drove on in silence for a couple of minutes, Warlow sensing that though Al seemed mollified by his response to the question, something remained between them. Something yet unspoken. It took another five miles before it emerged.

'What you said about Mum, it got to me.'

'What do they say these days? Should have come with a trigger warning, right?'

Alun did not respond to the joke, and so Warlow added, 'It wasn't meant with any malice.'

'I know. But since Eva arrived…' He shook his head. 'I'm still so mad at her. Mum, I mean. What she did to herself, what she did to us, to you…' He ran out of the right words but reset and started again. 'I know I punished her by not letting her come out here, but I had no idea she was… I had no idea she was going to die, Dad.'

Warlow heard genuine anguish in Alun's voice. Not something he thought he'd ever hear from his confident, determined number-one son. But guilt and regret were hard taskmasters.

'No one knew, Al.' Indeed, ruptured oesophageal varices and acute pancreatitis tended not to give a great deal of warning. 'Tom understands that better than us,' Warlow went on. Tom was the youngest, but also the medic. 'He has a better take on it. He's had the training, I suppose. What your mother had was an illness. The drink, I mean. Self-induced maybe, but still an illness. You can't guard against that. If what I said upset you, I'm sorry.'

'It did, but I needed to hear it. I needed to be upset. I'm still angry, but I hadn't felt sorry for Mum at all until that moment in the restaurant. She was too toxic. I didn't want that affecting me and Reba. But I hadn't considered that she might have regrets, too.'

'Oh, she did. Most of the time. Though, after sinking her morning's half a bottle of vodka, those regrets went into a vault. But, towards the end, while she was in hospital, there was no vodka and no vault.'

Alun sighed. 'We're a bloody mess, us Warlows.'

'We are. But less of a mess than some.'

Alun nodded. 'I was sorry to hear about Ronnie Probert, Dad. Is he okay?'

'Apparently not. Battered half to death and a nasty head injury.' Warlow shook his head.

'Bloody hell. That try he scored against the South Africans on the Lions tour. I must have seen that on video a hundred times. What year was that again?'

'1974. No live TV then. You had to listen to it on the radio if you wanted live coverage.'

The Warlows had all played some rugby. Warlow in school and then for a variety of police teams throughout his career. Tom and Alun played in school and university; Alun good enough to have gained a British Universities cap. All three of them had been backs, not forwards, fast and elusive. A bit like Ronnie Probert. Or at least, Warlow liked to think so. Though Ronnie's speed and elusiveness as a fly half, partnered with some of the great Welsh scrum halves, had given him the nickname of "Ghost". Because, to other players, he was never where you thought he was, or would be, such were his skills of deception with ball in hand.

'What sort of person would do that to Ronnie Probert? I mean he is the G.O.A.T.'

Warlow didn't answer because he couldn't. Many people did indeed consider him the Greatest Of All Time. In his position, anyway. Even if by now he was an old G.O.A.T. Hard to imagine Ronnie Probert as an old man since he had a special place in the nation's hearts. Almost as if any day he could don those boots and be the National Team's saviour once again.

But Al's question strayed into the realms of motivation, and Warlow knew better than to try to soundbite that one. If it had been Rhys Harries, his Detective Constable, in the car, they'd have run through the five p's of motivation for assault: passion, profit, panic, protection, psychosis. Sometimes one, sometimes more than one, played a part. Sometimes planned, often unplanned. But all that strayed close to work. And, the last time he'd looked, and while he still had the journey home to go, he remained on leave.

Instead, Warlow said nothing, sat back and watched the strange, sunny city roll by one last time. Soon, he'd be back in Wales, to a winter that, by all accounts, was turning out to be a cold one. Never mind. There'd be no sun there like this, but he'd be taking home a barrow-load of a different sort of warmth with him.

'Looking forward to getting back?' Alun read his mind.

'Looking forward to seeing the dog,' Warlow said.

'And work?'

'Double-edged sword, that one. And a sharp one, too.'

'You could always retire. Come out here for three months at a time. They allow that on visas.'

'I tried that, remember? The retirement bit. But I will when I'm ready.'

'I bet the team missed you.'

Warlow snorted. 'They'll have survived.'

'We have a saying at work. There's a difference between surviving and thriving.'

Warlow threw Alun a glance. 'Not bad, that one. I might use it.'

They said their goodbyes. This time, there were hugs and promises of WhatsApp video calls. Warlow wanted to keep in touch with the grandchildren.

He got through to the departure lounge and slowly, still in holiday mode, let his mind drift towards what awaited him.

It was nearing 6pm in Perth, 10am in the UK. Ronnie Probert would be a victim of GBH and aggravated burglary. DI Bob Salini might be his best bet. Warlow took out his phone and texted:

> Bob, in the airport on the way back from
> Australia. Rough news about Ronnie
> Probert.

> Evan, Lucky you. I mean lucky you to have been, not the coming back. Nasty one. He hasn't been able to give us much. One or many thieves. Masked. Claw hammer and a crowbar used. Made a mess of his place and of him.

Anything useful?

> We're still looking. We don't know what was taken. Probert not able to say much, sounds like they thought he was hoarding money.

Leads?

> A couple. When you back in?

Few days

> We'll catch up then.

Will do. How's Ronnie doing?

> They say he's stable.

Stable.

Bugger. Warlow hated that word "stable" with a vengeance because it meant sod all. But he would catch up with Bob in a couple of days' time, even if it would not quite be in the same capacity of a concerned individual only. Between now and the seventeen hours and some it would take to fly home, the four and something hours, depending on traffic, it would take to get to Pembrokeshire, and the day of recovery he'd need to deal with jet lag, a great deal of water would flow under the bridge.

Much of it murky and tainted with blood.

CHAPTER FOUR

DETECTIVE SERGEANT GIL – short for Gildas after a sixth-century monk and pronounced with a hard G, as in gullet – took the call first thing on his mobile. On reading the caller ID, his face lit up.

'If you're from a call centre, let's save us both some trouble. I already have loft insulation, never did PPI, and you know what you can do with your heat exchanger. Though I would not recommend it without lubrication.'

'Good to hear your voice, Gil. I'd forgotten how much I missed that sense of humour,' Warlow said. 'But then I forget how much I hate biting my tongue, and I still bloody well do it. Everyone ship-shape?'

'The Jones clan remains a fully functioning unit. As for the team, they've been a bit bored.'

'Nothing too onerous happening, then?'

'No. Apart from Rhys running straight into the rugby posts at his last match.'

'Serious damage?'

'No. All good. And Rhys is fine, too.'

Warlow tried to cover up an exhalation of amusement

and failed. 'You're telling me no one has seen fit to kill anyone on the patch in my absence?'

'Don't sound so disappointed, Evan. I have a sneaking suspicion you put an ad in the paper to say you were away, and the orcs all took a break at Disney's Mordor resort. You wait, now that you're back, there'll be a tsunami of crime, let alone a wave.'

'Nothing to do with me. It's the weather. Been cold, hasn't it?' Warlow paused for effect, before rubbing it in. 'So I've heard.'

'Yes, go on. Salt in the wound. You have enjoyed weeks of unending sunshine, no doubt.'

'You got my postcard, then?'

'We did. I presume you were drunk when you wrote it?'

'What was the giveaway?'

'The giveaway was the joke you wrote on it with no punchline.'

Silence as Warlow tried to remember.

'What do you call a tired kangaroo?' Gil reminded him.

'Oh,' Warlow said. 'I remember scribbling that on a giggly evening around the barbie.'

'Let's hope Ken doesn't find out. But I must congratulate you on the scribble because it took Rhys two hours to come up with pouch potato.'

'Because you banned googling it?'

'Of course. I mean, pouch potato is Roo jokes 101. But not if you're Rhys.'

'Glad to be of help. What has Buchannan had you doing?'

Gil sighed. 'Rhys did a course on the use of social media in dealing with the public, giving him even more reason to be staring at that bloody phone of his. Catrin has been elbows deep in trying to find Roger Hunt.'

'Good God, is he still on the run?'

'He is, and it's making Sergeant Richards very tetchy. Which, since she is usually wound as tight as a piano wire anyway, has made eggshell walking a thing I might take up professionally, considering all the bloody practice I've had.'

It was hard for Warlow to believe that his involvement with Roger Hunt, an escaped murderer who'd gone on the run after killing one man, injuring another, and attempting to murder a third in response to having been filmed illicitly at an Airbnb, had only been a few weeks ago, just before Christmas. Of course, he'd had the benefit of a complete change of scenery, allowing him to distance himself, both physically and psychologically, from the case. But for those left behind, it remained an open and unhealed wound.

'No sign at all?' Warlow asked.

'Of Hunt? None. All I can say is that Border Patrol are convinced he has not left the country.'

'And what about Jess? She okay?'

'I'd hand you over to her, but she and Catrin are at a meeting. Some new initiative regarding drug trafficking. DI Allanby has an interest in that, as you well know.'

Warlow did well know. Her daughter had been targeted in a County Lines operation not so long ago. One which Warlow helped extricate her from. No surprise that Jess would want to keep on top of things there. And Catrin was glad of the diversion. Having enquired about the team, Warlow turned his mind to less pleasant matters.

'Any news of Ronnie Probert?'

'You heard about that, then?'

'Bloody awful. I spoke to Bob Salini. He didn't say much.'

A familiar sound of a chair squeaking in protest came through the phone's speaker. Gil had shifted position. 'There's the usual stuff being batted around. Addicts from Swansea on the rampage looking for easy cash. Oh, and of course there's the psycho-cyclist theory. Someone claims to have seen a bloke on a bike with loaded panniers riding up and down the old railway line path close to where Ronnie lives. They think he's camped out in the woods or a derelict building. So, he's made the list, too. Of course, we all know that a mad cyclist only ever uses the psycho-path.'

'I'll wait for that tumbleweed to drift by before I book the next plane back to Perth,' Warlow muttered.

Gil ignored the insult. 'The press has latched on to that. They're calling him the Signalman because of the railway line. A reference to the Dickens ghost story of the same name.'

'With a penchant for aggravated burglary? I must have missed that one in between Bleak House and Oliver Twist.'

'Oh, don't go there.' Gil added a groan. 'I've already had to explain Dotheboys Hall to Rhys. He thought it was an adjective, not a noun.'

'What about you, Sergeant? What have you been up to?'

Warlow expected a pithy remark along the lines of not a minute to spare but picked up on the slightest hesitation tempering Gil's answer.

'Didn't tell you before you left, but the Buccaneer asked me to look at the files we found in that Airbnb case of Hunt's. The one marked chicken.'

Warlow didn't have to think that one through. The man Roger Hunt killed was a pervert, no doubt about that. He'd filmed unsuspecting adults in all kinds of situations. But he'd had cameras in all bedrooms. 'The one with the kids in it?'

'Yes. Filming kids is not acceptable at the best of times, but there was nothing awful there. Nothing overtly sexual, just some kids getting dressed and undressed. Bad enough, but there was one image, from a good three years ago, that bothered me. Still does. And I wanted to chase up that vague lead. I've been waiting for some records and guess what? They're flood-damaged from a storage unit over in Monmouth somewhere. They've been drying them out, so I am still waiting. Anyway, enough of the banter. Have you picked up the dog yet?'

'No. I rang the sitter, and apparently, Molly Allanby has the lurgy and is at home, so she's got the dog for company. I wanted to tell Jess I'll see her after work this evening when I pop along to Cold Blow to pick up Cadi before she forgets who I am.'

'Jess or the dog?'

'Both.'

'I'll pass on the message. When you back in?'

'Day after tomorrow.'

'Make the most of it, then.'

'I'm trying to. Sadly, my body clock tells me it's nap-o'clock, but I'm going to resist it and stay up until I can't stay up any longer. That's why I need the dog back. Long walks would help.'

Gil rang off. It had been good to hear Warlow's voice. He and the DCI were the senior members of the team by a considerable stretch and at least they could laugh at each other's bad jokes without the interminable explanations needed as replies to the blank looks they got from the youngsters, Catrin Richards and Rhys Harries.

He turned back to the screen and the email from Gwent Police apologising for the further delay, and how they'd called in an expert team to get the records dried out to minimise further damage. Of course, many forces had opted for digitising all records, but it was a rolling programme for most. And paper records still existed. Stored at remote sites.

But at least he'd been able to get a name. A name he remembered from his time on Operation Alice. A missing, dark-haired, blue-eyed boy of four called Freddie Sillitoe.

But he needed the files before he did anything. Needed

to put it all together in his head before he pressed any more buttons.

Rhys came into the room with two mugs of tea.

'You just missed DCI Warlow. Sends his regards.'

'I bet he's tanned, is he?'

Gil accepted the tea in a steaming mug, expressing his gratitude with a commendable lack of sarcasm as he said, 'Difficult to say over the phone.'

'I expect things will get mad again, now that he's back,' Rhys observed.

'Exactly what I said. He's a crime magnet, is DCI Warlow.'

Rhys removed a couple of fluffy looking, wrapped, circular biscuits from his pocket. 'I was rummaging around in the cupboard, and I found these. Fancy one?'

Gil took the biscuit and examined it, much like someone would a relic on the Antiques Roadshow. 'The orange Viscount. A splendid example of fruit-flavoured chocolate-coated snack that probably contains nothing remotely applicable to your five a day. I think they stopped making these a couple of years ago.' Gil turned to his desk and typed something on his keyboard.

'They'd fallen down behind an old sugar cannister,' Rhys explained.

'2014 is the last day of manufacture.'

'Wow. Real vintage. Can I tempt you, sarge?'

'No, you're alright,' Gil said, handing the biscuit back. 'But please don't let the sell-by date put you off.' He watched as the junior officer unwrapped the biscuit and stroked some white powder off the chocolate's surface before taking a bite. He chewed twice and then his expression took on that of someone suddenly aware that they'd made a grave error.

'This tastes funny,' Rhys said.

'As the clown-eating cannibal said to his mate.'

''ardon?' Rhys said through a mouth reluctant to close on a bolus of half-masticated flour, sugar and, very probably, rancid cream filling.

'If you're going to spit it out, do it in the men's toilet,' Gil ordered, and then added, 'Which is not a statement you're going to hear very often in Police Headquarters, even in these enlightened times.'

Rhys grabbed a tissue and held it up to his face. 'You 'ouldn't 'ay 'at 'uff about 'annibals and 'owns, 'arge. S'not PC.'

'Snot PC joined the same time as I did. Terrible thing, allergies. But more to the point, who the hell would be triggered by a joke like that? A cannibal? Or a clown? Admittedly, we've got several of the latter, especially in firearms licensing who all think they're Tommy bloody Cooper—'

''ommy ooh?' Rhys asked, through his half-full mouth.

'Never mind. All I'm saying is that if you spot someone chomping on a leg in the car park, you have my permission to arrest them. Cannibals are not the victims here.'

Rhys thought about a comeback, but the unpleasantness of what was in his mouth proved too much, and he hurried out.

Gil watched him leave with a shake of his head.

CHAPTER FIVE

WARLOW GOT to 2pm before it hit him. He'd slept little and fitfully on the plane thanks to a passenger in the middle seat who did sleep, loudly, with much of his corporeal self spilling over onto both the window seat, where a timid woman hid under a blanket and sleep mask for the whole journey, and onto Warlow, in the aisle seat.

More than once, Warlow's judicious elbow had jolted the middleman awake so that a flopping arm or leg could be replaced into the tiny space the airline had designated. A space not commensurate with the variations encountered in the human frame. Especially not the man in the centre seat's case, whose frame hovered very much at the extreme end of the bell curve.

Next time, Warlow would go premium economy, sod the extra cost.

Tiredness arrived like a sucker punch. As if he'd run into a wall of treacle. He caved in and perched in a chair in his sunlit room before setting the timer on his phone for forty minutes. As soon as he shut his eyes, he was dreaming about Rottnest Island and the tour of Fremantle Prison he'd made and of making sandcastles with Leo and watching the sun go down over the Indian Ocean at Cottesloe Beach.

When the alarm dragged him out of unconsciousness, he could have given in to the siren call of sleep again. But he fought it, forcing his eyes open and, because his head had fallen back, and he'd slept with his mouth open, running his tongue over the fur on his teeth.

He'd do something about that right now.

Teeth brushed, he finished unpacking, loaded a wash in the washing machine and drove to the Co-op in Fishguard. There, he stocked up on groceries and dog food, grabbed a coffee and headed off to Cold Blow. He'd planned on waiting until Jess finished for the day, but his need to see Cadi got the better of him.

No sooner had Warlow pulled in and opened the car door than a furry black missile, unleashed from the house, flew at him. He turned and half stumbled as the dog, in her abandonment, almost knocked him over. She yelped with pleasure, wriggling around Warlow's legs like a demented bee. He knew there was nothing for it other than to join the celebration, and so he dropped to one knee and let her do what she needed to do: attempt to lick every inch of bare flesh she found and be as much in contact with him as it was possible to be, while doing an impression of a perpetual motion machine.

All Warlow could do was laugh and try, unsuccessfully, some calming words.

'I think we'd put that under the heading of glad to see you,' Molly said from the doorway of the house. She stood in her usual jeans and sweatshirt with fluffy slippers, looking a little paler than Warlow remembered, but otherwise, beaming broadly.

'Is it safe to come in?'

'Yeah.' Molly nodded. 'Whatever it was I had has

passed. Through me, mainly. Literally. I'm eating and drinking now.'

Warlow made a sympathetic face as thirty kilos of Labrador tried her best to topple him over again. 'Any idea what it was?'

'A dodgy fish taco from a van on Newport Beach last weekend. Word to the wise, street food isn't always as wonderful as it's made out to be.'

'Oh dear. If you're feeling rough, I can just go.'

'Don't do that.' Molly's eyes doubled in size. 'Mum would kill me. She's on the way. Come in, and I promise not to touch you or anything you drink out of.'

'Will you carry a bell, too?'

'Yeah, laugh it up. You and Mum qualified from the same school of zero sympathy.'

Warlow shrugged. 'Alright. I'll come in. I come bearing gifts anyway. Be a shame to take them away again.' A wet nose touched his hand, and he knelt again to hug the dog. 'She looks fit.'

'Course she is. I keep my promises, Evan.'

They sat at opposite ends of the kitchen table. Warlow had a glass of water, filled by his own hand from the tap.

'How's college?' he asked.

'Same old.'

'And Bryn?' Molly's boyfriend would be back at university by this stage of the game.

Molly said nothing but offered a tight-lipped smile.

'Best not to ask?' Warlow said.

'We're taking a bit of a break. Mutual agreement. Long-distance relationships aren't that easy.'

'I'm sorry to hear that. I like Bryn.'

Molly nodded, and Warlow sensed that further discussion was best not pursued at this point.

Jess's car pulled in, and Cadi's ears pricked up. Molly spoke in an urgent whisper. 'Who is it, girl? Is it that woman who makes you tidy all your toys away every night and sighs when your hair gets all over the silly grey carpet in the lounge?'

Cadi responded to the voice with sped-up wags.

The car door slammed, and Jess's key in the door triggered a waddle forward from Cadi.

'Hello, girl,' Jess said and bent to fondle the dog as soon as she stepped inside.

One reason he liked the Allanbys was that they were people who had their priorities right.

Then Jess looked up. 'Evan. Oh my God. You do realise it's not normal to look so healthy at this time of year? It should be an arrestable offence not to be pasty and have the sniffles since it's a national winter pastime.'

'Good to see you, too, Jess.'

Out of the corner of his eye, Warlow noticed Molly assessing this little ritual with keen appraisal. Perhaps, under other circumstances, he might have walked across the room and greeted Jess with a hug. Just a friendly grown-up greeting. But he hadn't done that with Molly because of her illness, so Warlow stayed where he was, though he stood up from the chair.

'I'm merely here to say hello and pick up the dog. I've stayed well over two metres from Molly, too.'

'Just as well. If you'd seen the state of the toilet this morning—'

'Mu-um,' Molly interjected.

Grinning, Jess turned to her daughter. 'You look better. On a scale of ten, let's say five and a half now. You were a two when I left this morning.'

Molly shook her head in despair.

'You not staying for supper, Evan?' Jess turned to Warlow.

'No. I'm all over the place. It's 6pm here but the middle of the night for me. I'll need another day before I function properly. But I brought some presents. As a thank you for looking after Cadi.'

From a plastic bag he'd brought in, Warlow took out a black box, held it up, and put it on the table.

'Archie Rose Distiller's Strength gin. Thank you,' Jess said. 'You know me too well.'

'Had my share of this over the last couple of weeks. I think you'll like it. And for Molly.' Warlow handed over a wrapped parcel. Molly ripped the paper off and revealed a black t-shirt with the words,

CREATING MAYHEM since 2005.

'Since you are now eighteen,' Warlow said, in case Molly had suddenly developed dyscalculia.

'Love it,' she yelped and then frowned. 'You'll have to wait for a thank you hug, though.'

Warlow held up a hand. 'No rush.'

'I'll get Cadi's things.' Molly took the t-shirt and left the room, the dog in tow.

'How've you been?' Warlow asked Jess. 'How did the drug-trafficking seminar go?'

'Another new initiative,' was all she said by reply, but her one elevated eyebrow added the scepticism.

Warlow nodded. 'I haven't forgotten. I owe you a proper meal out.'

'Think I have?' Jess said. 'I want to hear all about Leo and Eva.'

'Lots to say.' Warlow studied his colleague. She may have been fresh home from work and dressed simply in a smart knitted top under jacket and trousers, but she managed, as always, to be elegant. And her grey eyes were full of amusement at this oddly awkward interaction they were having.

For once, Warlow let what was on his mind drive his voice. 'It's good to see you, Jess.'

'Good to see you too, Evan. We've all missed you.'

Warlow nodded as Cadi came back into the kitchen leading Molly, who held a bag in one hand and the dog's bulky, but light, bed in the other.

'Right, I'll get going.' Warlow took the bed from Molly.

'Can't we tempt you to a glass of something?' Jess said, walking him to the door.

'No. As I say, I'm all over the shop today. But I'll be back in to catch up on paperwork day after tomorrow.'

'Don't rush,' Jess said.

'Is Australia as brilliant as they say it is?' Molly asked as Warlow let Cadi into the boot.

'It's pretty special,' Warlow said. 'But I'll tell you all about it when you feel better.'

He drove away with the Allanbys waving him off.

It was well after dark by the time he got home. But it wasn't raining, and so Warlow dressed warmly, donned a headband torch, and took Cadi on a night-time walk to the estuary with the dog's glow-in-the-dark ball. The temperature had fallen to just above freezing, and a northerly wind, a feature of this bitter winter they'd had, made him keep his head down as he walked. Though physically tired, his mind was wide awake and in need of distraction. Throwing a ball into the wind for a prancing dog was about as good a distraction as he could think of.

Later, at home, he began wading through the pile of correspondence that had accumulated in his absence, finding nothing of interest in the circulars and cruise offers and financial advice until he came to a letter from Dyfed Powys Police reminding him he needed an annual review and that Superintendent Buchannan's secretary would be in touch to arrange a suitable date and time.

These things used to concern him. Not anymore. They'd asked him back on a renewable fixed-term contract. He could leave at any time if he wanted to. He already had his pension. Still, HR demanded that his competence be assessed.

He made it to nine-thirty before exhaustion turned his head to mush. He had the TV on and must have watched all of five minutes of a Harlan Coben adaptation before his head lolled forward on his chest. But falling asleep on the couch was not an option. He dragged himself to bed, got his head to the pillow, and, ten hours later, woke up with a headache and a fierce thirst.

He got up, drank a pint of water, fed Cadi, and went out for a brisk walk with the dog through the village and out parallel to the river.

He was putting the kettle on at a little before 10am when his phone cheeped twice. Two texts, one from Gil, the other from Jess. He opened Gil's first:

> Sorry to be the bearer of bad news. Ronnie Probert passed away this morning.

Warlow read the text, standing in his kitchen, the good feeling from the walk ebbing away as he reread the words. Then he opened Jess's:

> You may have heard about Ronnie Probert. Docs say he died from his injuries. Buchannan wants us involved.

There was nothing cryptic in the text, though Jess had not said it directly. If Ronnie Probert had died as a result of his injuries, then they were looking at murder. He texted Jess back:

> Any chance we could meet where the attack took place?

> Tomorrow?

Today.

One-ish suits me.

I'll see you there. Gather the troops.

Welcome back.

Warlow looked at Cadi. 'Good while it lasted, eh, girl?'

Then he rang the Dawes, Cadi's usual sitters, to ask if he might drop her off on his way into work.

CHAPTER SIX

WARLOW MET Jess at Branwen Morse's house. The titular village of Five Roads, *Pum Heol* in Welsh, had history.

Like a lot of other villages, the centre adopted the colloquial name, *Y Sgwar* – the square. From there, five roads led off, including Horeb Road – where Branwen Morse saw Ronnie's hand waving at her feebly – Heol Hen (old road) and the main B4309, which ran right through the middle, joining Llanelli in the east and Carmarthen in the west.

In the mid-nineteenth century, Turnpike Trusts were set up, ostensibly to maintain roads and bridges, but as so often the case with investments, the owners demanded profits. And since the owners were most often business-people from a long way across the Severn, one of the quickest ways to get a return was tolls.

That had not gone down well with the locals, especially in rural Wales, where a poor harvest meant subsistence farmers struggled to survive. Paying tolls to travel on the roads proved very unpopular. The resultant violent unrest became known as the Rebecca Riots.

Not that anyone called Rebecca had been involved directly. Wales saw nonconformity blossom from a century before. The scriptures provided a road map and inspiration for the struggles of daily life. Genesis 24, verse 60, contained everything the insurgents needed.

They blessed Rebekah and said to her, "May you, our sister, become thousands of ten thousand, and may your descendants possess the gate of those who hate them."

Five Roads, and especially The Stag, the village pub, had a reputation as a place where the rioters met and made their plans. For a long time, two bars were named after ringleaders. Though that nod to heritage had gone, a blue plaque commemorating the pub's role as a "meeting place of the Rebecca Rioters 1843" now sat on the pub wall.

Oh yes, this part of the world enjoyed its historical share of civil disquiet.

The Morse property sat in a pleasant spot within a development known as Clos Clement. Clos referred to an enclosure, a throwback here to the fields and farms that gave way to housing. Jess's Golf sat outside the detached house, where a half-built wall to the side of the garage suggested a self-build project, as yet unfinished, along a street of similar brick-built houses. She got out of the car as Warlow pulled up.

'Fancy meeting you here,' she said.

'No time like the present is my motto. Time waits for no… adult male person.'

Jess gave him a wry smile and walked up through the drive towards a brick pillar supporting a small portico above which a glass-walled balcony sported some winter plants.

'Nice,' Warlow said, noting a new Hyundai in the drive.

The woman who opened the door regarded the officers with a bright smile. She wore the kind of clothes that would not have looked out of place in a gym, but that also passed for leisurewear these days. But they suited her trim frame. Jess had her ID on a lanyard and held it forward.

'I'm DI Jess Allanby, Mrs Morse.'

'It's Branwen. And I know who you are.'

'And this is DCI Warlow. He's now in charge of the investigation into Ronnie Probert's death.'

Branwen nodded. 'Come in. I've cleared it with work. They've given me an extended lunch.'

Warlow followed her into a large open-plan kitchen dining area with a striking grey motif broken only by some pale wood on the kitchen table and the doors.

'You work from home, Branwen?' Jess asked.

'For the local authority, yes. I'm in Environmental Health. I have to go into Carmarthen twice a week, but it suits me. Still, they're quite keen. Check if I've logged on and such like. Count the mouse clicks, you know.'

Warlow didn't know, and it sounded a little intrusive to him.

'I've made the tea. The sergeant who called told me yours is milk and one.' Branwen nodded at Warlow. 'And yours is just a splish, no sugar.' She smiled at Jess.

'Sergeant Richards, was it?' Warlow asked.

Branwen nodded. 'Pretty with freckles.'

'That's the one,' Jess said.

Warlow filed that one away. Reducing the redoubtable Catrin Richards to pretty with freckles was like calling a Starstreak missile a shiny stick. It picked out the bright wrapping but said nothing about the pyrotechnics underneath.

Branwen motioned for them to sit on white-painted chairs around the table. The place had the feel of a show home in need of some personalisation, but a spotless show home, nonetheless. The only art appeared as finger paintings stuck on the fridge door.

'How old?' Warlow asked.

'Josh is seven, Rita is eight.'

'There's a school nearby, isn't there?'

'Brand new,' Branwen said. 'One reason we chose to live here. They can walk there and back in the summer.'

Jess got down to business. 'We realise you've talked to other officers about seeing Ronnie Probert call for help, but we're a different department, Branwen.'

Branwen nodded.

'This is now a murder investigation,' Warlow said. 'I've read your statement and you've been really thorough, but it would help us a lot if you went through what happened that morning, starting from the beginning. From why you were there.'

Branwen nodded. They all had identical mugs, and she picked hers up now and sipped. 'I run,' she said and explained her routine. Her run up the main road, cutting across to the cycle path and then back to Horeb and the home sprint past Ronnie's property.

'What made you look in?' Warlow asked.

'I always do. Ronnie is… was a treasure. We looked out for him. And sometimes, in the summer, I'd get a wave. It was a sort of routine. I looked forward to it. I liked to think he did. Just a neighbourly wave. But the wave I got this time wasn't neighbourly. Just his poor hand above the windowsill.'

'You went in?'

Branwen nodded. 'I found him. There was a lot of blood. His face was… that was after I called the ambulance.' Her expression registered the harrowing memory. 'It's awful what's happened.'

'And on your run, you came across nothing else untoward?' Jess asked.

'No. I saw no one on the cycle path. And the usual traffic passed me when I ran on the main road.'

'You say you do this three times a week?'

'More or less. I mean, if it's belting down, I'll give it a miss. I'm not a masochist.'

'We've had some reports of people seeing someone on the cycle path. Someone who travels by bicycle, who carries a lot of extra baggage with him, or her. Tents perhaps, or bags?'

'The Signalman?' Branwen nodded. 'We've all heard about him. But I don't know anyone who's actually seen him. There are stories of waving lights by the railway. And people say he, or she,' Branwen echoed Jess's correctness, 'travels mostly at dusk.'

Warlow sipped his tea. A good one. Just the right strength. He had missed his cup of English Breakfast in Australia. 'It's a small village. Forget your run for a minute. Any sign of anything else odd here lately?'

Branwen shook her head. 'It is a small village. And what's happened to Ronnie, it's shocked everyone. These things don't happen here.'

Warlow said nothing. He'd heard that a hundred times before. Crime, in his experience, had no respect for geography. Yes, there were places in the world where crime was almost non-existent, but in his mind, there were only two reasons for that. One was that in tiny communities, where everyone stuck their noses in everyone else's business, you stole, or lied, or threatened at your peril because if you were found out, you were ostracised and that could mean the difference between death or survival. This was how it worked in certain remote tribes in the Amazon.

Then there was the second reason. Where the punishment for the crime outweighed the benefit of committing the crime to such an extent, it made you think twice. It, too, was ostracisation. Only it might involve ostracising a part of a limb from its remaining appendage.

They hadn't adopted that as a deterrent in Dyfed Powys yet.

'No strangers about the place?' Warlow probed.

'There's still building work going on. Both here and in Clos Y Parc. You can see the scaffolding from the back of our house. So, we have construction workers and…' She paused, checking herself. 'Kevin would kill me. He is one of those construction workers. An electrician. He doesn't work here, but you know what I mean.'

Jess nodded. 'We'll be speaking to everyone, so don't worry.'

An unhappy-looking Branwen put her mug down. 'Anyway, because of the works, there are more people from away here than there would be otherwise. Trades, I mean. But most of them are like Kevin. Not afraid of hard work.' She shook her head. 'I've been racking my brain trying to work out who would want to do such a thing.'

There it was. The same question that Alun had asked him a couple of days ago as he drove Warlow to the airport. Why?

Jess offered a little relief. 'If this is a burglary gone wrong, then the reason is greed. Burglars want money. These days it might be tied in with drugs. An addict's need for money.'

'You don't think it's someone with a grudge, then?'

Warlow paused before answering. It was an odd question. 'Why would you think anyone had a grudge against Ronnie Probert?'

'I don't, but you think all sorts, don't you? Kevin said Ronnie's autobiography caused a bit of a stir.'

Jess's eyebrows twitched down a notch. 'How so?'

'That's a good decade ago,' Warlow explained. 'And you can't have a sports autobiography without a bit of scandal.'

'Do I need to read it?' Jess asked with something approaching horror.

Warlow shook his head. 'I've read it.'

'There was that thing about someone dying on a tour when he was just a kid,' Branwen said.

Warlow shrugged. 'A player. Nothing to do with the actual playing of the game,' he added. 'This was a post-match ritual. An unfortunate part of the culture. Ronnie was made the Judge on a night out. Players had to take part in silly games and forfeit through drinking alcohol. From what I can remember, the chap died of an alcohol-related death.'

'Was he prosecuted? Probert, I mean?'

'No. But it changed his life.'

'Probably changed the life of everyone related to the kid that died, too,' Jess said.

'Not the first and he probably won't be the last. Still, we're straying a long way away from the facts here.' Warlow drained his mug of tea and stood up. 'This has been useful, Branwen. If we need anything else, we'll be in touch.'

Outside, Jess and Warlow stood by Jess's Golf.

'I'll follow you to the Probert property,' Warlow said.

'Fine. Odd that she should bring that up, don't you think?'

'The autobiography? No, I don't think it's odd at all. This is a tight community. I'd say half the population, mostly male, will have read Ronnie's book. This is pure gossip and conjecture. Not our friend in a case like this.'

'But it's something we need to follow up, right?'

'Of course. But let's have a look at the house first. I've seen the photographs. Whoever did this left a mess.'

Jess nodded. And although she didn't say it, Warlow sensed that Branwen Morse's mention of Ronnie Probert's chequered history had piqued her interest. And, of course, it would be a thread that needed pulling.

But first things first. And that meant a half-mile drive through the Sgwar to Horeb.

CHAPTER SEVEN

THEY ALREADY HAD crime scene photographs stemming from the CID's investigation into the aggravated burglary. But, as always when a spark became a flame, everything needed to be looked at again.

Probert's sister, Gaynor, was listed as next of kin. Ronnie had been a widower and, apart from the sister, his only other living relative was a younger brother by some four years.

They'd need to be interviewed again, too.

Some crime scene techs were still on site. Povey, the CSI lead, needed more samples taken from the bedroom where the attack had taken place. Probert had disclosed that much, at least.

And so, Warlow and Jess explored the remainder of the house and left the techs to it. With time and losing his beloved wife, Ronnie's existence seemed to have shrunk to the living room, kitchen, and the one bedroom with a bathroom en-suite. The place was trashed but clean, the furnishings all polished wood and expensive looking, with trademark spindly legs that looked like toothpicks and leant the rooms a seventies vibe. Which, Warlow realised, was when the Proberts had likely been able to afford such things. Downstairs, a living room and a study full of boxed-up memorabilia looked as if a hurricane had blown through.

'All this needs to be looked at and catalogued,' Warlow said.

Jess nodded. 'There is a lot.'

They walked into the study where Warlow knelt and reached into a box tipped on its side. He took out a shirt. A red shirt with three feathers over the left breast. A note had been stuck to it with a pin. He unstuck the envelope and opened it, his nitrile-coated fingers fumbling with the paper.

'You're out of practice, Evan.' Jess fought a smile.

'Nappies aren't this difficult,' he muttered. He teased open the pinned envelope and slid out a sheet. Handwritten, it read – Wales versus Scotland. Five Nations – 1974.

On the back of the shirt, a sewn-on number 10 in white.

Warlow whistled softly. 'Bloody hell, there's a treasure trove here for collectors.'

'Why the hell did he keep all this stuff?' Jess asked.

Warlow shook his head. Around them, the flotsam of the burglary lay everywhere. A jumble of books lay on the floor, having spilt off a shelf where one or two still sat leaning drunkenly. Jess stooped to pick one up. She studied the hardback cover featuring a photograph of the young Ronnie Probert in full flight in a British Lions' jersey.

'*Nowhere to Ron*,' Jess read. 'Catchy. Is this the book that Branwen Morse mentioned?'

'It is.'

Jess nodded. 'Once the techs give us the all-clear, I'll borrow this and give it a read. There must be half a dozen here.'

'Do you have that CID report?'

Jess handed over a hard copy in a transparent-blue plastic folder. Warlow stood in the ruins of Probert's study and thumbed through it.

There'd been no sign of forced entry. But a ladder had been found across the lawn and the back-bedroom sash window stood ajar as if a half-hearted attempt to close it had been unsuccessful. Someone had added in a hand-written margin scrawl, "Stuck from paint". The investigating officer, a uniformed detective sergeant, suggested the ladder had been used to access the open window. Warlow saw no reason to doubt that assumption. But it also meant that whoever'd done this must have visited the property in daylight to find out likely entry routes and to check out alarms.

Alarms. Were there any?

'Apparently not a useful one,' Jess offered up the obtuse reply to Warlow's question when he posed it. 'There is one, but we think he only switched it on when he left the premises. It wasn't armed at night. His insomnia meant that he wandered about the house at night. At least, that's what he told his sister. It's what she said in her police statement. The thieves must have known about the open window, but took a punt on the alarm.'

His thoughts exactly. Warlow smiled. He and Jess had worked several cases together, but he'd forgotten how much synchronicity they had. He held out an image of the rear of the house with a sash window easily identified.

'After you,' Warlow said and followed Jess through the kitchen door into the rear garden.

Even in early February, with shrubs cut back and trees devoid of leaves, the contrast between the clutter inside and the neat organisation outside was stark. Slate paths led through borders where brown grasses and denuded dogwoods provided colour and structure. Along the edge, the white bark of a row of silver birches gleamed as a backdrop to pink winter heathers.

'Wow, looks like he knew what he was doing here.' Jess admired the view.

'It does,' Warlow agreed. He crunched along a path curving towards a water feature. A slab of rough slate pointing skywards like an exclamation mark. In summer, Warlow suspected that water trickled out of this slab like some impossible, mythical fountain. But water did not run uphill unless the gods miraculously decreed it, or there was a pump beneath doing the job. Still, he imagined the sound of burbling water trickling into the pond would add another dimension to this landscaped tranquillity.

But now his eyes drifted along the trail to the bottom of the garden and the willow hurdle fence distinguishing the boundary. Beyond, there were no more houses, and the land rose as a gradual slope towards a tree-lined ridge in between brown fields bordered by more trees. Somewhere, not too far away, the cycle path ran right through the middle of it all, making access to the rear of the garden easy. Without taking his eyes from the horizon, Warlow asked, 'By the way, where are Catrin and Rhys?'

Jess pointed in the direction Warlow was gazing. 'They're reconnoitering the cycle path. It would be useful to know if the rear of Ronnie's house is visible from there.'

'It would.' Warlow turned back to Jess with a grin. 'Think Rhys could borrow his mate's drone again?'

Jess's turn to smile. 'Do you need to ask? Rhys probably has a poster of Inspector Gadget on his bedroom wall. Or at least he did before he moved in with Gina.'

Warlow cast his mind back to the case they'd investigated up near Llyn Brianne. There Rhys had borrowed and used a drone to help survey the land, inaccessible by any other means. A procedure that ended abruptly when the drone had been shot down by a 12-bore shotgun.

Warlow hoped nothing similar would happen were he to deploy the same technology now.

He picked up his phone and dialled Rhys's number.

'Hello, sir.'

'Where are you?'

'Approaching the village of Horeb from the north, sir. On the cycle path.'

'Were you able to observe the rear of the Probert property?'

'Only chimneys, sir.'

'Any chance you could approach the back of the property?'

'No question, sir. There are trees, but you could get through once you're over the fence.'

'Okay. We need drone footage of that access. Can you organise that?'

'Already texted my mate Steffan, sir. He's bringing it across.'

'Full marks for initiative, Rhys.'

'Thank you, sir.'

'Is Catrin with you?'

'She is, sir. Want to say hello?'

'I do, but in person. DI Allanby and I are in the garden of Probert's house. How long will you be?'

'Ten minutes, max, sir.'

'Right. We'll be waiting.'

———

DS CATRIN RICHARDS waited while Rhys finished the call.

'That was the Wolf,' Rhys said.

'So I gathered.'

'He was asking if we could view the rear of the Probert property.'

They were standing on a path that wound north.

'He's wondering if that sash window was visible?'

'I told him no, but it's a green light for the drone.' Rhys grinned.

'Makes sense,' Catrin said.

'You ever do the whole ten miles on a bike, Sarge?'

'This route? No. I'm not big on cycling. I leave all that to Craig.'

Rhys paused. Though he was Catrin's junior, and she outranked him, he was not averse to a little leg-pulling when it came to Craig Peters, a traffic officer with the same force, Catrin's significant other, and a rugby player like Rhys was.

'I bet Craig looks good in lycra.'

Catrin decided to take the bait. Or at least nibble at it. 'He does. No hiding place in lycra, is there?'

Rhys thought about that, reddened, and said, 'No, not that Craig's got anything to hide… I mean… You know.'

'I know exactly what I mean. I also know that you're digging a deep hole for yourself, but that is by the by. You a cyclist, Rhys?'

'Nah. Not my thing. And I hate lycra.'

'Never say that to an armoured polar bear.'

'No.' Rhys uttered an uncertain puff of a laugh, which flipped into a frown. 'Why?'

Catrin came to a standstill and turned to him. 'You're not a Pullman fan, Rhys?'

'Oh, right, armoured bears and *Lyra*. Northern Lights. Got you. But no, I didn't get past book one. The TV adaptation was good, though. The recent one.' They'd arrived at the access point at the village, and Rhys led the way off the path to the roadway.

'No sign of the Signalman, either,' Rhys said as they stood against the bank to let a car pass.

'Is that a real thing?' Catrin asked. 'Or just an urban legend?'

'Maybe a drone will flush him out too?'

'Possibly. We'd better get a move on, or the Wolf will start to howl.'

––––––

THE BEDROOM HAD a double bed and framed photographs of Ronnie and Sian Probert on their wedding day. Warlow realised immediately that, unlike the rest of the house where printed images of Ronnie in kit and in action dotted the walls, here, there was none of that. The bedroom was a shrine of a different kind. To a partnership. A marriage that had its roots in a childhood romance that blossomed in adulthood.

Ronnie and Sian met in school when they were fourteen. Her death from bowel cancer must have left an enormous hole.

The tech had left markers for photographers everywhere. Indicators of blood spatter. Places where smudges had marked the paintwork. Blots on the cream carpet. But Jess read the initial interview report out loud.

'Ronnie remembered the clock read 2:09 when he was disturbed. They pulled off the bedclothes. He was struck with what he thought might have been a crowbar.'

The other members of the team stood in the room with Warlow. Their presence cast shadows over the floor and bed. This was not a room designed to accommodate four people. And Rhys, being the size that he was, almost made that five. No one spoke as they listened to Jess's commentary.

'Then they dragged him to the floor and stripped him—'

'That's the bit I don't get, ma'am. Why do that?' Rhys asked, his voice hoarse.

Warlow answered, 'It makes the victim more vulnerable.'

'The attack was prolonged,' Jess went on. 'They—'

'How many do we think, ma'am?'

'That we are not sure of. Could have been only one. Ronnie saw only one face, but he thought that might have been a mask that more than one person wore. Poor bloke was injured and confused. Impossible to say. But whoever it was demanded to know where he kept the money. He or they fractured his wrist with a claw hammer and did the same to his right tibia. Beat him unconscious with blows to the head, this time with a crowbar only. Ronnie had defensive injuries on both arms and a fractured radius. Other trauma included a fractured nose and skull.'

'Disgusting,' Catrin whispered.

Warlow glanced at her and read an echo of her words in her expression. It was impossible to be completely detached in situations like this. That would come later when they followed up the evidence and analysed it all. But now, he didn't mind that his team felt appalled.

Because he did.

'Right,' Warlow said. 'There's a lot to do. Any idea about the house's contents?'

Catrin spoke up, 'I'm getting CID and Uniforms to lend a hand. There's a community hall in Five Roads. I've called the booking secretary, and we're taking it over as a staging area for all of this. Get everything labelled up.'

'Great idea.' Jess nodded.

'It'll upset the heritage society and the badminton group, but that can't be helped.'

'That's a good plan.' Warlow agreed. He liked plans. He liked progress. 'So, let's get back to HQ, see what Gil has lined up for us.'

CHAPTER EIGHT

DS GIL JONES had the Incident Room set up. Two boards: the Gallery for photos, the Job Centre for actions and notes, and the inevitable timeline. All in the usual place at the head of the room.

Crime scene photos were already pinned to the Gallery: the bedroom scene, the sash window, and the ladder taking pride of place. And above them, at the very top of the board, Gil had a black-and-white image of Ronnie Probert at twenty-five years old. A proud product of the Welsh "outside-half factory," reaching his peak as a player.

He looked boyish, hopelessly lithe compared to the modern-day gym-tweaked monsters. But Gil had taken the image from the internet. An image frozen in time from the first move in that astonishing piece of play that resulted in Ronnie, a few seconds later and seventy-five yards further on, touching down under the South African posts. A try, and a passage of play, that had passed into folklore in a rugby-obsessed country.

That it was an iconic image, there could be no doubt. The joke was that Ronnie Probert had never bought a drink for himself since that day. A statement with more than a grain of truth in it. He'd been a national hero, recognised and lauded across the whole of the UK and indeed the rugby-playing world. Sponsorships followed, and ambassadorships with companies and sport associations, as well as radio and TV punditry.

Ronnie had made himself a small fortune at a time when the game had been stubbornly amateur. He paved the way for others to follow, and yet, no one had quite reached the status he enjoyed.

Gil had tea ready and the contents of the Human Tissue For Transplant box – a camouflaged repository for biscuits – on display. Ready for the team's and their leader's return. He'd timed it, too. Steam rose from the mugs when the door opened, and his colleagues entered.

They shed their coats, grabbed mugs, and stood or sat around in a semicircle for this, the first briefing of the New Year for the whole team.

Rhys's eyes drifted down to the wheel of baked goods on the tray, anticipation exposing the whites of his eyes. 'Are those…' He looked up, words draining away.

Gil dropped his chin. 'Fox's half-coated cookies. Well spotted, Rhys. Christmas leftovers, so one each – and I have counted – by way of celebrating DCI Warlow's safe return from shark-infested waters.'

'Five Roads isn't that bad,' Warlow said.

'Glad to see that jetlag hasn't blunted that sharp wit, Mr Warlow.' Gil offered the tray of biscuits he'd arranged up to the team but kept his eyes firmly on it as it reached Rhys.

'Did you miss us?' Gil asked.

Warlow paused before answering, 'There is only so much lazing about under a warm sun sipping cool beer while the sea laps against the sand you can take, right?'

No one answered. They were all too busy trying to pierce Warlow's smug armour with their barbed glares.

'But I am back now and keen to get whoever did this to Ronnie Probert locked up. I don't make New Year's resolutions, but I'll make an exception for this.'

Sage nods all around.

'Let's do the usual. Gil, fancy kicking us off?'

Gil put the tray down a good ten yards away from Rhys to make it inaccessible. Then he came back and took a stance in front of the Gallery.

'I've spoken to DI Salini, who was running the investigation into the aggravated burglary. You've all had copies of their prelim report. They've done some legwork. Neighbours, people at the pub, that kind of thing. So far, nothing.'

'What about social media?' Catrin asked.

Gil blew his cheeks out in derision. 'Ronnie was old school. No computer or laptop. No Facebook or Insta accounts.'

'Unusual these days,' Warlow observed.

'No kids. That's the answer,' Gil explained. 'Kids drag you along with them, don't they? Laugh at you when you can't text with two hands or refuse to do a TikTok dance with them. Buggers.'

'Next of kin?' Jess asked.

'A sister and a brother. From what I've learnt, the sister acted as a kind of buffer between Ronnie and his brother Terry. Not much love lost, apparently.'

Warlow considered this. 'We need to speak to them both.'

'The sister is expecting a call from us, sir,' Catrin answered.

'Let's not forget the brother, then. While the iron is hot, etcetera.' Warlow turned to Rhys. 'Right. That leaves the post-mortem.'

'Tiernon's done the report.' Rhys fetched printed sheets from his desk and stood before a series of images of Ronnie Probert in the hospital. The same images that had appeared in press headlines and that Warlow had seen in Alun's house in Perth. A bloodied and battered Ronnie Probert, his face looking like a lump of ground meat.

'Cause of death is listed as secondary cerebral haemorrhage consequent upon head trauma,' Rhys read on, using his laser pointer to highlight the fractures and skin damage caused by the attack.

'Bloody unpleasant, but black and white as to cause,' Warlow said and then glanced up at a series of Post-it notes running along the top of the Job Centre. Gil picked up on his gaze.

'We have a timeline for the attack. 2.09 in the morning. Then we have Branwen Morse calling us at 08:35.'

Warlow tried to imagine a beaten and semiconscious Ronnie Probert on the bedroom floor for nigh on six hours. It was not a cheery thought.

'Actions?' Warlow asked.

Catrin took a little step forward. 'As mentioned, sir, I'll get some bodies out and set up in the community hall. We'll shift the house contents over there and try to get them into some sense of order.'

Jess spoke up, 'I'll get the sister in today.'

Warlow nodded his head, deep in thought. 'Why don't you and Gil talk to the sister? I'll take Rhys and speak with the brother.'

Gil pointed to a list on the Job Centre. 'CID came up with a list of recent contacts. It's the usual stuff. Tesco deliveries, post, and Ronnie had some work done replacing soffits on the house back in the autumn. Company from Llanelli. They had scaffolding up for a good couple of weeks.'

'Enough time to notice a sticky sash window that

wouldn't close properly, then,' Warlow observed. 'We'll need a list of employees.'

'Still waiting for that. CID have done the soffit people. They all checked out right away, but the scaffolding company has been slow in responding.'

'Give them a nudge,' Warlow ordered. He couldn't help but feel a certain sense of satisfaction at the information spread out before him. Much more than he would normally expect at this stage of an investigation.

'Order of the day, then…' he began, but then his eyes lost focus. They didn't shift from the boards, but he folded his arms and let an intruding thought take over. 'Of course, there is the left field scenario.'

'What, sir?' Rhys asked.

'The double bluff.'

No one spoke for several long seconds until Gil muttered, 'I read that jetlag has been known to cause psychotic episodes.'

Warlow's eyes refocused. 'I'm talking about the faint and unlikely possibility that this was all set up to look like aggravated burglary when all along the plan was simply to beat an old man to death.'

'What films did you watch on that plane?' Gil asked.

But Jess was tuned in to his wavelength. 'He's talking about skeletons in the cupboard. Apparently, in his autobiography, Probert admits to being half responsible for the death of a player during an alcohol-fuelled drinking session when he was a kid.'

'Bottom of the list, surely,' Catrin said.

'Next to the Signalman. Our mysterious cycle path man,' Rhys added.

'Agreed,' Warlow said. 'But still on that list.' He unfolded his arms. 'Okie-dokie, late lunch and then off to work we go.' They turned away from the board as the Incident Room door opened, and Superintendent Buchannan walked through, followed by a balding, stocky man in full Uniform. Two bushy eyebrows fought with each other for position on a scrubbed face. He needed no introduction. Everyone knew Chief Superintendent Drinkwater.

'Evan,' Buchannan said. 'Good to see you back. Bleddyn wondered if you could have a quick word.'

'SIO's office?'

'No,' Buchannan said. 'Too cramped. Why don't we stroll upstairs to mine?'

And stroll they did. Upstairs, in Buchannan's office, the BSU commander took his seat at the desk, leaving Warlow to stand and Drinkwater to pace.

'Have a seat, Evan,' Buchannan insisted.

'What about you, sir?' Warlow directed his question at the Chief Super. Drinkwater, distracted by a photo on the wall, turned and shook his head.

'I see your team is up and running,' Buchannan said.

'Luckily, Bob Salini's lot have done a lot of the donkey work after the burglary—'

Drinkwater, who continued to study the photograph with hands clasped behind his back in a military stance, spoke abruptly. 'I know you've been on leave, Evan, so you're coming to this without having experienced any of the flack, as it were.'

'Flack?' Warlow asked.

Drinkwater went up on his toes and back down again with a sigh before turning to face Warlow. 'Ronnie was a good egg. I've known him… knew him, for years through golf and rugby.'

'It's very sad,' Warlow said.

That caused Drinkwater's head to shoot up. 'Sad? It's a bloody disaster. Ronnie was a national treasure. You've seen the headlines I take it?'

'I've seen some. But—'

Drinkwater reached for a sheaf of papers on Buchannan's desk. 'We expect the usual crap from the local papers, but this has gone national.' He read out some headlines.

'"Not safe in our beds", *The Times*. "The sad state of Welsh policing", *Observer*. "Drug gangs roam the valleys looking for easy pickings", *The Mirror*.'

He fixed Warlow with a glare, his eyes full of burning anger. 'Flack,' he said through gritted teeth. 'Exploding all around us. And it's slithered up to the local MP and Assembly Members, and now the first minister wants to be kept in the bloody loop over what we're doing about it. As it bloody were.'

Warlow narrowed his eyes. 'By it, do you mean the case or the press?'

'Both. The quickest way to deal with this is to get a result and show these bastards we're not a bunch of bloody hicks, as it were.'

'Agreed.'

'Good,' Drinkwater said.

Warlow had been around the block enough times to see that this was simply a senior officer letting off steam and wanting to make sure the lower ranks got the message. This was nothing but showboating from the Chief Super. And from the expression on Buchannan's face and the fixed grin under pleading eyes, he was praying Warlow would accept it. Nothing more needed to be said, but Drinkwater was not a man who could resist flexing the odd verbal muscle. He was venting a group anger, the voice of a nation.

Warlow had spoken at length to Tom, his doctor son, about this. A shared experience in professions where anxiety came with the territory. Tom knew all about how nervousness and tension could sometimes trigger responses in people. How those triggers sometimes possessed the inflammatory capability of burrowing deep under the sufferer's skin. Like the twitchy patient who felt the irritating need to ask, just before going into surgery, 'You will do a good job now, won't you, doctor?'

Of course, being a Warlow, Tom's immediate response to such a daft question, at least in his head, would be to say, *'No, not today. Today I can't be arsed. There's spag bol special on in the canteen, so I need to get there pdq, which means, for you, dear patient, an in and out botch up. Be prepared to have the odd instrument left inside, capisce?'*

Tom, or any of his colleagues, would never say that, because they knew such anxiety required reassurances, not pithy flippancy. It didn't take a psychiatrist to understand that trust was a prerequisite in humans prior to letting someone stick a knife in them.

But Warlow was not Tom.

'I know you're good, Evan. We all do. But this time, as it were, it's special.' Drinkwater laid emphasis on the last word. 'Ronnie was special. I need you to make a special, as it were, effort.'

Effort.

The Chief Super had leaned in, earnestness oozing from every open pore of this fully paid-up member of God alone knew how many old boys' clubs. Out of the corner of his eye, Warlow saw Buchannan wince on the other side of the desk.

Why was it that management, bad management anyway, always felt the need to state the bloody obvious and get everyone's goat in the process? For months, Warlow and his team had to put up with someone spouting the same brand of shite, stick and never carrot, micromanaging crap in the form of Superintendent Goodey. She, thank God, had been moved sideways. Disappointing to see that the same strain of unnecessary BS permeated the higher-ups.

Warlow nodded. A movement that presaged the calm

but blistering words that came out of his mouth in the next minute. 'I don't really do special, Chief Superintendent. I do consistent. Or at least, I try to. That way, everyone gets a fair shout. The dead all deserve that, don't they? Junkie or aristocrat. Makes no difference to me. Because if I didn't do things that way, what bloody use would I or my team be?'

Drinkwater's face changed colour, darkened to a blotchy mauve before he pulled back as if scalded, and cleared his throat.

'I would expect nothing less.'

'Excellent. Because you and everyone else will get nothing less since there isn't anything more. We approach every case the same way, full throttle, no preconceptions, and no varying levels of thoroughness. Unless it's a child, in which case I have to keep Gil Jones on a leash because he's apt to tear someone's head off and ask questions later. I was about to visit Probert's brother before you popped in. Mind if I get on with that?' He glanced from Drinkwater to Buchannan, whose smile had become far less plastic than a moment before.

Drinkwater took another step back. 'No, don't let us delay you, as it were.'

'Marvellous,' Warlow said and pushed back his chair before leaving the room.

As the door closed, he heard Drinkwater clear his throat, and a muttered, 'Jesus H Christ,' from the Chief Super, to which Buchanan replied, 'No, only DCI Warlow. I did warn you.'

But Warlow didn't linger. He had other bread to butter.

CHAPTER NINE

GIL SCROLLED through the burglary report on his screen until he found the witness statement of the UPVC window suppliers who'd fitted Probert's soffits. They were based in Cross Hands with a storage and preparation facility on the industrial estate there. Clarity Windows had three teams, according to the report. Gil dug out the names and statements of the two-man team who'd spent two days at Gorffwys, Ronnie Probert's house, in late October. Neither had previous entries on the PNC, and both had firm and corroborated alibis for the night Ronnie had been attacked.

He then dug out the address and phone number for Castell Scaffolding. The number indicated a Llanelli exchange with a location in Trimsaran. He rang, and the call went straight to the answerphone. Gil once again left a message. The second one for him, the sixth according to the records. He sat back, had a small brainwave, and found Ronnie's brother Terry's address, which he scribbled down before finding Warlow, who was with Rhys in the car.

'What is it?' Warlow asked. 'Did I forget to flush the toilet?'

'And a good afternoon to you, too,' Gil said. 'Judging by that response, clearly your meeting with the higher--ups ranked up there with banding of haemorrhoids as a fun-filled encounter. Let me cheer you up. Castell Scaffolding has an address in Trimsaran. I get no answer when I ring. I smell fish.'

'And you're ringing me to ask me to call to check on this fish?'

'Kind of you to offer, Mr Warlow,' Gil feigned surprise. 'Happens to be on the way to Probert's brother's house.'

'Barcelona is more on the way to Probert's brother's house than Trimsaran is. We're nowhere near it.'

Rhys joined the conversation with his usual candidness. 'It'll take us twenty minutes from here, sir, according to Google Maps.'

'You're in this together, I see,' Warlow muttered.

'I'm thinking of the carbon footprint, that's all,' Gil argued. 'Just trying to avoid another unnecessary journey… And since you're on the doorstep.'

'It'd be on the doorstep only if I was the BFG. And since when did you join the Green party?' Warlow asked.

'Since my granddaughter carried out a waste audit at her school and has demanded we have a compost bin and a wormery. The hole in the ozone layer has shrunk perceptibly above Llandeilo already.'

'I did not know you were so in touch with these pressing ecological and socio-political issues,' Warlow said.

'Oh, ye of little faith. And as for not flushing,' Gil added, effortlessly revisiting Warlow's initial quip. 'Some would say that's also an environmentally friendly way to go about things.'

'A fly-friendly way to go about things, certainly.'

'I don't mean when solid objects are involved,' Gil qualified his statement. 'We're not barbarians in the Jones' household.'

'Glad to hear it,' Warlow said.

'And you certainly do hear it when in the vicinity of DC Harries's toileting, eh, Rhys?'

'Me, sarge?' Rhys, put out at being dragged into the conversation, objected vehemently. 'What did I do?'

'Quite a lot, judging by the splashing I heard in the men's this morning. Sounded like a flock of penguins launching themselves into the Antarctic Ocean, followed by one very large orca. To be honest, the orca brought a little bile to my throat.'

Warlow looked away to disguise a snort.

'So glad you've overcome your constipation issues, Rhys,' Gil added.

'I never—'

'Took my advice, did you?' Gil asked.

'Advice?'

'When you're constipated, eat some alphabet soup and wait for the inevitable vowel movement.' Silence from the car.

'I'll leave you both to it, then,' Gil said quickly and rang off with a smile of immense satisfaction.

IN THE JEEP, Warlow glanced at Rhys and his quietly flabbergasted expression.

'What's up with you?' he asked the DC.

'I still don't understand how a conversation about an address for a scaffolding company ends up being about my bowel movements?'

'It's a skill. Designed to confuse the enemy. Any nosy bugger from GCHQ listening in would think we were mad.'

'Do they? Listen in, sir?'

'Wouldn't be surprised.'

'And are we, sir? Mad, I mean?'

'Don't ask me. Ask the giant white rabbit in the backseat.'

For one-half of a millisecond, Warlow thought Rhys might turn around to check. Mercifully, he didn't.

'Now, enough of your nonsense, Detective Constable. Ask that nice lady on Google to tell us the way to the scaffolders.'

It took nineteen minutes.

Castell Scaffolding had a yard not too far away from the racetrack at Ffos Las down a rutted lane. Said compound comprised a fenced-off area with a couple of large buildings, both open-ended, facing one another. One contained horizontally stacked metal poles, wooden boards, and ladders in three layers, and the other was an open barn with profile metal siding and roof as a garaging area for lorries.

The only vehicle parked there now was a purple Astra. At the far end, a steel container unit of the kind found stacked high on giant ships sat on a base of breeze blocks. A single lit-up window suggested occupancy, and there were wooden steps up to the door. A sign, Castell Scaffolding, with a turret logo and two phone numbers, had been bolted to the outside of the container unit. Warlow surmised this to be the office.

They parked up, took the steps, and knocked on the door.

A female voice chirped, 'Hang on.'

The door opened on a four-inch chain to reveal the made-up visage of a young woman in her late twenties with a bottle tan and lips so engorged with filler they looked like two overblown pink tyres.

'Can I help you?' No smiles, only unbridled suspicion.

Warlow held up his warrant card. 'DCI Warlow, and this is DC Rhys Harries, Dyfed Powys Police.' Warlow half turned to reveal Rhys looming behind him. He loomed well, did Rhys. Something he brought to the table with lanky ease on calls like this. Warlow noted how the woman's eyes went up and down Rhys's frame with a great deal more interest than they had when they'd taken him in.

'I'm not supposed to let anyone in. Boss's orders.'

'We're here on serious business, Miss…'

'Lorna.'

'Right, Lorna. Can you tell me why no one has responded to our calls about a serious incident?'

Lorna, chewing gum, ceased masticating for a moment as her brows furrowed. 'We've changed our numbers. Gone all mobile now. No fax anymore.'

'Then why is your answering service still working on the landline?'

Heat from inside the room washed over Warlow's face. From the limited view, the office looked in good order. 'You're supposed to give them notice. A month or something,' Lorna explained. 'But Barry said I should ignore the calls on that number now.'

'Barry?'

'Barry Kirkland. The boss.'

Warlow sighed. *Obviously not struggling for business, then.* 'And how do I get hold of Barry?'

From the lane leading to the yard, the noise of an approaching lorry drifted in on the breeze. 'He'll be here in thirty seconds. You can wait if you like.'

'Thanks,' Warlow said, expecting the door to open. When it shut with a click and stayed shut, he turned to Rhys. 'What happened to common courtesy, eh?'

'She's a woman alone out here, sir. I think it's very sensible she had the door on a chain.'

Warlow grunted out a 'Maybe.'

The lorry, a six-wheeler with an open-framed side which looked to be a cut-down version of the stacking system in the yard and similarly arranged in three layers, pulled up in front of the storage area. Two men jumped out. Despite the cold, both wore only polo shirts with Castell Scaffolding logos on their breasts. One, the older of the two, bald and bearded, one thick earring in his left ear pirate style, got to work unloading, ignoring Warlow and Rhys's approach until they were within a few yards.

'Not safe here, mate,' said the older man. 'These poles could do some actual damage if one fell on you.'

'Barry, is it?' Warlow said, ignoring the veiled threat.

'Who wants to know?'

Warlow repeated the performance with his warrant card.

Barry finished unloading the pole on his shoulder and came around to the front of the lorry. He wore heavy gloves on his hands, but above them, his forearms were sinewy and tattooed.

'What's this about?' he asked.

'Ronnie Probert?'

Barry frowned. 'Yeah, heard about that. Bad bloody news if you ask me.'

'You provided scaffolding for a job in the autumn. We've been trying to contact you for several days, but your phones—'

'Need sorting out, I know. Didn't think it through, did Lorna. She just got rid of everything and got a new system.'

'That's not what she told us,' Rhys said.

'Lovely girl, Lorna. Face of the company, but not the brains.' Barry tapped his head. 'BT needs time to switch stuff over.'

'Doesn't matter,' Warlow said. 'We need a list of your staff. The ones who worked at Probert's place.'

Barry frowned. 'That won't take long. There's only two crew. That's me and Lewis as one, and my brother Hywel and his mate John as the other.'

'Which one of you was involved with the Probert property?'

'Us.' Barry indicated to Lewis, who carried on offloading regardless.

'No one else?'

Barry hesitated. From the side of the lorry, Lewis answered, 'Jordan was with us, Bar. I remember that.'

'We sometimes call boys in. If we're busy,' Barry explained. 'Strictly cash, you know? Off the books, like. Just for a couple of days' work and that.'

'I'm not interested in employment law, Barry. But we need everyone's names and contact details so that someone can be in touch to take a statement.'

'About what?'

'About where you all were the night Ronnie Probert was attacked,' Rhys said from over Warlow's shoulder.

Barry looked up. Momentarily stunned, but then nodded. 'Fair enough.' He went back to the lorry's cab to fetch a phone and dialled a number. 'Lorn, print out mine and Lewis's names and addresses and phone numbers. And you'd better do the same for Jordan Nicholas. Nice old bloke was Probert,' Barry said, ending the call.

'Where were you on the night of 23rd January?' Rhys asked.

Warlow twisted partially towards the DC, who was unyielding.

'Can't tell you offhand,' Barry said.

'Try,' Rhys suggested. 'Doesn't look good you not fielding our calls. So, now that we're here, maybe you could spare a few minutes to get this sorted.'

'Bit of a tight schedule,' Barry replied, glancing behind at the back end of the lorry.

'It'll be even tighter if we have to take you in for questioning.' Rhys stepped forward.

'Alright, let's not get excited. Jesus. What was that date again?'

Rhys provided it, and the two officers waited while Barry, and then Lewis, tried to remember their movements of nine days ago. A task that seemed to take every inch of their mental powers. They conferred.

Barry eventually replied, 'I was playing darts at the Sheaf in Hendy. Lewis was at his girlfriend's all night. He's given me an address for that.'

'Where did you go after your darts?' Rhys asked.

'Home. We had a six o'clock start next day. Council buildings in Llandeilo. Big job.'

Rhys took the details down. When he'd finished, Barry said, 'Lorna will give you Jordan's details and all the rest.'

Halfway back to the office, Warlow turned to see Barry and Lewis back at it, offloading and stacking, handling the heavy poles as if they were straws.

'What do you think, sir?' Rhys asked.

'Don't look too bothered, do they?'

'No,' Rhys agreed.

Lorna opened the door four inches again and passed out the folded sheet.

'Thanks.' Rhys took it, and the door closed once more. 'Friendly isn't a word I'd use for this place, sir,' Rhys said as he got back into the Jeep.

'The police make people nervous, as you know. Ring all that through to Gil. Let's see what he comes up with.'

'Took a photo of it, sir, and WhatsApped it through. He should have it already.'

They'd gone a mile when Rhys's phone started belting out Dua Lipa's *Be the One*. Warlow sent him a pained glance. 'Gina's idea, sir.'

Rhys took the call and immediately put it on speaker, so the tail end of Gil's sentence came through.

'… tell him it's not that far.'

'What's not that far?' Warlow asked in a low rumble.

'Jordan Nicholas. The third member of the scaffolding team. His name rang a big bell when I ran it. He's nineteen but been in trouble for half of that. ASB, affray, spitting at police, anger issues, theft and, wait for it, burglary.'

'Lovely,' Warlow said.

'We could send some Uniforms around to pull him in,' Gil offered.

'What's the address?'

'It's in Carway, sir. Five minutes away.'

'Right. In for a penny. Stab vest under the seat, is it, Rhys?'

'Always bring it when I'm with you, sir.'

'Smart,' Gil said through the phone's speaker.

CHAPTER TEN

GAYNOR RICHMOND BROUGHT someone with her as support to talk to Jess. There were no smiles as the DI introduced herself and then Gil. The second woman turned out to be Ruth, Gaynor Richmond's daughter. Both shared the same fixed expression of miserable hostility, declining the offer of tea when Gil brought it up. If she had to score it, Jess gave Ruth the marginal lead in the truculence league table.

'What can you tell us?' Ruth began with a belligerent stare. 'I mean, you've dragged us in here, so I hope you've got something new to say, have you?'

'That's not quite how this works,' Jess said.

'Surely, you've made some progress?' Gaynor, a heavier, drabber version of her daughter, snapped.

Jess stayed relaxed. She'd been here before. Too many times to count. Grieving relatives were never the easiest of people to deal with. And these two were primed and ready not to make the police's life easy.

'We're at the beginning of our investigation, Mrs Richmond,' Jess said.

'Gaynor. Everyone calls me that.'

'It might seem that things stalled for a while—'

'What have you been doing for the last week, then?' Ruth demanded.

'Until yesterday, this was a burglary, not a murder investigation. Different team.'

Both women flinched at hearing the word murder, but they were intent on confrontation. 'So, what did they do, then?' Ruth asked. 'The last… team.'

Not as much as we'd have liked, Jess mused. But saying that wouldn't help the cause here. Instead, she said, 'A great deal. But now the emphasis has shifted.'

Ruth shook her head and clenched her jaw. 'We are toying with bringing in a private investigator.'

Jess wasn't fazed. 'That's your prerogative, of course. But I'd ask you to give us a couple of days. DCI Warlow is leading the team. He is a very experienced detective.'

'Where is he, then?' Ruth asked.

'Out doing his job,' Gil said.

Ruth inhaled through her nose and drew in her chin. All that was missing was a theatrical folding of her arms and a pushing up of her bosoms. Still, the day was young.

'I've told you everything I can,' Gaynor said.

Jess ran with this less aggressive stance. 'Ronnie said the burglar kept asking him for the money. Do you know what they were referring to?'

Gaynor wheezed out a thin laugh. 'He had money. Kept it all himself, mind. But he wasn't the type to stuff it under a mattress.'

'Though that was the rumour,' Ruth added. 'What people thought. All the idiots. An old wives' tale about how my uncle kept his money stashed away like that comedian. What's his name?'

'Ken Dodd,' Gil said.

Mr Dodd had famously been found with a third of a

million stashed in the attic of his house and that of the house next door in Knotty Ash.

'My uncle did like getting paid for appearances in cash,' Ruth added.

'How much are we talking about? How much is he worth?' Gil asked.

'A fortune,' Gaynor said. Though she tried holding back, the resentment shone through. 'He never told us how much.'

'Is there a will?' Jess asked.

Gaynor nodded.

'Do you have any idea who the beneficiaries are?' Gil tried to couch it as an afterthought, though it was far from that.

'No. It would be nice if he left something to the kids. That's all I hope,' Gaynor smiled at Ruth. 'But he was stubborn, Ronnie. My Graham tried to help him, talk to him about investments, but he wasn't having any of it. He said some of his old pals helped.' She looked up with a bitter smile. 'But what the hell do a bunch of has-been rugby players know about money?'

'He was really tight, too,' Ruth added. 'Spent nothing if he could help it.'

'Not a generous man, then?' Jess asked, recalling all the charity work.

'No,' Ruth said.

Something, guilt perhaps, clouded Gaynor's face. 'That's not strictly true. He helped you with your student loans. Paid that all off after a couple of years.'

'I suppose,' Ruth agreed, but reluctantly.

The implication, in Jess's head, was that Ruth was someone hard to please.

'And what about your other brother, Gaynor?' Gil asked.

'What about him?'

'How did he and Ronnie get on?'

'They didn't,' Gaynor said. 'Like cat and dog, were Ronnie and Terry. They haven't spoken to each other for twenty years.'

Gil wrote it down.

'Not since Ralph's wedding. Ralph, that's my nephew, Terry's boy. Ronnie and Sian bought them a silver tea set.' A bitter smile twisted one side of her mouth.

'What's wrong with that?' Gil asked.

'A silver tea set? Bloody insult. But Sian, Ronnie's wife, was old-fashioned that way. Ralph had been hoping for a honeymoon package.' She pulled a tissue out of her sleeve and wiped her nose. 'Terry never quite got over being jealous of Ronnie's success.'

Families, Jess mused. Bloody minefield.

'When did you last see Ronnie, Gaynor?' Gil asked.

'The Friday before the burglary. I called in every couple of weeks. Never stayed long. Ron is ten years older than me. Getting on a bit. We had a cup of tea and a chat. The usual. He had a hospital appointment coming up. I went with him the last time.'

'An appointment?' Jess asked.

'Leukaemia. Hard to believe in a rugby player. Harder to believe in Ronnie Probert. Everyone thought he was invincible,'

'What did Ronnie think of that?' Gil asked.

'Why are you asking?' Ruth interjected, still miffed by the line of questioning. Miffed with being summoned. Miffed in general. 'What does any of this have to do with my uncle's murder?'

Jess waited. Leaving a space allowed the heat to dissipate. Eventually, she said, 'It's clear that the motive for the attack was money. We're simply trying to establish who might have known or suspected there was some.'

'All of West Wales,' Ruth replied.

Gaynor toyed with the tissue in her fist. Pulling it out and pushing it back in again. 'Look, there was no money in the house. Ronnie wasn't stupid. All that is nothing but gossip.'

Jess watched Gil make a note. Gossip it might be. But gossip could get you into a lot of trouble. Jess knew that only too well.

———

WARLOW FOLLOWED the instructions and headed north to Carway, yet another village that had once provided labour to the coal industry. A village that, since the demise of that industry, now sat, purposeless, in the landscape. By way of excoriating the scars left by the vast opencast mines that had operated north and south of the village, a golf course and a racecourse had been built. All good on paper. Still, Warlow couldn't help but wonder how many miners it needed to run those facilities.

Not that many, he guessed.

As with all these villages, social housing played some part, and as Warlow took a right and drove down into one of the small estates, he guessed he'd found Carway's. Nicholas's address was on a street where an architect had decided it might be novel to have garages jutting out from the front of the blocks of terraced houses, as opposed to at the rear. The result turned out to be an ugly mess.

'Is this the back or the front, sir?' Rhys asked.

'There's no other road. This must be the front.'

'What number, sir?'

'Wind down your window and take a guess,' Warlow said.

Rhys did. Loud, heavy metal music blared out from the second block of terraces. The first two houses had fresh coats of paint, then one house had been boarded up with screwed-down marine ply over the windows and doors. A sure sign that neighbour relations had been strained. The end house, its once cream-coloured walls now marred by the damp fungal growth that made it look perpetually dirty, was where a brash guitar combined with a thumping beat and incoherent screaming pounded out from.

'That's loud,' Rhys said.

'Is that supposed to be music?' Warlow asked.

'Thrash metal, sir.'

'Right. Gives us cause to knock. I'm offended by that level of… noise, and I don't even live here.'

Warlow got out of the car, stepped across four feet of pavement, and opened a wooden gate next to the sloping roof of the garage. The music came from upstairs. Not quite from the room with an open window and a purple curtain hanging drunkenly off its rail, but somewhere else, probably a room behind. Several black refuse bags and a food recycling bin with bits of what looked like curry sauce – God, he hoped it was curry sauce – running down the outside, stood under a window next to a door leading into the garage.

'This the front door, sir?' Rhys asked.

'Weirdly, yes.'

Warlow rapped loudly. A single pane of obscure glass in the top half of the door had a piece of brown parcel tape running down its entire length as a repair to previous damage. Warlow knocked again. The music did not abate, but the sound of a dog barking, followed by a screeching female voice warning it to shut up, reached them.

'What do you think is in those bins, sir?' Rhys said, glancing down at the refuse.

'Body parts, probably,' Warlow said.

'Just what I was thinking.'

Warlow jutted out his lower lip and gave a slight nod. 'Good to see the training is paying off.'

The door opened; the sound of music got louder. Though this noise came about as close to The Sound of Music as dragging nails across a blackboard did to The Lark Ascending. Not that he enjoyed nuns singing about lonely goatherds. In fact, he, like Gil, had used Von Trapp as rhyming slang on more than one occasion. But the racket seemed not to bother the person standing there.

Judging from her appearance, it didn't look like she let much of anything bother her, including hygiene. As for age, Warlow guessed anywhere from fifty to mid-seventies. Her toothlessness did not help. Her hair might once have been blonde. Now the roots were reclaiming their true colour, and pink streaks at the tips of the wispy strands that hung down around her face from the scrunchy, trying in vain to contain the frizzy mess up on her head, spoke of some vague, failed attempt at caring about that appearance. The hand around the edge of the door showed unvarnished nails the colour of burnt wood, stained by years of contact with burning tobacco. Thin to the point of emaciation, the loose-fitting tracksuit in grey and red she wore hung off her. On her feet, she wore striped slides. The remnants of some long ago-applied nail varnish clung in geographic patches to her un-pedicured toenails.

''Elp you?' she asked, in a voice coarse from shouting, maybe at the dog, maybe at other people.

Warlow held up his warrant card. 'Looking for Jordan Nicholas.'

'Not here,' said the woman.

'You the owner?'

'Yeah.'

'Mind turning the music down?'

'That's not me, that's…'

Warlow was willing to bet 'Jordan' would be the next word, but the woman realised the error and let the sentence drift.

'Who?' Warlow asked.

'It is me. Forgot. I put it on and went for a fag.'

'Could you turn it down, then?'

'Alright.' The woman turned and took the stairs that ran directly up from the hallway. There may have been a runner on those stairs once, now bare wood augmented the noise of clattering feet. The woman opened the bedroom door just enough to allow herself to slip in. Fifteen seconds later, the cacophonous noise eased to a background annoyance as she walked back down the stairs with one glance behind her before re-joining the officers at the front door.

'Can I ask who I'm speaking with?' Warlow asked.

The woman shrugged.

'We're standing at your door. We know your address. It'll take us sixty seconds to find out,' Rhys said, phone in hand.

The woman considered this before shrugging. 'Linda Nicholas.'

'Are you related to Jordan, Linda?' Warlow knew the phrasing sounded off, but he was hedging his bets. This woman could be a mother, grandmother, even sister.

'He's mine, is Jordan. Him and Troy.'

'So, you have two sons?'

'Yeah. Two. Good boys, they are, too. Never mind what this lot think.' She moved her head up to indicate the estate, or perhaps the world in general.

'We need a word with Jordan, Linda. If he's here, it would make life much easier for us. Save us bringing him in.'

Linda shook her head. 'Come in and look.'

'Would that be okay?'

'Help yourselves. I'll be out here having a smoke.' She pulled the door open. 'Stay out of the kitchen. Grommet's in there. He's Jordan's Jack Russell. Not a big fan of strangers, is Grommet.' Linda stepped out, reached into her pocket, and took out a packet of cigarettes with an image of a cataractous eye on the front and the words "Smoking increases the risk of blindness" over the top half. She paused with a cigarette between her fingers and addressed the officer. 'Oh, and excuse the mess. I'd have dusted if I knew you were coming.'

With the door open, Rhys and Warlow exchanged glances.

'You heard the lady, Rhys. After you.'

CHAPTER ELEVEN

PROBERT'S TREASURE trove of memorabilia began arriving at the community hall mid-morning. By one-thirty, they'd put up trestle tables and began labelling the evidence. To that end, Catrin had enlisted the help of Sandra Griffiths, whose experience as a Receiver and Evidence Officer, though extensive, would be stretched in this case.

'I considered putting things in chronological order, trying time-related links, but that wasn't working. So now, we're adopting a dual labelling.' Sandra wore thick-rimmed glasses that lent her a fussy librarian air. 'One is for type: personal, sports, business, financial, etcetera. The other label shows where in the house it was found.'

'Show me,' Catrin asked.

Sandra walked her around the quadrangle of circular tables she'd arranged, pausing at one. 'This is all his rugby-related stuff.'

Catrin picked up a box labelled Barbarians 73 to 79. The clear-sided box contained black-and-white striped jerseys, programmes, newspaper cuttings, letters of invitation, and other bits and pieces. A separate label had been stuck on the lid, showing that the contents of this box had come from bedroom two and the living room. 'He had stuff all over the house. Not quite a hoarder, but close.'

'I noticed,' Catrin said.

The two officers did a sweep along the rest of the tables, which were slowly but surely filling up with items and papers.

'Are you interested in anything specific?' Sandra asked.

'That's the trouble. I'm not. But it'll all need sifting through.' Catrin glanced up at a corner where a series of photographs were stacked on the table.

Sandra followed her eye-line. 'That's going to be for personal stuff. Did you know there was an attic?'

'No.' Catrin sent Sandra a sideways glance of cringing surprise.

'It's a big one, too. God knows what's up there.'

'No money, I hope.'

'Why do you say that?'

'Because if there is, then the smart thing to have done was own up to it. He'd have saved himself.'

Sandra hoisted an eyebrow. 'Some people might consider not giving in brave.'

'Some people might consider it stupid. Often, the difference between the two is a thin line. One step in the right direction, and you could end up on the podium with a gong around your neck. One slip in the other, and you end up getting battered to death in your own bedroom.'

The door opened, and three officers entered, carrying more boxes full of more stuff. 'Right.' Sandra waved them towards a holding table at the front. 'I'd better see to this lot. There's tea brewing out the back if you want a cup?'

'I'm fine,' Catrin said.

'By the way, there is a reporter outside looking for a quotable source.'

'Really?' Catrin shuddered. They'd been warned not to engage. They had departments for that, or, as in Warlow's case, a look that made most reporters wish they were somewhere else, or at least hadn't asked the question that triggered the look in the first place. Relations between the public, the press and the police were, if you believed the hyperbole, "The worst they have been for decades." Commissioned reports on sexism and racism, high-profile cases of rogue officers given almost carte blanche to continue with their egregious behaviours seemed to be everywhere you looked, and not only in the big cities. And a case like this, involving a well-known and well-loved personality who'd held a place in the hearts of a nation, the crime, though a reflection of today's society, always somehow ended up being, "A failure of policing".

As if having more bobbies on the beat would have stopped this calculating robber, or robbers, from doing what they had done. She knew of no beat, on foot or in a car, that encompassed an isolated property on the edge of a village in the middle of Carmarthenshire. Yet, the press were hungry for any little snippet they could misquote or skew out of context.

Not today, though. And certainly not from DS Richards.

'I might be better off finding a quiet spot and diving headfirst into one of these boxes.'

'Take your pick,' Sandra said.

Catrin looked around. The hall was just one big open space. She pulled up a chair to the nearest table, grabbed a box and began sifting through the contents, all the while imagining telling her partner Craig all about her glamorous day chasing down a killer. Luckily, since he was on the job, too, he knew better than to buy into the fiction about the detectives' car-chase lifestyles. This was where you found out the truth. Sitting on your bum in a community hall, trawling through the bits and pieces of an old man's life.

Maybe she would have that cup of tea after all.

———

WARLOW MADE Rhys wait in the hallway while he went upstairs. His feet echoed on the wooden treads. He kept his hand away from a banister that had enough grease marks and stains to start cultures for a dozen brands of yoghurt, kefir, or kombucha. On the landing, Warlow took in a violently yellow bathroom and three doors. Two were closed, one stood ajar; the one he'd seen Linda come out of, from where the more muted, but still crass, sound of thrash metal still emerged. Warlow walked forward.

'Jordan, it's the police. We need a chat.'

He pushed the door open with his foot. It swung inwards to reveal a room that still had the sweet aroma of a burnt weed, one that was most definitely not tobacco, in the air. The unmade bed had sheets that might once have been green but were now a murky grey. A white tubular skeletal clothes rail held fewer clothes than were scattered, crumpled or rolled up on the floor. The walls of light blue looked in need of touching up. Two large posters, one for a rock band called Megadeth and the other, Anthrax, took up most of the wall space. This second one dated 2022 and showing a group of four with only one grey beard amidst a sea of black dyed hair.

A melamine-topped table masquerading as a dresser bore half a dozen empty cans of so-called energy drinks with lurid-green and black colouring, an ashtray with several used cigarette ends, and a battered laptop. Next to that sat three canisters of deodorant spray packaged to imply their use would turn the bearer of the aroma into a wild animal, and a bottle of similarly sourced aftershave. The room otherwise was both cold and empty.

Warlow walked across to the wide-open window over

the bed, through which a steady draft blew. Looking down into the rear garden, he noted a ladder tied to a downpipe by some bungee cords. It might have doubled as a quick-fire escape, but he doubted this was in any way connected to fire regulations. More likely a means of rapid exit when the situation demanded it. Situations such as a couple of police officers turning up at the front door.

'Gone,' Warlow said, loud enough for Rhys to hear. But he got no acknowledgement by reply.

The DCI retraced his steps and opened the other doors. One opened into a bedroom marginally less untidy than Jordan's. This one with a double bed. But the presence of female underwear hinted at this being Linda Nicholas's room, though that, in this day and age, could be a dangerous assumption.

But his guess was reinforced when he opened the last door. This room, painted green, looked very different. It was neat, clean with a made-up bed. One wall had two brightly drawn Manga posters and on the other, above a wooden-topped desk, was a poster of a video game called Ghost Reign Crusade. On the desk, books sat neatly stacked.

Warlow picked up a copy of Aldous Huxley's Brave New World on top of a well-thumbed pure maths textbook.

Returning down the stairs, he expected to see Rhys, but the DC had gone. Warlow followed the sound of voices and found a door under the stairs opened to a room behind the garage. In it sat two people in wing-backed chairs that Warlow recognised from various locations he'd visited where someone under thirty lived, as gaming chairs. High-backed, with armrests, on wheeled bases. Light came from a couple of desk lamps. The desk itself was curved, with two large monitors facing the door. Rhys was standing, chatting to the people in the chairs. A girl of perhaps fifteen or sixteen, blue earphones displaced around her neck, glanced up at Rhys with an expression of mild annoyance.

A glance she redirected towards Warlow as he appeared in the doorway, and Rhys made the introductions, wearing an animated grin.

'DCI Warlow, this is Lola Danes, and the bloke killing it in the uncharted plane is Troy Nicholas.'

Warlow glanced over at the second monitor. The boy in front of it had a mop of brown hair and his blue earphones were clamped onto his head.

His fingers jerked and twitched over a controller in his hand. On screen, a caped figure, sword in hand, rolled, dodged, and skittered over the screen while something twice its size and with a twinned stone head, cast red beams of power from sightless eyes. The boy, of about the same age as Lola, didn't look up.

Probably don't even know we're here, Warlow surmised.

'What's he playing?' Warlow asked.

'That, sir, is Ghost Reign Crusade. And this is a masterclass.'

Warlow turned his face back to Rhys. The light of admiration burning in the DC's expression faltered. 'He's almost finished this level, sir. Not long.'

'Oh, well, if he's almost finished this level, we'd better wait.'

Rhys grinned. Or at least showed his teeth. Warlow leaned against the door frame and folded his arms. 'In the meantime, Lola, any idea where Jordan might have got to?'

Lola, short black hair, and dark makeup around her eyes, shrugged. 'Could be anywhere there's some free weed or a fast car.'

On screen, the stone-headed foe evaporated in a swirl of green smoke and the caped, sword-wielding hero turned and bowed. The screen paused, and the boy in the seat swivelled, stood up, blinked as the normal world impinged, and glanced at Lola for an explanation.

'Cops,' she said. 'Looking for your brother.'

Troy swept the mop of hair that had fallen forward over one eye out of his face, smiled the smile that made a pleasant face good-looking, and pressed a button on his phone. The room lights came up, revealing a small kitchenette area behind.

'Nothing new there, then,' Troy said. 'Cup of tea, gentlemen?'

CHAPTER TWELVE

WITH RONNIE PROBERT's sister and niece finally gone, Gil and Jess sat in the Incident Room over a cup of tea.

'Knives were out there, ma'am.'

Jess wrinkled her nose. 'They're hurting. I probably would be too. Going over old ground is only ever going to rake up misery.'

'Had to be done,' Gil said. 'And always useful. Certainly doesn't seem to be any love lost between the two brothers.'

'Family dynamics, Gil. Can't beat them.'

Gil, his mug held in both hands, glanced over at Jess with his best old-lag-being-inquisitive expression. 'Hope you don't mind me asking, ma'am, but there seemed to be an added bit of weight to that last sentence you spoke.'

Jess grinned. 'No flies on you, Gil.'

'No, Ma'am. My deodorant has that added capability. Jungle strength, as always.'

Jess's smile was muted. 'I don't bring Allanby dirty laundry to work, but there's not much laughter at home now. Molly's going through a break-up. And I know what that's like having worn the t-shirt for too long myself.'

'She's young.'

'That's the trouble. Not much perspective at that age, is there?'

Gil, the father of girls himself, remembered those teenage years only too well.

'And add to that the saga of her father dropping off the face of the earth,' Jess muttered.

'You still have no idea where he is?'

'No. And I'd sooner not. The few messages we've had from him haven't exactly been cheerful. Warnings about keeping our eyes and ears peeled.'

'For what?'

'You tell me! I don't know who he's got in with, and I'd rather it stayed that way.' Rick Allanby's recent dive into undercover work in Greater Manchester was an experiment that had all the hallmarks of his mid-life angst not having been assuaged by the affair with a colleague that led to Jess saying bye-bye.

'She'll bounce back,' Gil said. 'Molly, I mean.'

Jess nodded. 'I'm sure she will. Evan coming back hasn't helped.'

Gil kept his eyebrows raised.

'He's taken Cadi back, hasn't he?' Jess explained. 'That's a twist of the knife.'

'Ever thought of getting a dog yourself, ma'am?'

'Molly has. But then, in nine months she'll be at uni and guess who'd be the dog's keeper?'

They lapsed into pensive silence. Jess's mobile buzzed a notification. She glanced at it and said, 'Catrin says she's found at least five signed rugby balls in Probert's effects. She wants to know if she should put an armed guard in the community hall.'

'If they're signed, those will be worth a few bob. And that's what might be behind Ronnie's sister's anger.

They've not been allowed into the place since the burglary. Not had their hands on the treasure. From what I'm hearing, Ronnie couldn't remember half the stuff he had there and there'll be rich pickings. There's going to be a TV special about his life and career next week. That'll up the ante, no doubt. The jerseys and the balls at auction would fetch thousands.'

'Perhaps you should go over there and help Catrin sort things out. You'll have a handle on that side of things. Much more than I do since rugby seems to be the religion here, and I am an agnostic on that front.'

'Rugby is an interesting one, ma'am. A conundrum we've never quite unravelled. I mean, we don't always win, but when we do, it lets everyone celebrate the tribe without the nuisance of arguing about what it means to be in that tribe. Like how Welsh you really are. A lot of crap gets talked about the language or what part of Wales you were born in by the pompous few. Fact is, when it started here, rugby was as much a reaction to repression as it was a game. I mean, it's a lot more enjoyable than sermons in the chapel and doesn't require that you speak the language. Both stifling influences in their own way in times past.'

'I'm from Manchester, so I understand tribes. It's just that the ball is a different shape, right? Plus, Catrin says there's a press hyena lurking. She sent me a photo.' She held her phone up.

Gil got to his feet and examined the screen. A man in a waxed jacket sat sideways in the front seat of a car with the door open, outside the hall, eyes peeled for the comings and goings. He had a hooked nose and eyes a little too small for his face.

'Geraint Lane. He does the odd topical piece for both the English and Welsh channels sometimes. A lot of online stuff. Pops up when something major occurs. Floods, fires, murders. All the happy events. Slippery little sod. Has an agenda he tries to shoehorn into his pieces so that he politicises everything.'

'Catrin doesn't want to speak to him, but Buchannan has said we should at least explain what's happening at the hall. Otherwise, the made-up stuff will be worse.'

'I could give DS Richards a hand in the sorting and chat with Mr Lane.'

'Two birds and all that.'

'If Geraint Lane is a bird, ma'am, he'd be a red-necked vulture. And I've got plenty of stones for him, plus a sling.'

––––––

WARLOW TURNED down Troy's offer of tea. Instead, he stood inside the doorway of the room, looking around. 'This is… nice.' He tried to keep the surprise out of his voice but failed.

The room was painted dark navy. Apart from the gaming desk, chairs, monitors and associated gaming equipment, the place had a couple of easy chairs in front of the sink and worktop, but no window.

'My game room,' Troy said. 'There's a lock on the door. No one allowed in but me. I painted it. All the equipment's mine.'

'We're here to talk to your brother,' Warlow said.

Troy nodded.

'Did either of you see him leave? My guess is he got out by the bedroom window.'

'Does that a lot,' Lola said. She had a quick smile that dimpled her cheeks. She made no attempt to disguise the natural tone of her skin, pale and emphasised by the hair and eyeliner. Her complexion bordered on a sickly colour. But then, Warlow thought, spending your time indoors in a room like this would do that to you. She sported a sweatshirt, dark and spacious, with a logo on it which, Warlow speculated, could have been that of a Games maker. Her black jeans were baggy, and she wore a pair of Converse on her feet.

Troy, having stood up, was about average height, thin and with an intense and edgy look about him. He wore a burnt-orange hoodie and some brown chinos.

'Do you have any notion of where your brother may have gone?' Warlow kept probing.

Both youngsters shook their heads.

'Is it only with Castell Scaffolding he works?'

Troy gestured no idea with both hands palms up. 'Says he's a free spirit, does Jordan.'

'And your mother—' Warlow began.

'Linda's a mess,' Troy pre-empted Warlow.

But the DCI heard no rancour there, only a kind of sad acceptance. 'She gets her methadone every day from the pharmacy in Kidwelly. But then, you probably guessed that.'

Warlow could only begin to wonder how Troy had got to this point in his life as unscathed as he appeared to be under the circumstances. Perhaps, having dealt him a bum hand, the gods blessed him with intelligence and insight. And perhaps a bloody good social worker. Warlow had seen stranger things. Though not that many.

'Are you still in school, Troy?' Rhys asked.

'Sixth form college in Gorseinon. Me and Lola get the bus.'

'What are you doing for A level?'

'Double maths and computer science plus a bit of English at AS,' Troy said.

'The plan is to escape from here. We've already done coding courses online. Troy's much better than me. And he's ace at GRC.'

'GRC?'

'Ghost Reign Crusade.' Lola pointed at the screen and the game Troy had been playing.

'Not much better,' Troy said.

Warlow watched the exchange and the little smiles of mutual respect that followed.

'Jordan wants to get away, too,' Lola added. 'But he's trying to do it by being an idiot, like jumping out of the window when you lot turn up.'

'Jordan has trust issues,' Troy said as if that explained the ladder and the disappearance with no need for further discussion. It could have sounded snide, but neither of the kids laughed. Lola turned to Troy, as if to add to his comment, but then nodded instead and said nothing. These two were friends who locked themselves away from the noise and whatever else had caused their neighbours to up-sticks and the council to board the place up. They'd created a little haven in a house where pride in surroundings did not seem to be a factor high on the adult Nicholas's scale of importance.

'If Jordan comes back, tell him to give us a ring.' Warlow left his card on the table. 'It's important.'

'What's it about?' Lola asked.

'We can't say. But it's serious enough for us to have come out here. Better that he contacts us than we come looking again. I don't care if he smokes a bit of pot in his bedroom. That's not why we were here.'

Linda Nicholas was still outside, smoking legally. Warlow wondered if this was the same cigarette she'd begun minutes ago, or the second or even the third. 'Find him? Jordan?' Her sunken cheeks flapped as she spoke.

'No. Something must have spooked him, and he bolted out of his bedroom window,' Warlow said.

'Bloody headstrong, is Jordan. Reflex, him running off with strangers at the door.'

'Why?' Rhys asked.

Linda shrugged.

'We met Troy, too,' Rhys said. 'Bright kid.'

Linda smiled. If there were any teeth left in her head, they must've been hidden at the very back. But the pride was obvious to see. 'His grandma helped a lot when he was little. Now he says he wants to live with me, so…'

'Nice set up he has there.'

Linda's smile faltered. 'He works hard. He deserves it. And he's not Jordan,' was all she said in reply.

In the car, Warlow waited for Rhys to find the quickest route to Ronnie Probert's brother's house on Maps.

'What's your assessment of the Nicholas household, Rhys?'

'Big surprises there, sir. With Troy. That game, it's hard.'

'It's a game. How can it be hard?'

Rhys, a half-smile on his lips that strayed dangerously close to being condescending, sent a questioning glance over to the senior officer before he explained, 'Ghost Reign Crusade is huge, sir. There are world championships. Televised gameplay. Massive in Asia especially. You can get people who spend their whole lives playing these games eighteen hours a day. People win an enormous amount of money. Millions sometimes. And other people, fans, shell out money to watch these things.'

'Pay to watch people play video games?'

'It's big money.'

Warlow sighed and shook his head. Yet another fact of modern life that had passed him by. 'I was mean at Space Invaders at one time,' was all he managed to say.

Rhys nodded. 'That's cave painting compared to these games, sir. Especially GRC. It's a different world. A virtual world. You can live in it if you want to. Some people have actual addresses there. They barter, work, swap weapons, even pay for things sometimes with real and virtual money. As I say, it's a whole different world.'

'Well, good for him, I say. I may not know much about games, but I know that computer science might be a ticket out of Carway.'

'Pleasant surprise, though, seeing that.'

'Maybe. But perhaps Lola has something to do with it. It's old-fashioned to say these days, but sometimes the love of a good… partner is all it takes.'

'Didn't have you down as a romantic, sir?'

'I see what I see, Rhys. And you're on thin ice when it comes to romance. I saw those flowers you bought for Gina on her birthday.'

Rhys blinked a few times, sighed, and then nodded. 'Mea Cooper, sir.'

Warlow toyed with correcting him, but let it pass. For all he knew, Rhys might know the correct phrasing, and this was simply a Gil-ism. He would not have been at all surprised.

'How is Gina, by the way?'

'Good, sir. Bit of a New Year fitness thing going on. She's threatening to do an Ironman with some of her mates.'

'That's running, swimming, and cycling, right?' He was only making conversation here. He knew full well it was all three, having investigated the death of a colleague in Tenby whose body was found by two women who'd been training for a triathlon on a Pembrokeshire beach, and whose goal had been the Tenby Ironman.

'It is, sir.'

'You helping?'

'I follow. She waits for me to catch up.'

Warlow grinned. 'Still, a change from getting battered at rugby. Tell you what, why don't you add the cycle path between Tumble and Swiss Valley on your training schedule this weekend? See if you can find the Signalman.'

'I'll talk to Gina, sir.'

'I already have. She said yes.'

Rhys opened his mouth to say something but wisely and promptly shut it again.

CHAPTER THIRTEEN

JORDAN NICHOLAS KNEW the paths through the fields and coppices behind his house well enough to have made the journey in the dark. Something he'd done many times. In both directions. More often when he was younger, sneaking out after dark when Linda had confined him to his room, supposedly. These days he stashed an e-bike he'd bought off a mate for fifty quid. The bike must've been worth twenty times that, but the mate, more an acquaintance in a pub in all honesty, just wanted the cash and quickly.

He hadn't asked why.

Jordan had added his own custom light-blue paint job to the front forks of the bike in an attempt at making it a little less conspicuous. His hiding place was under a tarpaulin at the rear of one of the storage sheds around the edge of the newly built racecourse at Ffos Las. So remote that they even had some outside electrical points there with no covers. That meant he could charge the bike overnight with no problem.

As for the cops, "You couldn't be arrested if you weren't there" was his creed. And you couldn't lie if you couldn't be questioned. If he'd heard of the Scarlet

Pimpernel, Jordan would've been a shoo-in for the movie. But his literary dalliances never got as far as an actual book, let alone Baroness Orczy. He preferred films. Or at least anything with "fast" or "furious" in the title. That and YouTube stuff. Things that made a lot of noise and moved quickly.

But the cops.

Again?

That he was a target and on the list for any theft that took place anywhere within a twenty-mile radius was obvious. It had been only a matter of time before they turned up to ask him about the theft at the Probert property. The text from Barry at Castell Scaffolding had been a heads up and then his mother's nod had sealed the deal.

Now he was on the back road heading towards Lenny's place. Lenny owed him big time and the very least he could do was to let him lie low for a while. Jordan had fixed Lenny up with a twelve-speaker sound system for his motor. A Panasonic job thanks to another friend who boosted cars for laughs and could strip them in under a day.

Lenny had been beyond grateful and said all the right things. Anything he could do, any time. Now was the right time. Jordan had picked up a snazzy bike helmet from a table at Caffè Nero whilst its owner had slipped to the bog. He'd done that the day after he got the e-bike so that he was geared up. He wore it now as he pedalled. Better he looked the part.

The cops would talk to Linda, but she would refuse to speak, even if she knew where he was going. And as for Troy… Jordan shook his head and smiled to himself. The kid was smart when it came to tech. Sorted out Jordan's wonky laptop like it was nothing. Troy knew about Lenny, but Troy wouldn't say anything either.

They were blood.

Somehow, they'd bonded since Troy'd come home. And the kid was a certified genius; there was no doubting it. If Jordan recognised the irony of this admiration after years of slagging off his luckier younger brother who had received the better deal of having his upbringing supervised by a grandmother in Kidwelly, while he'd had to tough it out with zombie Linda, he dismissed it.

After all, Troy was three years his junior, and he'd had no choice. But he was smart. And Jordan had stowed his jealousy and felt something akin to pride. Troy even said anyone could learn about computers and crap. There were ways you could do it all without shelling out by going to university. Even if you only had two crappy GCSEs. And Jordan believed him. He'd done nothing about it yet, but he would.

One day.

But he couldn't with the filth breathing down his neck.

He slipped through Furnace on the bike and headed into Llanelli.

Lenny's place was a ground-floor flat in an area known as Capel. An area where Jordan would have to lock the bike indoors for any of it to be left, even after removing the battery and front wheel, when he came back to it. And even then, in Lenny's flat, that could not be guaranteed.

Jordan used to hear the old men in the pub talk about Llanelli from the old days. When it was full of work, and steel, and a rugby club with a world reputation.

That was then. He knew it was a very different place now.

Maybe remnants of that time still existed on some of the outer edges. But not in the warren of streets that riddled the centre. And if he'd ever bothered to look it up, he'd have found his impression reinforced by statistics that showed it to be the fifth most dangerous town in the whole of the UK for its size. And that included places like Bristol and Coventry. Jordan didn't need that spelled out, not after having spent nights in the town centre.

Plus, the place was full of thieving bastards with one eye on "his" bike, no doubt. He'd have to be careful.

And so, Jordan powered through the streets, blissfully lacking any insight into the idea that he was one of those thieving bastards himself.

———

TERRY PROBERT LIVED at an address in Hendy, close to Pontarddulais, on the eastern fringes of the Dyfed Powys area with the River Loughor as the natural boundary. A place known for its choirs and a once-thriving cricket club.

Warlow's route from Carway took him cross-country, through Sylen, across acres of open countryside heading east along single-track roads.

'What do we know about Terry Probert, Rhys, apart from the fact that umbrage was taken after his son's wedding?'

Rhys checked his notebook. 'He's four years younger than his brother and works as a bookkeeper. Has his own business.'

'Still works?'

'As far as I am aware, sir.'

'Chartered or otherwise?'

Rhys made a face. 'I'll have to look that up, sir. What's the difference?'

'Qualifications. You can hang your shingle up as an accountant with only a calculator. But if you're Chartered or Certified, you're a member of a professional body and all that palaver.'

'So that they can charge more?'

'Got it in one there, Rhys.'

'Like I say, I'd have to—'

'Sport?' Warlow was enjoying firing off questions. And seeing Rhys squirm.

'Again, I'd have to—'

'I'm only asking because if you have a brother like Ronnie Probert, either you try to emulate him, or you hide what little skill you might have in a box and never take it out. Sometimes you hear of siblings who have been successful… who are those New Zealanders? You know, the three brothers playing in the All-Blacks? Incredible. But they are one-offs.'

'As far as I know, Terry Probert never played, at least for any big clubs.'

Warlow pondered the matter as the fields rolled by. Eventually, he said, 'Must be hard, being the brother of a phenomenon. If you play yourself, I mean. Everyone expects some of the magic to have rubbed off and everyone, including the poor bugger who everyone expects it from, is usually let down. Most of these one-off stars are freaks of nature.'

Rhys twitched an eyebrow.

'In a way that makes someone unique,' Warlow explained. 'Whether it's physique or an ability to react with lightning speed, fool a player, dink, dribble, you name it. It's something you can't teach. You may well be able to hone it, but it's nothing you can bottle. When you're related to someone like that, people can expect what they want, but they're never going to get it because it's fairy dust.'

Rhys nodded as the idea sank in. 'Never thought of it like that, sir. Fairy dust.'

'Well, think on, Detective Constable.' They'd finally arrived at a junction with an A road. Warlow paused with the engine running. He was safe to do so because there was nothing behind him. 'If my geography's right, somewhere not more than a couple of miles away is the M4, the Pont

Abram services, and a Costa. Before we speak to the grieving relatives, I think coffee is in order. And where there is coffee, there is also the means for you to fuel up on something terrifyingly calorific at exorbitant prices.' Warlow glanced across at his junior colleague with suspicion. 'Are we going to find a chair with your name on it there?'

'Not yet, sir. I'm working on it.' Rhys grinned. 'I have lots of bean stamps in my book.'

'Fine. But none of your cream-topped monstrosities. It'll be a flat white or an Americano. That's as elaborate as I'm willing to go.'

'Got you, sir,' Rhys said.

'You'd agree to anything so long as you had access to a flapjack. In the meantime, look up Probert's accountancy business and see what you can learn.'

CHAPTER FOURTEEN

There was no doubting the family resemblance. Terry Probert had been cut from the same cloth as his famous, now dead, brother. Except that Ronnie's amiable smile and open manner had been replaced by a taciturn, jowly glare and a ruddiness that made Terry look as if the thermostat inside him was set permanently to boiling point.

The house looked neat enough. A detached sixties-built property in a quiet close of half a dozen little boxes. Nothing ostentatious either outside or in. The one interesting feature in the sitting room that Warlow and Rhys ended up in being naval-themed art hanging on the wall. Men'o'War and galleons, many of them in tempestuous seas, sailed from one side of the room to the other.

Warlow sat on a settee of many patterns, realising he should've recognised at least one of these reproductions. Something struck a vague chord. He knew Turner had dabbled. But that was about his limit in terms of naval artists. Still, it made him wonder if the man opposite him had ever been in the services and this little artistic quirk had its origins in a personal history. Now, though, was not the time to ask.

They'd declined the offer of tea, having topped up on coffee at the service station, but also because the offer had been perfunctory. The host and his wife made no pretence of finding the visit a comfortable one. Though they hadn't said as much, it was clear they both resented Warlow and Rhys's presence. Rhys had asked about other relatives, a bit of history and background. Nothing too probing.

Yet.

'You'll have spoken to my sister?' Terry Probert asked.

'Not personally, but one of my colleagues has,' Warlow said.

'Then you have discussed us, the family. So, you know we weren't on the best of terms, Ronald and me.'

'You hadn't spoken in a while?'

'Years.' Terry sounded adamant. 'Words were exchanged. Words I could not forget.'

'These things happen.' Warlow flattened his mouth in sympathy.

Probert glared at him. 'Do they? You may think I'm a petty man, Mr Warlow. You may be right. But Ronald wasn't the saint people made him out to be.'

'Saints seldom are,' Warlow observed. *Or if they get to be it's because they're at the epicentre of some violence or persecution.*

'When we had Ralph, when he was a baby, Ronald and Sian were all over us and him. They had none of their own. Too busy bloody gallivanting to dinner engagements all over the world, long after he'd retired from actually playing. But by then, they probably thought they were too good for us. It all fizzled out. They stopped coming. Always some excuse or other. They distanced themselves. I didn't care, but their nephew did. Ralph loved Ronnie. And then when Ralph got married and they bought him a bloody tea set—'

The woman sitting next to Terry, already introduced as his wife, Arlene, put a hand on his arm. The look she gave him was severe. It made Warlow wonder if Terry's blood pressure needed an eye kept on it. That might be Arlene's job.

Terry took some deep breaths. 'But that's water under the bridge.'

'Is there any point in us asking if you knew of anyone who might want to do Ronnie harm?' Warlow asked.

'Harm? What do you mean? This was a burglary. Some thief seeing a red mist—'

Probert's words ended there as the front door opened. Both he and Arlene turned as a man ushered in two young pre-teen children, a boy and a girl. They both wore coats with slung-on backpacks, the girl holding something in her hand that looked suspiciously like some artwork. The door between the sitting room and the hallway stood open, revealing this little family unit.

Arlene got up, all smiles, and ushered the children through the hall towards the rear of the house and probably a kitchen. The man behind the children, late thirties, losing his hair and paunchy, was obviously a Probert. He had the same trademark snub nose that both his father and uncle had. He looked in through the open door with a quizzical expression.

'*Heddlu*,' Terry Probert used the official Welsh word for police before adding. 'This is my son, Ralph.'

Ralph looked up and nodded an acknowledgement before saying, 'Here about the Great Redeemer, then, are you?'

'If you're referring to your Uncle Ronald, then yes,' Warlow said.

'No doubt there'll be a load of wailing and black armbands this weekend. And all the old tries on TV again. If only they knew what a bloody miser he was.'

So, no doubt what side of the fence Ralph Probert sat.

Terry looked from Warlow to Ralph. 'They're saying that maybe it wasn't a burglary.'

'What?' Ralph spat out the word.

'That's not quite what I said,' Warlow began.

'There are certain aspects of the case,' Rhys said, taking everyone by surprise, 'that support the theory that whoever did this was after money. Burglary, yes, but with a... purpose. We are trying to ascertain where such a rumour might have originated.'

Ralph shook his head and trumpeted out an unfunny laugh. 'Everyone thought he had money. And he did. No doubt about that. But keeping it hidden under the floorboards in the shed or in the attic?' Ralph rejected the idea. 'That was just talk.'

Warlow nodded. People talked. But he wondered what sort of naïve person might believe such talk. A naïve or a desperate person, perhaps.

'Whatever your relationship with Ronald Probert might have been, this is still a murder enquiry,' Rhys said.

'And we will do our utmost to bring that killer to justice,' Warlow added.

'Hang on. The burglary was days ago,' Ralph said. 'All this talk about murder…'

'Your uncle died of his wounds,' Rhys said. 'A secondary haemorrhage. That makes it at least manslaughter if not murder.'

Harsh, but true. And Rhys stating the blunt facts triggered a change in Terry Probert's expression. When he next spoke, it was with a trembling lip. 'Bloody Ronald. Couldn't do anything by halves.'

He turned away, dabbing at his eyes, and leaving only Ralph to continue glaring at Warlow and Rhys.

Warlow asked them questions, Rhys wrote down their answers. He left a card and phone numbers, but eventually, both officers left the Proberts to it, none the wiser than when they'd arrived. Whether it turned out to be grief or recrimination they left behind was difficult to say.

Outside, as they hurried through the growing gloom of the afternoon to the Jeep, Rhys turned to Warlow.

'Were we supposed to establish movements, sir? For the brother and the nephew.'

'Hardly the time,' Warlow said. 'Why? Do you have Terry Probert on your list of suspects?'

'No. If anything, I'd say Ralph Probert seemed the more…' He trailed off as the word he sought escaped him.

'Bitter?'

'Yes, sir. That's how he came across.'

'Then that's your homework for tonight. Let's have a shufti at Ralph Probert, see what he's up to. Social media, where he works, circumstances. You know the drill.'

'I do, sir.'

'Oh, and by the way, I forgot to say that you did well with the Nicholas boy, Troy.'

'How do you mean, sir?'

'Establishing a relationship quickly. On his level. You play some of those games yourself?'

Rhys inclined his head. 'We've been known to. Gina likes a bit of Mario Kart now and again.'

'Don't tell Gil that.'

Rhys laughed. 'I won't, sir. But I've done my share of Call of Duty and that over the years. But this GRC, Ghost Reign Crusade, it's been hyped to the gills. And for once, the hype seems justified. People have gone nuts over it. Partly because it's been co-authored by that Science Fiction author, J C Mistral.'

'Even I've heard of him. Behind the Star Sage franchise on TV?'

'That's him.'

'Right, well done anyway. Finding common ground, that's half the battle. And Troy ended up providing the only sensible intel we got from that visit. Make sure you write it all up.'

'Where to now, sir?'

'Back to HQ. Some paperwork and then an early start tomorrow.'

'Sounds good to me.'

'Think you can avoid starvation for the duration of the drive back to Carmarthen?'

'Got a Snickers bar in my pocket, sir.'

Warlow gave up a wry smile. 'I didn't doubt that for one second. We'll put some music on so I won't have to listen to your impression of a horse.'

'What impression, sir?'

'AKA you eating a Snickers.'

'Harsh,' Rhys said, but his hand strayed to the inside pocket of his coat to make sure the prize was still there.

Warlow scrolled to a playlist. He'd collated some of Led Zeppelin's more mellow tracks. Trips in the car with Rhys were always a learning opportunity for the younger officer, and that tuition should, in Warlow's mind, extend to music.

That's the Way's melodic opening bars took Warlow's mind off the rustling of the confectionery wrapping.

'We used to consider Led Zeppelin the heaviest of the heavies,' he mused.

'Good tune,' Rhys said after a few bars. 'But hardly heavy these days. Jordan Nicholas wouldn't approve.'

'Exactly.' Warlow turned up the volume.

––––––

GIL GOT to the community hall in Five Roads mid-afternoon. The temperature had failed to creep above five degrees, and the morning rain still hadn't evaporated off, with the low cloud providing a blanket of humidity. These damp dull days were enough to drive you into thinking about the sun and summer.

Already, the Lady Anwen had the brochures out. If it wasn't for the grandchildren, of course, they might already be flitting off to the Canaries for a blast of winter sun. But then, he wasn't much of a sun worshipper. Though he was happy to sit on the beach under a sun hat for an hour with a good book, or in a café with the sun on his face and a thick coffee you could strip paint with. Or even do some walks in the hills…

'Well, well, Sergeant Gil Jones. I see they've brought in the big guns.'

Gil hadn't been expecting anyone to speak to him as he got out of the car. He swivelled to see Geraint Lane, barely recognisable in a hooded anorak, striding towards him.

'Mr Lane. What a pleasant surprise.'

Lane's grin was a sardonic one under his hooked nose. Both men knew Gil was lying. 'You've come as back-up for the vital transferring of chattels from Ronnie Probert's place. Excellent use of police resources, that. Any deep, dark secrets you can give up?'

'Anything deep or dark, you'll be the first to know. Be careful you don't fall into it, that's all,' Gil said.

'Ah, I didn't realise you were a joker.'

'Not much to joke about the last time we met.'

Lane had been a freelancer who'd latched on to Operation Alice and written a long, and negative, piece about the use of resources with no real clue about what Alice had been looking into. If he'd seen one-hundredth of the sort of things Gil had seen, he might not have been so critical of the money spent in tracking down child traffickers. He'd angled to look, of course, he had. Wanted a fly-on-the-wall approach, afflicted, no doubt by the trend in all things reality-related so that he might offer a, "truth". But the powers that be quashed that idea unceremoniously. And at the back of Gil's mind was the unhealthy little niggle that there just might have been an ulterior motive in someone wanting access to the imagery that he and his colleagues – two of whom had taken early retirement since – had been tasked to examine.

Gil knew he had no real grounds for those suspicions. But after one day in that viewing room with just him and a screen in front of him, the suggestion that anyone, journalist or not, might want to see anything remotely like those images, unless they were paid to as part of an investigation, rang a dozen alarm bells.

'How much did they spend on Op Alice in the end, three-quarters of a million?' Lane dangled some bait.

'Don't forget the twenty-five arrests, two rings broken open, fifteen convictions,' Gil said. 'Fifteen vermin off the internet. It would have been worth ten times the money.'

'In your opinion,' Lane said, his smile never slipping.

'Indeed. Mine and every right-minded person in the country.'

'Oh, I wouldn't say that.'

'Then don't.'

'Oh, come on. Look, forget Alice. We'll agree to differ.'

'No, we won't.'

'Please,' Lane said with a dismissive head shake. 'This case is front and centre of people's minds now. It's Ronnie bloody Probert. It's in the public interest. What are you guys thinking? Burglary gone tits up? A stranger attack? This weird bike thing with the Signalman?'

'We're making enquiries into several potential leads. There, have that.'

Gil turned and started for the entrance, only to feel a tug on his sleeve.

The sergeant stopped, pivoted, looked down at Lane's hand, and laughed. 'You really do not want to do that.'

Lane dropped his hand. 'Sorry, but it's bloody cold out here. Any chance I could come in for a warmup?'

'What's wrong with your car?'

'Petrol's expensive.'

'Then bugger off home.'

'I've been here for hours—'

The shout from behind Lane drew Gil's attention. It also drew the attention of the Uniform stationed outside the hall doors. Lane pivoted, too, but it was Gil who spotted the cyclist, helmet on, haring towards the Uniform.

'Can you help? We think we've got him.'

The Uniform had his hands up, bidding the cyclist stop. He did, with a screech of rubber and a skid on the damp floor, until a foot found the ground. Male, thin, lycra shorts over leggings and a red and blue cycling top under a black helmet.

Gil started across the car park. Lane followed. Gil turned on him. 'Stay here. This is none of your business.'

Lane's lips thinned to a slash of frustration. But he didn't move when Gil did.

'What's all this?' Gil asked as the cyclist, out of breath and animated, spilled out the story.

'We got him. We spotted him, the three of us. He buggered off into an old factory, but we cornered him.'

'Who? What the hell are you talking about?'

'Him. The Signalman.'

Gil exchanged glances with the Uniform. 'Get a response vehicle out here.' He turned back to the cyclist. 'And what's your name?'

'Paul.'

'Right, Paul. You've chased down and cornered a man, is that right?'

'Yeah. Old guy, panniers stuffed with all sorts. Wild looking.'

'And he's told you he's the Signalman, has he?'

Paul guffawed. 'No. Course he hasn't.'

'Right. Well, I don't have a bike, but I'm going to follow you on foot. How far?'

'About a mile.'

'Right.' Gil turned again to the Uniform. 'Make sure laughing-boy doesn't follow us.' He threw a thumb toward Lane.

The Uniform grinned. 'Happy to do that, sarge.'

But as Gil walked quickly with the cyclist pushing his bike, he risked a glance at the reporter. And got a huge and leering grin in return.

CHAPTER FIFTEEN

RHYS TOOK the call from Gil shortly after they'd passed the Pont Abram roundabout on the A48 on their way back to HQ. That call resulted in DCI Warlow circling the roundabout at Cross Hands and heading back the way they'd come, to Five Roads. They arrived to not so much a circus as a mini carnival outside the community hall.

Three response vehicles no less, a small knot of onlookers, and a huddled group of very sheepish-looking cyclists shivering together and looking very sorry for themselves. An hour later, with the evening now fully dark, Warlow sat in the hall's kitchen making a call to Jess.

'So, have we found our man?' Jess's face peered out of the phone's screen. Warlow had set it up to lean against a silver kettle with a plate in front of it to prevent it from sliding down. He recognised the crack high up on the wall behind Jess. And so he should. Corkscrewing around in his chair to stare at that crack was one of his favourite pastimes when he retreated to the SIO room at HQ for a bit of cogitation during a case.

'We found *a* man, that's for certain. One Patrick McMartin, mid-seventies, about the same era as Ronnie

Probert. Ex opencast miner, long retired. Still has a County Mayo accent as broad as shomeone who shall remain namelesh's backshide. He came over here to work and stayed. Lost his wife, family moved away, and now lives alone just off the cycle path at Cynheidre.'

'So, why did whoever catch him think he was the Signalman?'

Being it was a video call, Warlow felt enabled enough to roll his eyes. 'Because the sodding press has put the idea into everyone's heads. Admittedly, Patrick looks a bit like a down and out. Never looked up the word barber in the dictionary, doesn't shave, wears a striped-brown suit under a navvy's jacket that Noah's chief zookeeper wore on the Ark, and cycles every other day to visit an old pal in a nursing home between Horeb and Sylen. He does half of that route via the cycle path to stay off the roads. You've heard of beachcombers?'

'I have.'

'Pat is a cycle-path comber. That means his panniers are stuffed with half-empty shopping bags and an umbrella and a variety of things that make him look as if he's on the way to a camping site for tatterdemalions.'

Jess raised her eyebrows.

'One of Gil's words, and it's a good one. Had Rhys searching for tattered medallions for ten minutes, though.'

'Oh dear.'

'Yes. The three musketeers on bikes followed him to an old railway siding shed. He was brandishing a fence post and threatening to take on all comers when Gil arrived.'

'What a waste of sodding time. No injuries, though?'

'Nothing serious. Gil calmed things down. The cyclists, three kids from the CCTA at Llanelli on their way home to Tumble, apologised. But Patrick had fallen off his bike and hurt his shoulder. He's been whisked off to Glangwili.

Catrin is with him now. His bike got a bent front fork, but the boys will fix that. Least they could do.'

'Think he'll press charges?'

'No. He's old school. Gil said his war cry when he appeared was, "Come near me, and I'll *shtick* you with my *shpear*."'

Jess huffed out an almost silent laugh. 'What is it with the Mayo accent slurring the s's?'

'All to do with their long shea shore, apparently.'

Jess smiled. A tired thing, but it lit up the afternoon. Warlow, meanwhile, massaged both temples with his fingers. 'And to cap it all, that hyena, Lane, was here in the middle of the scrum, lapping it up with a grin like a cat from Cheshire. Catrin says he's been hanging about all afternoon and, while everybody was distracted, she saw him at a hall window taking photos of the interior, the shit. With the lights on, it's like Santa's grotto.'

'Bloody press,' Jess said. 'How did it go with the brother?'

'It didn't. Terry Probert is a bitter man. But we'll keep all that for tomorrow if nothing earth-shattering is happening on your end.'

'No, the earth remains in one piece.'

'Molly, okay?'

'Lovesick. Mainly for Cadi, not Bryn.'

'I'll bring her over on the weekend. But, for now, I'm sending the troops home.'

'Good idea. I'll monitor social media for Lane's big size tens.'

Warlow signed off the call and walked into the hall. The tables groaned under Ronnie Probert's flotsam. He glanced again at the windows. Anyone could see what was on display from the car park. He walked to the door and stared out into the damp gloom. A van, driven by one of the cyclists' fathers, was picking them all up.

Warlow had chatted with the boys. He did not dress them down; that would've been unfair. Instead, he thanked them for being good citizens but warned them about vigilantism. That kind of thing only ever got you into serious trouble. But he also told them not to worry too much about it, and he was sure that Patrick was going to be fine. They seemed like good lads, uncomfortable at finding themselves in a situation that had quickly soured.

The report from Catrin at the hospital was that Patrick had a bruised acromioclavicular joint, but nothing serious. Rest and then a bit of physio was all that was needed. She also said that Patrick told her he was glad Gil turned up because he hadn't wanted to get into trouble for banjaxing one of the boys. Warlow'd liked that. Not of this generation was Patrick, where clamping on to victimhood and compensation was more often than not priority number one.

From the hall doorway, he waved to Rhys. The DC jogged over.

'Ready? We can leave all the rest to Uniforms. Someone is going to be here all night, I take it?'

'Yes, sir. We've got a night watchman.'

'Right, home it is, then. You'll have the drone footage for us to look at tomorrow, right?'

'Yep, Steff's uploaded it.'

'Good.'

They walked to the Jeep, and Warlow fired her up. 'We'll have a lot to sift through. It'll be a busy day.'

'I wouldn't have said today was exactly quiet, sir.'

Warlow glanced over at Rhys as he tried to find room for his long legs. 'Still have that Snickers bar?'

Rhys grimaced. 'No, sir. Polished that off.'

'And I didn't even get a bite.'

Rhys flinched. 'I didn't know you liked the caramel, nougat and peanut combo, sir.'

'No, well, you never asked.'

'Next time, sir,' Rhys said, genuine remorse on his face.

'Never mind next time. Open the glove compartment, Detective Constable.'

Rhys did and murmured, 'Wow,' as he reached in and removed a four-bar multipack of the aforementioned confectionery.

'Now, if you'd be so kind as to unwrap one for me… and one for yourself, of course,' Warlow said. 'And then find something decent on the radio so I can chomp in peace. That is if you're up to it. Two Snickers in one day might be—'

'Nothing, sir. Five's my record. On a camping trip once. I'd eaten all my sandwiches by half ten in the morning.'

'A graph of your insulin levels must look like the Himalayas. Right, open away. Sugar may be bad for you, but by God, sometimes it's the only thing that hits the spot.'

———

GIL MET Catrin in the A&E waiting room at Glangwili Hospital. The unit was a more recent addition to a hospital in dire need of a revamp. Plans for a new billion-pound build further west had been circulating, like the smell around a leaky drain, for years.

Whenever Gil drove in through the hospital entrance, he could almost hear the sound of the can rattling as it was kicked yet again up the road by whichever Welsh Assembly department held the purse strings. He'd lost count of the number of public consultations he'd had through the post. It wasn't as if the Assembly had any excuses. There hadn't been a change of party in Wales since dinosaurs walked the Earth. In the meantime, while stegosaurus yelled at triceratops across the floor at the Senedd, the old hospital was left to creak along.

Gil found Catrin sitting on one of the plastic chairs at the back on the right of the reception area. Away from the more infectious occupants, sniffling and coughing a concoction of viruses into the air. A child with its arm in a sling wailed quietly at the front.

'Funny thing,' Gil said as Catrin looked up from her phone. 'My daughters asked me if I ever got to watch that series, The Walking Dead on Netflix. I said no, but I've been to Glangwili A&E several times. Same difference.'

'Thanks for coming,' Catrin said.

'No problem. You get off. I'll run Patrick home.'

'I could have done that.'

'I know, but I found him, so I'll deliver him back to the bosom of his bungalow. Finders keepers.'

Catrin stood up. 'What a disaster.'

'Could have been worse. Could have been someone else who found him and decided on a citizen's arrest. And Patrick could have been carrying a concealed weapon. Come to think of it, that umbrella he had had several loose spokes.'

Catrin nodded. 'How did the Wolf take it?'

Her reference to Warlow held no malice. Wolf stemmed in part from the DCI's tendency, in an investigation, to be alone. Either at the crime scene or even in the SIO office. As he so often pointed out, there was a lot to be said for simply sitting down, or walking about, and thinking. That, plus the link with his beloved property in Nevern, made the analogy an easy one.

'Oh, you know him, stomped about for a bit, but he was good with the kids who wrongly singled out Patrick as the Signalman. Wasn't too hard on them.'

'Well, he's had two boys of his own. He knows what they're like.'

'Indeed. Now, where is the man of the moment?'

Catrin nodded towards reception. 'Just waiting for discharge. They're writing a letter to his doctor for him to take along when he makes an appointment.' Catrin shook her head.

Gil picked up on it. 'What?'

'That bloody Lane bloke. I hope he didn't take a photo of Patrick. He's been through enough.'

'Is he with a newspaper at all now, or freelance?' Gil asked.

'He does a lot of online stuff. There's a ton of that these days. Instant as opposed to yesterday's news.'

Gil groaned. 'Jess said she'd keep a weather eye on things.'

'She means Molly will keep a weather eye on things.'

'Having a Gen alpha to hand has its uses.'

The secret door that led to the innards of A&E opened and a brown-suited Patrick walked out, the jacket hanging off his left shoulder with that arm in a sling, the other linked in with a nurse in blue scrubs.

'There you are, Pat,' Gil said. 'We thought they'd sold your body for dissection.'

The nurse glared at Gil. 'Don't say such a horrible thing.'

'Ignore him,' Catrin said. 'Pat, how are you feeling?'

'Good. Do you have my bike, by any chance?'

'It's being repaired,' Gil explained. 'Not that you'll be able to ride it for a few days.'

'A week,' the nurse added with a note of admonishment. 'Got a bit shaken up, didn't you, Pat?'

'You should see the other blokes,' Gil said.

'So, how'm I gettin' home?'

'Your carriage awaits,' Gil said. 'I'm running you back.'

Patrick looked into Gil's face and then into Catrin's. 'If

I had a choice, now, I know which of the two of you I'd be pickin'.'

Catrin grinned and turned away. 'See you tomorrow, Sergeant Jones.'

'Indeed.' Gil watched her leave before turning back. 'You're stuck with me.'

Patrick nodded and dropped his voice. 'Truth be told, it's you I'd have chosen. She's a bit stern, her.'

'Still working on her standup routine, is Sergeant Richards. Heart's in the right place, though. Even if it is made of stone.'

The nurse supporting Patrick grinned. 'You're terrible.'

'Car's outside, if you're happy to help him out?'

'Of course,' the nurse said.

'Let's get this show on the road, Patrick. And on the way, we might even call for some fish and chips for your supper.'

'What'll it cost me?' Pat asked with a sly look at the nurse.

'Nothing more than a chat. No singing involved. I'm sure you could write a book about the odd things you see on that cycle path.'

'I've seen my share of strange things. Once saw a fox carrying a child's toy in its mouth.'

'Great.' Gil turned to the nurse. 'Sounds like the meds you gave him were the good ones, not the European imports.'

The nurse, still grinning, shook her head.

Gil crossed to the car park and opened the car door. Once Pat was seated, Gil thanked the nurse and got in himself. 'Now, one question before we set off. The fish and chips. Cod or hake?'

'Quite fanshy a bit of both,' Pat said.

'Well said that man. We'll go for a child's portion of each, a full size on the chips, and don't spare the vinegar.'

CHAPTER SIXTEEN

WARLOW PICKED Cadi up at seven-thirty from the Dawes. The welcome he received was, as usual, effusive. Only a notch or two below that of a few days ago, on his return from Australia. He often wondered how dogs measured time if they did at all. Being a Labrador, Cadi had an inbuilt clock that told her when food was due. But during his weeks away, had she scratched the days into a wall with her nail? Six vertical strokes and one diagonal to mark off the week? Or had time flown by like the wag of a tail.

He'd tried asking her but got only a look from those soft brown eyes. A look from a brain wondering if there had been any hint of a 'walk' or 'food' (*bwyd*) anywhere near the vicinity of the words that Warlow had used.

Winter was a sod for dogs. February had demonstrated nothing perceptible as an extension of daylight hours, though glib terms like 'the nights are drawing out' were often bandied about. Warlow still got up in the dark and came home in the dark. Added to that was the fact that the weather was wet more than it was dry, or so it seemed. Of course, there was always the beach to walk on. There, wet was a part of the deal, anyway.

But that would have to wait for the weekend. The Dawes would've taken Cadi out with their Lab, Bouncer, but still Warlow hankered after a stroll to stretch his legs almost as much as the dog.

Not tonight.

'Right, what can we rustle up for supper, eh, girl?'

He'd done some shopping but had not yet organised much. Tom had bought him a great cookbook that only used roasting tins, but this evening he didn't want to fuss with much preparation, so he stole a recipe for baked avocado, substituted Roquefort with Perl Las – a creamy Welsh blue – and used pecans and hazelnuts instead of walnut which he found bitter. He added raisins to the mix, then stuffed the lot into the hollows of a halved avocado and stuck the lot in the oven. Fifteen minutes later, when the topping had browned, he drizzled a little olive oil with lemon juice and paprika over the top and added a couple of crumbly crackers on the side.

A little after 8pm, with Cadi sitting at his side and a small lake of dog drool accumulating between her paws, Warlow ate under the watchful and ever hopeful dog's gaze as she sat two metres away. He rarely gave her titbits but occasionally gave in and yielded up a morsel. In return, she'd learned to be patient and look pretty.

Two things she did very well.

He made some tea and retired to his sunroom, now a dark room, with a notebook, to make sense of the day's events. Or at least attempt to. He managed one headline after five minutes.

BURGLARY or NOT?

That was when Jess's text came through via WhatsApp. The message was one word:

Hyenas.

But with it was an image, barely recognisable because of its size in the app window, and a link beneath. He held the phone up to look closer at it. There was the Five Roads Community Hall, and there were the three response vehicles and there, walking through the little melee, was Gil Jones helping Patrick McMartin along.

With an already sinking heart, Warlow clicked the link. It took him to the page of the West Wales Post. A newspaper Warlow remembered being in existence for as long as he could remember. But the little mini billboards advertising the physical newspaper with headlines pasted on a swing board outside newsagents and garages, he had not seen for many years. The explanation for that he found on the website where it announced that the West Wales Post was now a digital-only news outlet. The page was simple, a white background and front and centre, an advertisement for equity release. He scrolled past that and was glad to see the ad not following him as he did so like so many bloody did.

Beneath that were columns of images and brief headlines outlining stories. Warlow found the one he was after right underneath the leader about how putting out too many rubbish sacks for collection might end up in a fine.

But there, below, sat the image Jess had sent him and next to it, the text.

"Police waste time on innocent cyclists in hunt for Ronnie's killer.".

Warlow cringed. 'Christ, Lane, you utter…'

Next to him, Cadi tilted her head. The movement was enough to make Warlow bite his tongue. Something he had to do more than once as he read the story.

In an attempt at finding the people responsible for the death of rugby hero Ronnie Probert, police today brought in a suspect for questioning to the Inquiry Room set up at Five Roads Community Hall. Throughout the day, officers ferried evidence for inspection from

Probert's house a short distance away in Horeb. It is understood that detectives were hoping to find some clues that might link the pensioner's death to the burglary, where he was brutally attacked and left severely injured. Ronnie Probert died from his injuries five days later.

But today, in a bizarre twist, officers were called to the disused railway line that is now a cycle path running from Tumble to Swiss Valley, where cyclists had spotted a man acting suspiciously. Police reacted by rushing to the scene, and the man is seen here being brought in for questioning by a detective.

Warlow looked again at the image and clicked it open. Gil was in shot with his arm holding onto Patrick McMartin as they walked towards the hall. Gil appeared to be grinning, not an unusual expression for the sergeant, but unfortunate in the context of this image. In short, it looked like Gil was having a rare old time of it. Perhaps someone had asked him a question, or said something, and he'd responded to it in his usual bluff way. Warlow was also pretty sure that this would not have been the only image Lane, or the editor of this clickbait, could have chosen.

There was more drivel further down.

A police spokesperson later said that the man was released without charge and thanked the public for their vigilance. The community hall has become a museum of memory for Ronnie Probert, whose legendary exploits on the field led to an OBE in 1991. But after losing his wife some years ago, he had become increasingly reclusive.

Another image had been posted up. Catrin had been spot-on in her concerns over Lane. This, a grainy shot of the trestle tables inside the hall, laden with boxes and papers and jerseys in untidy heaps. With the caption: *Ronnie Probert's treasure trove of memories.*

Warlow shook his head. He, like Lane, knew what effect this would have. The magpies would come and gawk, hoping to catch their own glimpse of something… anything, titillating. He was glad they had some security in the hall and that the house was still a crime scene. He turned his eyes down to the last paragraph.

Chief Superintendent Bleddyn Drinkwater, responding to questions, said, 'Everyone involved is one hundred percent committed to finding whoever did this and bringing them to justice. Ronnie Probert was a much-loved member of the community, and this was a brutal and prolonged attack that resulted, ultimately, in Mr Probert's death. We're exploring several lines of inquiry, but if anyone has any information, please contact the hotline we've established.'

When asked if these lines of inquiry included patrolling the cycle path on the lookout for the mysterious Signalman, Superintendent Drinkwater refused to comment further. The officer involved in apprehending the suspect shown in the photograph, Sergeant Gil Jones, was not available for comment either. The community remains shocked and disappointed by the lack of progress. One resident said, 'Dragging people in from the cycle path sounds a bit desperate to me. We had some thefts from the shed last year, and they were reported, but nothing came of it. Could be those same thieves came back for more. Either way, I'm locking all my doors from now on.'

The hunt for those responsible continues.

Dyfed Powys Police Hotline number is 08081 570336

Warlow blew out his cheeks. He toyed with contacting Gil, but instead contented himself with returning Jess's text:

Journalism at its finest

Might as well have waved a red rag.

I'm too polite to use the words that come to mind.

Bet they're not as bad as mine.

At least they got the number out.

Can't wait.

THERE WERE advantages and disadvantages to providing a contact number. It increased the response rate, but it also gave trigger-happy idiots another number with which to complain about next door's cat defecating on their lawns.

Hard to believe, but all too true.

Warlow abandoned the notebook and found some telly to watch. No wine tonight. He'd made a promise to himself to limit consumption to the weekends after over-doing it on holiday. But after reading Lane's trite crap, he had to make a genuine effort to avoid pouring a glass of Appassimento.

He flicked through the channels but didn't fancy any drama this evening. He'd had enough of that all day. He settled instead for a catchup of the weekend's rugby on iPlayer and a roundup of the Six Nations' competition from the weekend. Hardly likely to cheer him up, given the National Team's performance; still, he'd not seen all the games.

But, after the first set of highlights, the presenter put on her serious face and turned her attention to the death of Ronnie Probert. Ralph's prediction was spot on. There could be no escape from this outpouring of grief. The next thing Warlow saw was the "try" from that "game" all those years ago, before the presenter chatted to some of the remaining players from that era in a glut of reminiscences.

Here was Warlow, trying to forget, only to have the case rammed right back down his throat. Still, cases tended to be all-consuming, and this one especially. He watched for a while, fetched his meds from the box he kept them in in the kitchen and threw down his Anti-Retroviral.

Just the one pill still.

'Belt and braces,' as his HIV doctor, Emmerson, liked to quip. 'To keep you suppressed.'

He was a lucky man. To have been diagnosed and treated early and with modern drugs. There was every chance he'd remain unaffected.

Physically, at least.

But it never left him, that knowledge, like the virus itself, lurking at the back of his mind. He recognised it as a psychological barrier to… what exactly, Evan?

Other people?

He motioned Cadi to him and fondled her ears. There was a time before he'd gone to Australia when he thought he'd clambered over that barrier. But time away, perhaps too much time to think, had let him slip back on the wrong side of it. No reason for that. Simply his own demons.

'Or maybe the jet-lag, eh, cariad?'

The dog licked his hand.

'Right, let's get you a supper *biscuit,*' he used the French version of the word, brainwashed by Gil, 'and out for a pee and then, I think, we hit the farter, as they say where I've just come from.'

Alun's coarse slang for going to bed had caused great jollity when Warlow first heard it. That a bed, these days thanks to duvets, was indeed a "fartsack" which the Australians had transmogrified, in that way they had, into something even slicker like "farter" simply made it more hilarious.

Cadi got up, tail wagging, and followed Warlow to the back door while he watched and let the February air kiss his face with its cold, dark promise.

CHAPTER SEVENTEEN

WARLOW THOUGHT he'd be the first one in the following morning. He got up early, left early, but ambled into the Incident Room to discover Gil already there. Jess arrived two minutes later.

All three officers stood in their coats until Jess said, 'Right. Should we discuss the elephant in the room?'

Gil dropped his voice. 'Oh, ma'am, that's Magda, one of the secretaries. They say it's hormonal.'

Jess shifted her lower jaw to one side and sighed. Gil's attempt at deflection wasn't bad, and of course, there may well have been a Magda, but she was most definitely not in the room at that moment. 'I'm talking about the West Wales Post, as if you didn't know.'

'Admittedly, not a very flattering shot of me, I'm afraid,' Gil said. 'Lighting was all wrong.'

'You don't seem anxious about it, Gil.' Warlow shrugged off his coat.

'What's there to be worried about? I was there, and so was Pat McMartin. At the instant of that image, the bugger had just told me, out of the blue, that you should never ask a man from Mayo to teach a dog to sit.'

Warlow fought a grin. 'That's why you were grinning?'

'Shertainly was.'

Warlow sighed. 'The fact is, Lane is an arse, end of. We can only hope that something else happens on the patch to pull the misery-chaser away.'

Nods all round. Schadenfreude be damned.

'But you and Lane have history, don't you?' Jess asked.

'We do,' Gil said. 'He's always had a thing about the money we spent on Op Alice.'

'What the hell did he find to criticise in an operation to flush out paedophiles and child abusers?' Jess looked incredulous.

'Resource allocation was his schtick. He's like a dog with a bone. Sees us as capitalist stooges to beat the Assembly with, and by proxy, Westminster. Touch of the Bolshevik about Lane. But he loves the sound of his own value for money, fishwife voice, too. He considers himself a champion of the people. And yes, I am surprised he doesn't wear his underpants over his trousers.'

'Still an arse,' Warlow said.

Right at that moment, and as if on a cue from the gods, given the content of Warlow's last sentence, the door to the Incident Room opened and in walked a uniformed Chief Superintendent Drinkwater with a face like loud and bone-shaking thunder. He stood, gave Jess a curt nod, glared at Gil, then nodded towards the SIO room.

'Quick word, Evan.'

Warlow followed the Chief Superintendent through the Incident Room to the slightly larger-than-a-cupboard SIO office.

'Close the door,' Drinkwater said, already with hands clasped behind his back. Warlow complied and sat in his usual chair with Drinkwater facing him on the other side of the desk.

'You saw the news, I take it?'

'That earthquake in Turkey? Yes, bloody tragic—'

'I meant the local news. Your sergeant out there laughing like a bloody demented horse, as it were.'

Warlow quirked an eyebrow, knowing full well he'd be using that phrase before the day was out, and toying with asking the Chief Super if he minded.

'McMartin, the man Gil was helping, he's a bit of a comedian, sir.'

'I don't care if he is Michael bloody Macintosh.'

'Tyre, sir.'

'What?' Drinkwater blustered.

Warlow shook his head. 'Not important.'

Drinkwater's glare burned with fury. Warlow wondered how far someone's eyes could move forward in their sockets before popping out. 'What is important, my reason for being here, is to state that you do not laugh like a bloody baboon in front of a camera. Those are not good optics.'

Warlow couldn't help but grimace on hearing the word optics, even if he just about kept his face straight. He despised it almost as much as the word "stable" which, when used in a hospital setting, always set his teeth on edge.

'Gil wasn't expecting anyone to take his photograph at that point,' he explained.

'Christ,' Drinkwater spat. 'It looks like he was bloody enjoying himself. We need to take this seriously.'

'We do. Of course, we do. And one candid shot by a parasite like Lane—'

Drinkwater interrupted Warlow with a harsh whisper. 'Upsets people. Upsets me. Upsets everyone.'

'Other than clapping Lane in irons…'

'Can we?'

'For being an annoying git? No.'

'Is your sergeant likely to bump into him again?'

'I expect he'll make a point of it.'

'Then, for God's sake, tell him to be less… in your face, as it were.'

Warlow thought of the big sergeant sitting outside. 'Gil doesn't do unobtrusive very well, sir.'

Drinkwater's lips moved, but no words came out. Eventually, what emerged was a harrumph. Warlow couldn't remember, other than in books, ever hearing anyone do that. 'Are we making progress?' Drinkwater asked then, in a more conciliatory tone.

'Several leads. We're about to do a briefing. You're welcome to stay.'

'No. I have fires to fight. The local Assembly Member is due in at nine. I need two coffees before that.' He turned, opened the door and, without looking back, said, 'Keep me updated.'

'Will do,' Warlow said and added, in a voice only he could hear, 'I'll put a Post-it note on my screen to remind me.'

————

AFTER THE INTERLUDE WITH DRINKWATER, Warlow checked his inbox, found nothing of interest, and walked back out into the Incident Room to find the team assembled and tea brewed. Everyone appeared to be busy, eyes on the screen, or scribbling on pads, except for Rhys, whose eyes kept flitting down to his mobile face up on the desk next to him. As if he was willing it to ring.

'Chief Super lending his support, was he?' Jess asked.

'Discussing the colour scheme for the new meditative room on the third floor.'

'Meditative as in a space for employees to relax in when irritated by coworkers' distracting whistling, loud phone conversations, or chewing gum,' Gil asked.

Warlow nodded. 'You read the article in The Times on

the weekend too, I see. Soothing workplace angst, I think the headline was. Meditative rooms, my arse.'

Jess chortled. 'You'd never be out of it.'

Warlow caught a smile from Catrin and had half expected Rhys to pipe up with a naïve question like him not having heard of a meditative room. Or why had no one told him, and what colour was it really going to be? But the DC kept quiet. In fact, he didn't even look up. Warlow felt slightly irked.

'Okay, let's get this show on the road,' he said. 'Jess?'

The DI pushed back from her desk and held up a copy of *Nowhere to Ron*. 'I am aware that this is not a primary concern, but I have contacted the sister of the player who perished during the drinking game where Ronnie Probert was the games master.'

'And?'

'We have a Zoom call booked this afternoon.'

'How did she seem when you told her about Ronnie?' Catrin asked.

'She already knew. She lives in Warwickshire, so it's reached there. Since it's national news, that's not surprising. If you're asking if I sense any inappropriate jubilation, the answer's no.'

'As you say, not top of the list, but if you talk to her, we can tie off that thread.' It was way too early for biscuits, but the tea was hot and satisfying when Warlow sipped at it. 'Gil? I think everyone knows about McMartin. Lessons learned?'

Gil looked up. 'A couple. One is to avoid the bloodsucker Geraint Lane at all costs. The second is that Pat, who is a frequent flyer on the cycle path, actually believes that there is a Signalman.'

'What?' Jess barked out her disbelief.

'Pat's on that path three times a week and on weekends. He says that sometimes towards dark he's seen him.'

'Photos?' Catrin asked.

Gil's glare of scepticism told her that Patrick McMartin was not a camera-toting, or even a mobile-phone-toting, kind of guy.

'What about a description?'

'Nothing much. Dark figure usually spotted in poor light. Sometimes Pat says a red light moves in the darkness.'

'But couldn't that be any cyclist?' Catrin sounded unimpressed.

'Pat said the red light is a warning signal for the trains of the past.'

'I'm not buying it,' Catrin said.

'I'm only telling you what Pat McMartin told me.'

'Funny things can happen to your imagination in the dark, though,' Catrin observed.

Gil hummed a few bars of the Twilight Zone theme tune under his breath.

'It's a sizeable area to search. I don't mean the path, but the land either side of it,' Warlow said. 'But it's something we can consider if our other leads go nowhere. Catrin, what have you got?'

'We've almost finished getting everything out of Ronnie's house, sir. There's a lot. I think they're in the attic today. I've already begun cataloguing with the help of Sandra Griffiths. She's a godsend. Gil said he'd help, too.'

'And I will. Got side-tracked by Pat McMartin and Lane yesterday.'

'Yes, Lane,' Warlow muttered. 'I don't need to tell you, no contact after yesterday. He is officially persona non grata. If he asks you anything, refer him to the press officer. Otherwise, Catrin, hopefully by end of day, you'll have got stuck into Ronnie's stuff?'

'With Gil's help, I'm sure we could make good

progress.' She affected a bright smile. 'Oh, and we've requested the usual phone and banking records.'

Fishing. He didn't like it. He much preferred a targeted approach, but fish they must here.

'Okay. Let's consider our prime suspect.' Warlow walked to the Gallery and the image of Jordan Nicholas, nineteen years old, taken eight months ago during an arrest for affray during the hot weeks of July.

It was not a flattering photograph. Jordan's hair was plastered to his forehead with sweat, his eyes glazed, his cheeks flared red by acne. Apparently, he'd decided, after some recreational drugs, to turn the garage at the front of the house in Carway into an impromptu rave and attacked a neighbour who had the temerity to complain.

'Jordan was not at home when we called. Or rather, was not at home when we eventually got to his bedroom, though I suspect he was until his mother gave him the heads up. What we now need to do is dig up a list of known associates, girlfriends – although I think that's unlikely – haunts, the usual. The mother is a registered addict, but there is a brother who has moved back to the house and somehow seems to function amidst the chaos that is the Nicholas family unit. Jordan Nicholas was present at Probert's property while scaffolding was erected, that we've had confirmed by Castell Scaffolding who employ Jordan on an ad hoc basis.'

'I have his file, sir,' Rhys said in a subdued voice.

'Okay, we'll develop a plan of attack. Talking to him is our key priority.'

'What about Probert's brother?' Jess asked.

'Good question. Bad blood. But I think it's worth looking at the nephew, Ralph Probert. Something about him felt a bit off. Agreed, Rhys?'

The DC, whose eyes had drifted down to his phone yet again, looked up. 'Yeah, sure, I can do that.'

'Do what? I haven't asked you to do anything yet.'

'I thought you were discussing Ralph Probert, sir.'

'I was. And by some miracle, you've tuned in to that. But I was going to ask DI Allanby if she'd lead on that since you're going to be too busy chasing Jordan Nicholas. When you finally decide to join us.'

'Sorry, sir. Something's come up.'

'Not team selection again, is it?' Catrin asked with a tilt at Rhys's rugby woes.

'No, sarge,' Rhys said, his voice unusually flat. 'It's my dad. He was rushed to hospital last night. He's on the coronary care unit at Glangwili.'

A very long five seconds of silence followed.

'Bloody hell, Rhys,' Gil said. 'Why didn't you say?'

Rhys looked around at the team's faces, all registering the same shock and concern until he settled on Warlow's. 'Sir, you always said we had to leave our baggage outside the Incident Room door. I didn't think it was appropriate to bring it up.'

Warlow, still standing, nodded slowly. 'You're right. And you sitting there is probably the most professional thing I've seen in months. But there is baggage and there is family. Never the twain. Not when it comes to illness. Now get off your arse and get down to Glangwili.'

But Rhys didn't move. 'Sir, my mum's there. They don't allow more than one visitor, and the fact is he's okay, just waiting for a bed in Morriston. They're going to do another scan there and decide what needs to… be done. At the moment he's quite—'

'Don't say it, the "s" word,' Warlow warned. 'But he's okay?'

'Yeah, just come as a bit of shock, you know. 3am phone call from my mother. But I'd rather keep busy. They say he might be in CCU for a couple of days until Morriston calls him down.'

Warlow stared at him for several long seconds, toying with the idea of sending him away, but then, sometimes being alone could be worse than being around people. Distraction was often a useful medicine.

'Right, your shout. You leave whenever you want to. Meantime, what about this drone footage?'

CHAPTER EIGHTEEN

THE DRONE TOOK off from a part of the path a hundred metres north of the property, rising above the fields and the small patch of forest before travelling south over the house itself. Warlow asked for the footage to be paused several times, but it was clear after only a few moments that access along the side of an enclosure and under the cover of trees led to a hedgerow and some rough land directly behind the garden of Gorffwys, Probert's house. Warlow had already heard Gil explaining to Jess the irony of the translation being 'resting place' and the pronunciation as Gor as in gorgeous, ffwys as in foo-ees. Next to it, another patch of land looked ripe for development at some point.

The drone then flew east over the village of Horeb itself, picking up the cycle path south of Horeb Road. The drone followed the cycle route as far as a brick tower.

'What's that?' Jess asked.

'Horeb brickworks,' Rhys said. After unburdening himself of his concerns over his dad, Rhys had recovered somewhat. 'Built in 1907, ma'am. Listed building.

Chimney stack and kiln still there, plus lots of cooling chambers.'

'Good place to hide out,' Gil said.

'Not the only place along this route.'

They watched the footage twice until Warlow called it. 'Rhys, good work. Please thank Steffan for us.'

'Since we got him that souped-up model, sir, he's happy to help anytime.'

'Good to know,' Warlow said. 'But what this tells us is that if I was burgling Probert's house, that is the way I'd come in. From an unlit cycle path that would be deserted that time of night, across the empty fields, in through the rear and back out the same way. No one will have seen anything.'

'Implies a bit of local knowledge, though,' Gil said.

'There is that. So, no change in our approach. Gil, you and Catrin get back out to the hall. I'm going to have a chat with Bob Salini about Jordan Nicholas after I've made a few calls. Weekend is looming. I'd like another Vespers before we all shoot off to our villas in the Riviera this pm.'

He left them to it and retreated to the SIO room. The first call he made was to Rhys's mother.

'Mrs Harries, this is DCI Warlow. Rhys has just told us about his dad. How is he?'

It wasn't a long conversation, and Mrs Harries confirmed everything Rhys had told them with little to add. Warlow clarified that Rhys was free to go whenever he wanted to, but she, like her stoical son, insisted there was no need and that it was a waiting game. Now that they had Meirion Harries's blood pressure under control and him on a monitor, he was sitting up in bed, feeling bored. Warlow told her to ring him if she needed to and hung up.

Rhys's parents had him when they'd been older. That put his mum in her early sixties and his father a little older. Warlow remembered when his parents were alive how his own father, his health blighted by pneumoconiosis at an early age, succumbed to the cigarettes he'd smoked for forty years, and his mother just a few years later, to a heart condition. Both had suffered chronic illness, and the strange sensation he'd experienced of being in the middle, worrying about your kids on the one hand, and fretting over your parents on the other, had left him emotionally exhausted. And that was before having to deal with Jeez Denise, his alcoholic wife. So, he felt for Rhys, who at least didn't have any kids to keep him up at night.

That done, Warlow searched for Bob Salini's number and sent him a text.

———

GIL LET CATRIN DRIVE. Not much point in taking two cars.

'What about Rhys, then?' Gil said as they headed south off the A48 towards Five Roads. 'Such a dark horse.'

'Really. I think the exact opposite. He's an open book.'

'Let's agree to differ. How about Black Beauty? That's a book about a dark horse. Win, win.'

'I don't think we can go around calling him Black Beauty,' Catrin said. 'You'd get into all kinds of trouble saying that.'

'Don't you start. My daughters give me enough grief. They've bought into the let's-not-risk-offending school of thought for kids' books. They're buying the nice-nice versions of Roald Dahl where they've banned words like horse-faced? Come on… I know many people who are exactly that. There's John Shergar for a start, not to mention Winnie Red Rum. Fat? No, now it's "affected by obesity". Blue men have to be blue people. I call Foxtrot, foxtrot, Sierra.'

'You don't think the world would be a better place?' Catrin asked.

'What? If we all tried to be nice to one another? I'll try that next time I'm in Llanelli city centre at two in the morning and some scrote high on speed calls me a fat, old, ugly charlie, uniform, November, tango. I'll take them to one side and explain that what he should have said was: affected by obesity, temporally challenged, plain-featured organ of reproduction. Though, of course, that's up for grabs, too. Not that I'm suggesting anyone should grab their, or anyone else's organ of reproduction.'

'I'm so glad I asked.'

'Pandora's box. And that's not a euphemism for an organ of reproduction either.'

When they got to the car park at the community hall, as well as a response vehicle and the Uniform guarding entry, a couple of white vans had their rear doors open facing the hall's open doors. Across from them, as before, on the far side of the car park, Geraint Lane sat sideways in the front seat of his Renault, phone in hand, observing.

'Can we insist he doesn't take photos?' Catrin asked.

'Don't think so. But we could pour petrol over him and set fire to the bugger.'

Catrin shot him a warning glance.

'Only kidding. That must have been a dream I had. Ignore the organ of reproduction and walk in, head held high.'

'I always walk like that,' Catrin said.

'You do. I, on the other hand, prefer the Columbo slouch. I feel it has more gravitas.'

'More gravity, I'd say, in that you're having to fight it.'

'Very good, Sergeant Richards. Glad to see you're responding to the challenge of attempting to match wit with wit.'

'Matching wit with something that rhymes with wit, definitely.'

They pulled up, parked, and got out of the car. Neither

of them acknowledged Lane. Inside the hall, the tables were now officially overflowing.

'Christ, it's like a jumble sale in Bedlam. Would you like me to start anywhere in particular?' Gil asked.

'No, dive in,' Catrin said. 'Let me know when you come up for air. I'm heading for the stuff that's come in from the attic. Who knows what secrets await?'

'You've been reading too many books, that's what I think.'

————

JESS REREAD the chapter in Ronnie Probert's autobiography where he described the tragic details surrounding the death of Charles Unsworth, the player who succumbed to alcohol intoxication. It made for uncomfortable reading.

At the time it happened, Ronnie had not yet broken through into first-class rugby and was still playing for local teams. An end-of-season tour had taken him across the border to Gloucestershire and Warwickshire.

After playing a team known as Old Rutherians in a friendly, both teams took over the players' bar in the club-house with drinking games and a mock court empowered with inflicting fines.

And Charlie's fine had been to drink a double vodka, a double rum, and a double whiskey. All that after several pints of bitter. Other people had paid similar fines for such crimes as having a bad haircut, wearing too flashy a shirt, or scoring too many points during the game. That had been Charlie's crime at the kangaroo court.

He'd paid his dues, throwing back the alcohol. Some of his fellow players had thrown up after theirs. Paradoxically, had Charlie, he might still be alive. Unfortunately, he had not regurgitated what he'd drunk. The alcohol had stayed in his system and had, instead, suppressed his respiratory system enough so that he did not wake up from sleep the next day or ever again.

The coroner's report showed a blood alcohol level of 410 milligrams per 100 millilitres. Five times over the legal drive limit. The cause of death was hypoxic brain injury brought on by cardiorespiratory arrest.

Charlie's sister had been ten when her brother died. Nine years younger than him and nine years younger than Ronnie Probert.

The face that appeared on Jess's screen when the Zoom call connected showed an attractive woman with fashionably cut grey hair, styled and coloured so that the grey looked almost like a fashion decision rather than yielding to the march of time.

'Thanks for talking to me, Mrs Lock,' Jess said.

'Josie, please.'

'Josie, thanks for this.'

'That's alright. You said it was about Ronnie Probert?'

'Your brother, Charlie. His death features in Ronnie Probert's book. I presume Charlie wasn't married or had a partner when he died?'

'No… he was just a kid… … That's a bit of an odd question, isn't it?'

Jess knew she had to tread carefully here. 'It is, and I'm sorry to have to ask.'

'Charlie was only nineteen. He had a girlfriend but no children. Obviously, not at that age.'

'How about you, Josie?'

'I'm divorced. Two daughters…' Irritation clouded Josie's features. Behind her and in shot was a window. The daylight haloed her head and threw her face into shadow. But not enough to blur out the change of expression. 'Hang on, what is this really about?'

'Due diligence, I'm afraid,' Jess said. 'Ronnie Probert was murdered, and we are exploring all angles.'

Josie exhaled a sigh of disbelief. 'Do you seriously think that an Unsworth might be involved in any of this?'

'We have to ask.'

'My God,' Josie whispered.

'We're not accusing anyone of anything,' Jess added quickly.

'Glad to hear it.'

After a few beats of awkward silence, during which Jess wondered if she'd blown this interview, Josie spoke.

'We were devastated when Charlie died. My mum, nor my dad, ever fully recovered. It was just us two in the family, my big brother Charlie and me. What it doesn't say in the book is that Ronnie came to see us. Apologised. He was really upset. But of course, we knew it wasn't his fault. Charlie couldn't say no to a challenge. And he liked to drink, too. Even at that age. Rugby club culture isn't the healthiest at grassroots level. Ronnie almost gave up playing then. Did you know that?'

'No.'

'It was my dad who convinced him to carry on. That Charlie would not have wanted anyone to take the blame. And those drinks were only one batch of many rounds that night. They had trebles and doubles on offer for just a couple of quid. Rugby club culture, as I said. These days we'd have added a toxic to that sentence. And Ronnie wasn't the only Judge at the court.'

'I'm sorry to drag it all back up,' Jess said.

'Over the years, Ronnie came back to visit. He gave us shirts and balls for auction in the school my dad taught in. Charlie's old school. It ran to thousands over the years.'

Another pause followed. 'Ronnie wasn't guilty of killing my brother, DI Allanby, but he acted as if he was.

No one in the family blamed him, but he didn't shy away from what happened. He wasn't that kind of man.'

Jess thanked her, ending the call with a click of the mouse. She got up and walked to the board and put a line through the name of Charles Unsworth. As she turned back, she saw Rhys busy at his desk.

'How are you holding up, Rhys?'

'Fine, ma'am.'

'No change at the hospital?'

Rhys shook his head.

'Okay. I've just gone down a blind alley with Charlie Unsworth's sister. So, let me help you with some digging. What was the name of Ronnie's nephew again?'

'Ralph Probert, ma'am.'

'Right, let's have a look at what we can find out about him.'

CHAPTER NINETEEN

Warlow found Bob Salini in an open-plan office with three other CID officers. Bob was a few years younger than Warlow, and though not having quite the same paunch as Gil, the belt of his suit trousers still strained over a taut shirt that left no room for manoeuvre. He sat at a desk with his suit jacket off and no tie.

'Evan, welcome to Shangri La. You know Sara and Tim?'

Warlow didn't, other than to nod at in the corridor. But that was enough; they knew who he was. He raised a hand and got smiles and nods in return.

'Busy?'

Bob didn't answer. The look he bounced back was enough. 'Last week, we had a visit from the Commissioner waving a report. A heads up on something he'd dragged up from somewhere. Sixty percent NSIs in theft. And another twelve percent lost to evidential difficulties.'

Warlow nodded. Theft, including burglaries, was the bane of CID's lives. NSI, no suspect identified, made everyone look bad. The cross-over with rural crime, and thefts from remote places like farms, were on the up.

'Our detection rate shows a seventy percent NSI rate for vehicle thefts, non-domestic burglaries, and bikes, and around forty percent for car theft.'

'About the same as everywhere else, then.'

'Exactly. But of course, no one cares about that. The Assembly is bloody soft on theft. They prefer to push money and bodies towards hate crime prevention and awareness.'

Warlow nodded again. It all came down to resources and prioritising. It made victims of theft feel abandoned and made the police look uncaring. But then, you did not do this job if you wanted to be liked. Everyone deserved protection and a right to live in a country where the laws were obeyed and upheld. Truth was, criminals knew what they could get away with. And, as everyone kept being told, there was never enough money to go around.

'Anyway, that's enough of my bleating. You're here for Jordan Nicholas.'

'Don't tell me you've got him in that desk drawer?'

'Hah. I take it you haven't found him, then?'

Warlow outlined his trip to the Nicholas's house in Carway and the empty bedroom.

'Slippery bugger, is Jordan,' Bob said. 'You met his mother?'

'We did, and his little brother.'

Bob's eyebrows went up. 'So, he's back, is he?'

'Is Troy on your radar?'

'Only because of the domestic setup. But I guess he's sixteen now and beginning to have his own voice. Last we heard, he was living with the grandmother.'

'Well, not anymore. He's moved back, and from what I saw, lives in a room he's taken over there. Big on video games, apparently.'

'Good for him. So, what can I help you with?'

'Jordan buggered off as soon as we turned up. We need

a list of associates. Any intel on where he's likely to hang out.'

Bob turned to his monitor and began typing. 'I will not ask if you enjoyed your trip to Carway. We're aware of what a delight Linda Nicholas can be.'

'She was pretty subdued.'

'Then you caught her on a good day. Admittedly, she isn't as bad as she used to be. Is the house next door still unoccupied?'

'Yep.'

'Hardly surprising. She used to terrorise that entire block. High as a bloody kite, dancing in the road, screaming at all hours.'

'What about the father?'

Bob slid his mouse around, clicked and clicked again. 'GBH with intent. He's been in for ten already. He'll do another six as a minimum. I doubt she'll be there to welcome him home.'

A sad story, but one depressingly common. 'The grand-mother is whose mother?'

'Linda's. The courts stepped in after social services saw what was going on. Custody was applied for and given to the grandmother. Surprised to see that's ended.' Bob's screen filled with writing. 'Okay. Known associates. Most of them are in Llanelli. I can see two or three likelies we could try. A couple of our people are at an industrial break-in over there. I could ask them to call?'

'That would be a great help,' Warlow said.

'He rides a bike, does Jordan. You could get the word out to Uniforms. They might spot him out and about.'

'Good idea.'

Bob printed out a list of names and handed it to Warlow. 'Got to say, Jordan doesn't normally work with a partner.'

'How definite was Ronnie that there was more than one?'

'Not at all definite,' Bob said. 'They, or he, or she, wore masks, we think. Ronnie was very confused. Said the all had the same face.'

Warlow tutted.

'You know that Jordan running off proves bugger all,' Bob added. 'It's his way. Runs from everyone and everything. But I'll keep my ear to the ground, too.'

Warlow thanked the DI and headed back to the Incident Room. He got a thumbs up from Rhys and a nod from Jess, both of whom were busy on their computers.

When Warlow got to his, he pulled up the National Database and found Linda Nicholas and her arrest record. But what he was really interested in was her mother.

Sylvia Reeves was listed, but only as Linda's birth mother. She appeared to be as clean as a whistle. She had a Kidwelly address, a town no more than a couple of miles from Carway. Everything he'd learned so far hinted at a connection between Sylvia Reeves and Troy, not Jordan. But you never knew. Worth posting on the Job Centre as a thread.

———

JORDAN'S "MATE" in Capel had given him short shrift.

'No way can you stay here, man,' had been his response. 'I've got my girlfriend and a baby, man. No, not even in the fuckin' shed.'

He hadn't quite slammed the door in his face, but as good as. Jordan hadn't even had time to finish his piss-off-and-thanks-for-nothing sentence. 'Last time I do you any fav—'

Bang.

The door shut.

Jordan got back on his bike and headed into the town, hood up, head down. He'd stay away from the town centre. Too much filth around there. Too much aggro. Besides, the places he knew from spending long days and pissed-up nights weren't places you wanted to be after dark, alone, on a bike. His best bet might be to get down to the dock. He could grab a coffee from the café and get warm, maybe ride down to Burry Port, and hang about there for a few hours. Always loads of people on bikes on the coastal path. He wouldn't be out of place. And then, once it was dark, he could get back up to the tracks and maybe head home again.

Yeah. That would be a brilliant plan.

The filth had been and gone. The last place they'd expect him to be was back in Carway. And he could text Troy to make sure the coast was clear. Not Linda. Her head was permanently in the sodding shed.

Troy was a different matter. He was never keen to be involved in anything dodgy. Not even when Jordan had tried to get him to ask around the college he went to for anyone interested in the odd bit of weed or some Wizz. He knew a couple of mailmen who could deliver, though he wasn't himself a dealer. Jordan was not averse to making a bit of cash on the side. But Troy had blown him off. He had no interest in it and didn't know anyone who did.

Fair enough.

Playing games was his jam. Jordan did a bit of gaming, too. But he was more into GTA than anything else. Except for this new one that Troy was into. Ghost Reign Crusade was effing amazing. And when Troy was AFK – away from the keyboard – he was into school stuff. At least computing school stuff.

Bloody amazing that he could do all that.

Jordan called into the convenience store on Marine Street, bought sandwiches and stole a can of Coke and some crisps before heading down to St Elli's Bay and the coastal path. He bought a coffee there and hung about out of the wind, looking out over the Loughor towards the humpback of the Gower Peninsula across the grey waters of the estuary before heading north and west to Burry Port and the marina. He'd kill some time there before giving Troy a buzz to make sure it was safe to head back.

It was a Friday, and he guessed the filth wouldn't be working balls-out on the weekend. That would buy him some time. He could lie low until they lost interest. Would not be the first time. He could do it again.

The tarmac millennium coastal path caterpillar'd up and down parallel to the railway line, winding west towards the Burry Port lighthouse. A few other cyclists and some dog walkers were the only people he saw on this drab, chilly February afternoon. Come the weekend, the stretch would be teeming. But not today.

Jordan's mistake was to let hunger drive him.

By four, the light changed. Not by much, but the shadows along the paths where it slid between trees and bushes became denser, and the sky above seemed to get lower. On a sunny day, maybe there'd be another hour, but today there was no sun. Just lowering cloud and damp.

His plan was to get to Swiss Valley by maybe 4:30. It would mean getting back to Carway in full darkness, but he had his phone light. He'd used it before with the bike. He'd wedged it so it acted like a lamp. But overall, once he was on the path, he'd be alone. No one else used it much after dark.

But, despite the sandwiches and crisps of earlier, the bike ride had left him hungry.

Jordan took a minor detour to a different convenience store from the one he'd stolen from earlier. This one on Station Road. He pedalled around until he discovered a hiding spot behind some bins on an alley off Pemberton

Street. He didn't know this part of town that well, but who cared? All he wanted was a drink and a pasty.

The shop was crazy busy. Children journeying back from school buying Sherbert Fountains, Drumsticks, and Whizzers. It took him five minutes to buy what he needed. Still, he managed to slide a KitKat up his sleeve. When he came out, busily attempting to free the pasty he'd bought from its paper package, he saw them. Three blokes. Three clones. Dark hoodies, joggers, three stripes on their trainers.

He dropped his eyes, but too late not to have made eye contact with one of them. Jordan turned and hurried the other way. It wasn't more than fifty yards to the bike, ten yards to the turnoff on Pemberton Street. He got halfway there before he heard the shout.

'Oi, where the fuck are you off to?'

He had two choices then. Turn and confront them, explain why he was there and who he was, that he wasn't meaning any harm. He wasn't selling, nor buying. Just stopping off for a pasty and a drink. But he knew the type. He had friends who were Collie men, and without thinking, he'd stumbled into the wrong corner here.

Then there was the second choice. The one he chose.

Jordan went from stroll to a full sprint in an instant. He turned left into Pemberton Street, sprinted twenty yards past a pub, then left again to the dumpster where he'd stashed the bike. There, he ducked and got down on his knees, eyes shut, trying not to breathe. He heard them before he saw them. The rapid noise of trainers hitting pavement. They ran past. Two soldiers in pursuit of him. Stupid. He'd been bloody stupid.

Crap. He should have known they'd be out now, catching the kids on their way home from school.

And there he was, bold as fucking brass, dressed the same way they were.

Competition.

They didn't need to put two and two together. He'd be surprised if any of them could count. This was turf protection, and he'd put his foot in the wrong place at the wrong time.

Jesus. From behind the dumpster, Jordan peered out. They'd gone. Sprinting one hundred yards down to Charles Street where they'd no doubt split, one left, one right to complete the square. Hunting for him. This was tribal stuff. He willed himself to wait.

He counted to ten, wheeled the bike out, and got on. The lane ran parallel to Station Road. If he could get to it, he'd be away. He made it to Paddock Street, his heart racing, eyes peeled. To the right, fifty yards away, he saw one of his pursuers walking now, tired from the run. But as soon as he spotted Jordan, he began running again. Jordan took a left towards Station Road and pulled up at the T junction, hardly believing his luck.

Then he saw the third man.

The one that had stayed behind. The seller.

'Oi, you prick,' the guy yelled and came for him.

Traffic had picked up. There was no gap. Jordan pushed off anyway. A car screeched as he shot straight across. Someone yelled. The third man had his hand out, reaching for him. Jordan glanced down, the wind whipping at his hood, tugging the tied cord tight again around his neck, and saw the Stanley knife moving through the air. He felt contact on his thigh and almost lost control.

Almost.

But the e-bike sped away. Cars honked, someone else shouted, but Jordan didn't look around. Didn't dare. All that mattered was that he'd got away.

His leg stung. He looked down to see a purple patch spreading across his grey joggers.

'Shit, shit, shit,' he muttered. But he didn't stop. Not

even when he got to the Texaco garage on Felinfoel Road and veered off to join the old railway and the cycle path. He only stopped when he'd passed the reservoir in Swiss Valley. There, on a sheltered stretch, he got off the bike and pulled down his trousers to inspect the damage.

Even in the oncoming gloom, he could see that it was a clean cut against his pale thigh. But a cut that was still oozing. Still, it could have been worse.

He looked up at the sky and let out a groan of frustration.

This was all the filth's fault.

The cycle path was empty. Jordan got back on the bike and headed north, back to Carway.

CHAPTER TWENTY

'SOME OF THIS stuff is worth an absolute fortune,' Gil said for the fifth time, his gaze drifting from table to table like a kid in a sweet shop.

Catrin looked up, preoccupied with what she'd been looking through – some end-of-year reports from a financial adviser.

'Hmm?' she muttered.

'There are Triple Crown jerseys here, even Grand Slam jerseys.' Gil sounded animated. 'All signed from the seventies. Fans pay silly money for this kind of stuff.'

'Glad to hear it,' Catrin said. Of course, she knew that the Triple Crown and Grand Slam referred to the International Rugby Tournament held every year between the home nations, France and now Italy. She'd grown up in West Wales. How could she not?

'What about you? Anything interesting?' Gil asked.

'Financial reports. He was well off. There's no doubt about that. He may well not have been online, but he used a financial adviser. Everything is on paper. Old school.' Catrin glanced across at the untouched boxes from the attic that had come in that afternoon with a lost expression. 'I haven't even started on that lot yet.'

'Perhaps we should get someone in to value all of this.' Gil smoothed out another red jersey and shook his head.

'That's the thing, isn't it? There's a small fortune here, but it isn't liquid. I'm not even certain there is a black market for international signed jerseys.'

'There probably is, but I know what you mean. Burglars want readies or at least things they can sell readily.'

'Well, I haven't found a locked box full of fivers yet.' Catrin glanced around at the boxes as yet unopened. 'But I'll keep looking.'

Gil glanced at his watch. 'We need to get moving if we're going to make Vespers.'

'I could come in on Sunday and make a start on those other boxes.'

'Overtime? You're keen.' Gil fetched his coat and Catrin's from where they'd been left on a chair.

'Craig's working. I might as well.'

'I'll have a word with the evidence officer. I'm not sure how secure this place is. The last thing we need is some idiot breaking in.'

'That would be ironic, wouldn't it?' Catrin slid her arms into her coat. 'Double burglary.'

'With cheese.' Gil added an extra, 'Mmmmm.'

Outside, in the late afternoon gloom, Lane's car still sat parked in the car park. 'Think he's filming us?' Catrin said.

'I bloody hope not. I didn't do my hair before I came out.'

Catrin glanced up at the mad dance Gil's thinning hair was doing.

'For God's sake, don't smile,' Gil said. 'Drinkwater will have you court marshalled… as it were.'

Catrin turned away to hide her smile. 'Forgot about him. What do you think Lane's doing all this time?'

'Wondering where he's going to get his next drink of blood from, I expect.'

'As in, you think he's a vampire?'

'Blood sucker, definitely.'

Catrin blipped the key fob and the Focus's lights flashed. The officers got in and stared across at Lane's car. 'He looks pasty the times I've seen him in the flesh, I have to admit.'

'There you are, then. He's probably rigged up a coffin in that car and now that the sun is going down, he'll be up, fangs akimbo.'

Catrin pressed the ignition and rolled the car forward slowly, fighting a smile. 'Fangs akimbo? I'm not going to be able to look at him now without my eyes straying to his incisors.'

'They'll be filed for penetration. You mark my words. Always make sure you have garlic when you meet him.'

'That's disgusting.'

'It is, I apologise. Let's not talk about Lane. Let's talk about something marginally less disgusting. How's the old IVF going? Craig must be bloody exhausted.'

This time Catrin did laugh. And out loud.

———

RHYS HAD the tea ready for when Gil and Catrin got back. In a re-run of the morning's meeting, Warlow kicked things off. He tapped his pen on Jordan Nicholas's image.

'Mr Nicholas remains our key person of interest. I have spoken to CID colleagues, and they have visited some known contacts this very day on our behalf.'

'Very generous,' Gil said.

'They were out there anyway,' Warlow muttered.

'However, no joy. He was not there, and the people they interviewed denied contact.'

'Is it worth us watching the house in case he returns, sir?' Rhys asked.

'Good idea. But we don't have the manpower. Besides, the house backs on to open countryside. We'd need a team. And we do not have enough evidence to justify that. In fact, we have no evidence at all except for circumstantial.'

'And his previous criminal history, sir,' Rhys said.

'Indeed. But I would like to speak to his grandmother. She lives in Kidwelly, only five miles from the Nicholas house. Well within striking or biking distance. My understanding is that she was actively involved in looking after the younger Nicholas, but who knows if she has a soft spot for Jordan? She's on my list for Monday.'

'Sir, I've been thinking, what if it wasn't Jordan Nicholas's mother who tipped him off we were calling? What if it was the scaffolders?'

'How many sugars in that tea, Rhys?' Gil sounded impressed.

Warlow let this idea bounce around in his head. It made sense. 'I like it, Rhys. I think we ought to take a punt and have a proper look at the depot, don't you?'

'A warrant, sir?'

'Why not? We have reasonable grounds given that Jordan Nicholas is an employee. Plus, I'd like to see their bloody faces when we turn up. He could even be holed up there somewhere.'

Rhys got up and posted the action on the board.

'Catrin, Gil?' Warlow looked at the other two officers.

'It's a treasure trove,' Gil said. 'Mucho memorabilia. Enough to make your knees weak and press all your nostalgia buttons. You would have a field day.'

'Anything useful though?'

'He has a filing system of sorts for his paperwork,'

Catrin said. 'Bank statements, utilities, council tax. He also has a financial advisor. I'll go through these, and if need be, I'll visit the IFA.'

'Okay, I like that too. Slim pickings, but someone must've planted the idea of this mysterious money, so follow that through. See where it takes us.' Warlow regarded Jess and raised both eyebrows in invitation. She got up and waved to a Uniform at the back of the room. In return, the officer held up one hand, fingers spread to show five.

Jess nodded before holding up a copy of *Nowhere to Ron*. 'The autobiography thread goes nowhere. Probert may have felt guilty about what happened, but he wasn't remotely responsible for the death. Except in his own mind. I spoke to the dead player's sister. Probert visited the family afterwards. He apologised and almost gave up playing. But Unsworth's father convinced him otherwise. Ever since, he's supported them, donated prizes, spoken at the father's school at events to raise money. I think they have an Unsworth Cup they give every year. I sense no burning need for vengeance here.'

'Huh,' Gil said. 'That wasn't in the book. Him visiting the family, I mean.'

'No. Too much like trumpet blowing. That wasn't Ronnie's style.' Warlow wrinkled his nose.

Jess turned to a different photograph on the Gallery. 'So, then we come to Ralph Probert. He is Ronnie's nephew. Estranged. And I think we were led to believe that was all because of Ronnie's arrogance.'

Warlow nodded. 'That's how it was couched.'

'Ralph, though, has a chequered history. He went to college, qualified as a surveyor. But he never held a job for more than a couple of years. He's divorced. I'm awaiting the CAFCASS report.' She glanced again towards the back of the room. The Uniform, grinning, had her hand holding up some papers. Jess met her halfway across the room, exchanged a few words and a smile that made the young officer's weekend, and came back with the papers, one finger up demanding patience as she read and walked in silence, nodding slowly.

'I have three County Court Judgements here and the CAFCASS report.'

'CAFCASS, ma'am?' Rhys asked.

'Children and Family Court Advisory and Support Services,' Gil explained. 'Called in to arbitrate between warring couples. The CCJ's are probably fines for non-payment of something or other.'

'The report pulls no punches,' Jess said. 'Our friend Ralph Probert has lost more than one job, and his wife, to debt.'

'Debt?' Rhys sounded confused. 'Why would his wife leave because of debt?'

'What DI Allanby really means, unless I am very wrong,' Warlow said, 'is that Ralph Probert is an addict. That's why he's in debt.'

'I'd never have said he was into drugs, sir—'

'Not drugs, Rhys,' Jess said. 'He's a gambler. Some of this stuff are transcripts from online betting companies.'

'*Scheisse*.' Gil threw in a little German. Foreign swear words were always the best.

He was right, of course. This was a steaming pile of effluent. And sometimes hearing it in German added gravitas.

'That explains why he's living with his parents,' Rhys said.

'He's sharing custody, according to this.' Jess waved the papers. 'But the order is that this has to be at the grandparents' home.'

'So, we've got someone else to add to our POI list,' Gil said.

'I think we do. And I think, come Monday, we need to have another little chat with Ralph Probert. I heard his mother mention that the kids were with them for the weekend. Let's not ruin that. Our major thrust still must be Jordan Nicholas. And with that in mind, I think it might be worth revisiting the scaffolders. As mentioned, it would be an ideal place for Jordan to hide. Let's get a warrant and have a proper look around.'

'Agreed,' Jess said.

'Right. Rhys, anything happens, any change in your dad's situation, I want to know. Otherwise, we'll let the Uniforms search for Jordan, and we'll be back here bright and early on Monday. Agreed?'

Nods from the troops.

'Anything planned, sir?' Rhys asked.

'I have one or two things up my sleeve, yes.'

Rhys waited politely for a reply, but what he got was the usual enigmatic Warlowism.

'For me to know, and you to find out, DC Harries.'

CHAPTER TWENTY-ONE

A Saturday morning in February. Warlow got up, fed
Cadi, made fresh coffee, and checked the weather. And yes,
he was of the school of thought that accepted a quick peek
out of the window was better than any app. But he was
more interested in the afternoon. The forecast, when he
brought it up, had everything except sleet due over the next
eight hours of daylight. But then this was West Wales. And,
between 2pm and 5pm, it looked reasonable. Or at least
not sheeting it down. He'd promised Molly a walk, and he
was a man of his word.

After lunch, he picked her up from Cold Blow at
around one-thirty, and they drove up the coast to Porthgain, parked outside the brick hoppers of the old harbour,
and climbed up the steps to the coastal path to head south
towards Abereiddy.

Warlow had dressed warmly, and so had Molly, which
meant only her eyes were visible under her bobble hat and
above a muffler which rode high up over her nose.

Here, on the coast, the wind came rushing in off the
Celtic Sea, which joined the Irish Sea at just about the
exact latitude where dog, girl, and man stood on that

windswept western edge of Wales. Collectively, these waters made up the St. George's Channel, linking the Irish Sea to the Atlantic. Here it was at its narrowest, hence the ferry from Fishguard to Rosslare that would wind its way across later in the day.

Molly had Cadi on a lead. As usual, Molly had asked for a quick pronunciation lesson from the Welsh-speaking Warlow. Porthgain. Warlow suggested pore, th- as in theft, and gah-een. For Abereiddy, he went for Ah-bear-eye-thee. Which was more or less how she'd pronounced it herself at the first attempt. Warlow gave her a 9 out of 10. He did not believe in buttering people up.

The cliffs here were high, and though Warlow was confident the dog had enough sense not to stray too close to the edge, a startled seagull could prove too tempting, so he had Cadi on a lead.

They walked without speaking, the odd wary glance from Molly suggesting that perhaps this had been not such a good idea when the wind threatened to rip her hat off, but Warlow ploughed on.

People attracted to walking the coastal path justified its attraction in many ways. A closeness with nature as the birds wheeled and fought the gusts just feet away. Its stark beauty. The raw elemental nature of the wind, and yes, the danger. Because take a wrong step, slip, or get hit by a freak gust, and the rocks below, many feet below, made a hard and unyielding bed to land on.

The path brought you closer than anything Warlow had experienced to being alive and being in nature. You needed your wits about you on a day like today. And, notwithstanding those Molly glares, he knew she loved it, too. A mile and a half along, they came to Traeth Llyfn. A secluded, isolated beach accessed only by steep steps from the coastal path. It looked tempting, the sand smooth as the name Llyfn suggested, but when Molly turned with a questioning glance, Warlow cupped his hands around his mouth and said, into the wind, 'Let's press on to Abereiddy.'

They did that, crossing open grassland and winding down to the shingle and sand beach, now with Cadi off the lead. Off the path the wind dropped, and, as hoped Warlow and Molly could at last have a conversation.

'Wow, that's blown the cobwebs away,' Molly said.

Cadi, already at the water's edge, waited for Warlow to throw a ball. He duly obliged.

'We can go back to the car inland, make a circuit.'

'Good idea,' Molly said, her cheeks red from the walk. Warlow had enough insight to realise he looked much the same. 'I haven't done the path when it's blowing like this.'

'Sorry,' Warlow said. 'I was in two minds.'

'No, it's brilliant. I was worried about Cadi, that's all.'

'I know. Some of it's high. But she's sensible.'

'Mum would have loved this,' Molly said.

'She's shopping?'

'Yes. I said we could go tomorrow, but she wanted to get it done and said she needed a bit of RT.'

'Retail therapy?'

'Well done, Evan.'

'Never saw the attraction myself.'

'No? Well, you are a bloke. And anyway, it's more distraction therapy, I'd say.'

Cadi came back and presented the ball. Warlow gave the chucker to Molly, who launched the ball towards the water.

'From what?' Warlow asked, sensing that Molly might want to expand on the hints she'd already given.

'Me, work… other things.'

Warlow waited but didn't pursue any further. Molly would say what she needed to say in due course. They watched the dog splash in the outgoing water as a wave retreated before she arced back towards them. 'She loves this, doesn't she?' Molly said.

'Easily pleased, is Cadi.'

'Like you?' Molly, her face covering rolled down, grinned at him.

'Simple man, me,' Warlow said. A thought struck him. 'Aren't you getting your university offers round about now?'

Molly sighed. 'Yep. They're dribbling in. Three yesses so far. Leeds, Sheffield and Swansea.'

'Swansea to be near to Mum?'

'No. Definitely not. I wouldn't be staying at home, anyway. But it ranks high for criminology and psychology. They do a combined BSc.'

'So, you've stuck with that as a choice, then?'

'Yeah. Anything Mum can do, you know?'

'You on track?' Molly was bright, organised, and focused. He hardly needed to ask.

'Yep.'

They threw the ball another half dozen times before Warlow pointed to the south where the sky had darkened. 'I reckon we should head back before that comes too close. We'll leave the blue lagoon for another day. Summer's best.'

Molly slid her muffler back up. 'Lead on.'

Their path climbed through the car park to a broad footpath with views up the valley. Warlow lifted Cadi over a stile and led the way over fields towards a farm. It wasn't as windy here, but it took until they were at the kissing gate leading to the track back to Porthgain for Molly to say anything more about her mother's "distraction therapy."

'Has she told you about Greater Manchester Police getting in touch?'

'No.' He wanted to add that they'd had little time to

catch up since he'd come back. 'Job offer?' he asked, wondering why his pulse had suddenly ratcheted up.

'No. She won't go back there. Nor me.'

Warlow held the kissing gate open for her as Cadi wriggled through.

'This was something else,' Molly said. 'Something to do with my dad. Again.'

Warlow stopped walking. 'Is he okay?'

'Yeah. He's fine. But it looks like whatever he was involved in has gone belly up. I wanted to say tits up, but Mum said it lacks decorum.'

Warlow let slip a lopsided smile.

'Anyway, he's had to be brought in. That's what they say, isn't it? Brought in, like a spy from the cold. You read Le Carré, Evan?'

'Several.'

'I'm reading one now. But I prefer Slow Horses. Mick Herron's a bit more contemporary.'

'But your dad is okay?'

'He is. But they think he's going to have to transfer out to a different force. Not here, don't worry.'

Warlow understood well enough how this sort of thing could happen. There were rules associated with infiltrating organised crime gangs. Drug taking was never acceptable as a means of ingratiation. Nor was forging sexual relationships. Warlow wondered which of these cardinal rules Tricky Ricky might have broken. Having said that, a palpable threat to life was always grounds for removal.

'And you don't know where?'

'Not yet. The GMP guy wanted to keep Mum up to speed. Tell her Ricky might not be in touch for a while. I said try seventeen years.'

Nothing more was said on the walk. But when Warlow delivered Molly back to Cold Blow, Jess's Golf was parked outside.

'Come in for a cup of tea, or Mum will tell me off for not asking.'

Jess was unpacking Tesco bags when Warlow followed Molly in.

'Good walk?' Jess smiled at them. 'I've got the kettle on.'

'Where's Cadi?' Molly asked.

'I've left her in the Jeep. She's muddy and—'

'I have the warm water watering can technique all sorted out at the back. Let me fetch her, and I'll give her a wash and a rub while you make the tea,' Molly said.

Warlow handed over the key. 'Yes, ma'am.'

Molly fetched the dog.

'And before you say it,' Jess said. 'I know I have only myself to blame.'

'Apple, tree, fall. That's all I'm saying. Good retail therapy?' Warlow asked as he sourced cups and tea bags.

'Not bad. Got a new cover for the ironing board. That is the extent of my success.'

Outside, girl and dog walked around the side of the house to the rear. Warlow found Jess in the kitchen. 'Sorry about Ricky,' Warlow said. 'You should have told me.'

'I was going to. Haven't had much chance.'

Warlow took a breath. 'I owe you a night out.'

Jess tilted her head. 'You do.'

'I am a man who keeps his promises.'

'Glad to hear it.'

'It's just that I haven't even unpacked all my bags from Australia yet.'

'Evan. I'm not going anywhere.'

Warlow nodded. 'But Ricky is?'

'Don't. That man just can't help but bugger things up.' Anger flared in her cheeks.

Warlow made the tea. Five minutes later, a clean black Labrador, fur still fluffy from the rub down, came in and made a fuss of Jess while Warlow drank his tea. Molly took hers upstairs. 'I'm jumping in the shower to warm up and clean up. Cadi gave me a mud shake before we got started.' Footsteps clattered up the stairs.

'Oh dear, I hope I haven't put her off the coastal path,' Warlow said.

'You're kidding. Next best thing to canoeing in cold water, she told me.'

'She's had some offers from uni.'

'Yep. Now she just has to get the exams.'

'She will.'

Jess held up crossed fingers.

'Heard any more about Rhys's dad?' Warlow leaned against the sink.

'No news. Rhys is pretty upset about it.' Jess put away a couple of boxes of granola.

'Wears his heart on his sleeve. Bit like Molly. Is Bryn…'

Jess shrugged. 'Not been mentioned. I think she wants to keep her head down until the summer. There'll be a trip to sunny Europe after the results, no doubt. Her mates are already planning. That'll be a week of fun for her and worry for me.'

'But it will be summer.' It came out wistful. Largely because the squall he'd seen an hour ago to the south began hurling rain at the window next to him like an angry water god.

'Maybe we'll have had our night out by then,' Jess said.

Warlow turned to stare at her in horror.

'Only kidding,' Jess said.

'After this weekend, I should be straight.'

'What are you now, then?'

Warlow sipped his tea. 'I think you've been spending far too much time in the company of Sergeant Jones.'

———

JORDAN HAD WATCHED ENOUGH Amazon Prime to know that you could seal wounds with super glue. He'd got home and climbed into his bed via the ladder, disturbing no one. There were noises and he'd heard Troy's door opening late that night. Probably needing a pee after too much of the old Krank juice to keep him awake for the PS5, but Jordan had been up and out of the house before anyone else was awake.

On the bike again, with the sunrise still a good while off, he rode smoothly through Carway to Ffos Las Woods. From there, he took paths and farm lanes across to the cycle path at Cynheidre, avoiding major routes where possible.

He bought the super glue in Home Bargains at Cross Hands and slipped into the toilet at McDonald's. He cleaned the almost surgical cut first. It had oozed overnight, but he'd grabbed tissues and wrapped them around using an old towel to keep them in place so as not to soil the sheets.

Now he wiped the four-inch slash dry, squeezed on some glue and held the edges together. The powerful smell of cyanoacrylate ester burnt his eyes and made him turn his head away. Partly to avoid the fumes, partly not to look at the slash. But when he eventually did, the wound glistened a bit, but all the oozing had stopped.

He walked out, head down against the fierce wind and made it to Greggs, where he bought a chicken bake and a Coke. He needed a shower, but with his leg like it was, he could wait. Maybe wrap some cling film around it. Yeah, that sounded like a good idea.

He whiled away the hours back in Home Bargains and checked out the sports equipment in Leekes. Then he wandered up to B&M with another Greggs' lunch. When it got dark, he got back on the bike and headed back to Tumble and the cycle path. It was a Saturday, so Troy would sod off over to Lola's. That would mean he might sneak onto Ghost Reign for an hour. He wouldn't make it back now much before six. By that time, Linda would be half a bottle of Buckfast in at least. She wouldn't remember if he breezed in wearing a lime-green gorilla outfit.

Jordan had his phone at the ready, but it had started spitting rain and he didn't want to get it wet by using it as a lamp unless he had to. He hit the path in Tumble in semi-darkness, but there was no need for speed. It was only seven miles. He saw a couple of lights coming towards him and pulled off the path until they passed.

Late cyclists.

After that, he saw no one.

Until he got to the quietest and most remote stretch between Cynheidre and the Sylen Road. He wasn't sure what he was seeing at first. A bobbing red light way ahead of him moving back and forth. As if someone was waving a lamp. It got brighter the further south he went. Jordan remembered someone telling him that the path followed the old railway line and this, ahead of him, looked how someone might signal a train.

For a moment, he lost concentration. Difficult to judge how far ahead the light was in the gloom and it was almost fully dark now, the path a dark ribbon against the margin-ally lighter surroundings. But the contrast was fading into a nebulous and dangerous uniformity. When he mistook a corner and braked sharply, the noise of rubber brake biting against the metal screeched. It was no good. He'd have to switch his sodding light on.

He fiddled with his phone and slid it into the slot he'd fashioned.

When he looked up, the red light had gone.

It did not appear again in the time it took him to get to the Hebron Road and the track that took him past a farmhouse and along the edges of fields to the woods at Ffos Las and his house. And all the while he wondered if he'd really seen that light up ahead.

Or if the Signalman was nothing but a figment of his imagination.

CHAPTER TWENTY-TWO

CATRIN DID as she'd threatened to do. Armed with earbuds and a playlist, she returned to Five Roads on Sunday and attacked Ronnie Probert's financial file. Hours of wading through years of bank statements and letters, some from financial advisors, some from solicitors, yielded one or two little gems. Warlow spoke to her on Sunday evening. The upshot being a follow-up call to Ralph Probert, inviting him in for a chat the following morning.

At 9:30am that Monday, while Rhys did the necessary to get a warrant for Castell Scaffolding's depot and Jess watched from the adjacent observation room, Warlow and Catrin sat Ralph Probert down in an interview room.

Catrin followed PACE guidelines, explained again why they wanted to speak to him in relation to Ronnie Probert's death, how he was not under arrest, cautioned him, explained how he could leave at any time, and that he was entitled to a solicitor.

Ralph, with the constant irritation he viewed the world with simmering away like school dinner cabbage, simply said, 'Let's get on with it.'

'First, thanks for coming in,' Warlow began.

'I don't know what more I can tell you.' Ralph wore a shirt and tie but had taken off his anorak. Two moons of sweat bloomed beneath his armpits.

'You told us you had not seen Ronnie Probert after your wedding to… Angela?'

Ralph nodded.

'It would be better if you vocalised your response, Mr Probert,' Catrin said.

Ralph cleared his throat. 'That's right.'

'So, you never saw him after that date?'

'As I've just explained, no.'

Warlow raised a hand and glanced at Catrin. 'And to clarify, I suppose, if you peel it all apart, what Ralph here says might be strictly true. Not seeing him face-to-face, I mean.'

'I don't follow.' Ralph turned up the irritation.

Catrin answered, 'What the Detective Chief Inspector is saying is that on asking you if you ever saw your uncle after the wedding, you have answered truthfully.'

'Like I say—'

'But it's a question of semantics,' Warlow intervened. 'Seeing is not the same as contacting. Not quite.'

Ralph went on. 'We fell out. My dad… he got upset every time we talked about it. Still does. You saw what it does to him.'

Warlow nodded slowly. The epitome of understanding. Sympathy even. But with a sting in its tail. 'The trouble is, Sergeant Richards here has been trawling through some paperwork of Ronnie's. She's been looking at his bank statements.'

Ralph became tight-lipped.

Catrin slid a typed sheet of paper towards Ralph. 'You ought to know we've accessed information from your bank as well, Mr. Probert. This is a summary sheet of money paid out of Ronnie Probert's account to yours over a ten-year period. Twenty-eight thousand pounds in total.'

Ralph said nothing.

'We also have a list here of County Court Judgements against you. Two from finance companies and one from a builder. One debt was for non-payment of a credit agreement for a washing machine, one for the finance on a car, and one for work done on a house by a building firm. These debts were cleared by payments to your account from your Uncle Ronnie. Shortly after the last one, you and your wife Angela separated.'

Ralph began to tremble. 'My dad… my father doesn't know about the payments.' His brow crumpled into deep lines of desperation. 'Does he need to?'

'I'm right in assuming these accrued debts, and I suspect there are many others, are because of your gambling addiction?' Warlow asked.

Ralph nodded, his eyes dropping away to the hands he'd clenched on the desktop.

'You lost your job after the last court appearance, am I right?' Catrin asked. 'As a surveyor with Calasco Construction?'

'I did.'

'And what is it you do now?'

'I work in the office at a builder's merchants.'

'Why haven't you told your father about your uncle's generosity?'

Ralph looked up at the ceiling, his lower lip trembling. 'Have you any idea how humiliating this has been? How degrading? To lose my job, my family, almost my kids. I've got that back. But I'm compelled to attend an addiction clinic. I get CBT… cognitive behavioural therapy. It's helped. But what helped more was Angela letting me have access to the kids at my parents' place.'

'That is where you live now?'

'I pay some rent,' Ralph said indignantly. 'I'm almost forty, and it's all I can bloody afford.'

Warlow leaned forward. 'Still doesn't answer the question of why you haven't told your father.'

'Because… because it would break his bloody heart. It works, being able to blame Ronnie for it all.'

Warlow shook his head, and Ralph pounced on that. 'I realise how it sounds. Ronnie didn't make me gamble, but… … Oh God, my dad needs a reason to explain how it all fell apart, and using Ronnie as the monster was an easy out.'

'Do you still think that?'

Ralph squeezed his eyes shut.

'We haven't finished going through all of Ronnie's papers. There may well be something we need to ask your father about,' Catrin said.

'This may be a chance to pre-empt all that.' Warlow would not back down, but neither officer wanted this family to suffer any more because of one man's pride and foolishness.

Catrin slid the papers back towards her. 'You're still in debt, Mr Probert?'

Ralph nodded, the bluster now replaced by misery. 'I pay for the kids and the courts let me pay off some fines at a monthly minimum.'

Catrin nodded. 'You see our problem here? Here's evidence you had money from Ronnie Probert in the past. You were aware he had money. You have debts.'

'Wait, wait.' Ralph put his hand up. 'What are you saying here? That I… … No, no way. That crap about him having money at home, it's all nonsense.'

'We will need to confirm your whereabouts on the evening of the attack, Mr Probert. It might be useful if you could give us a written statement.'

'I was at home. I don't go out.'

'Then we will need to interview your parents.' Catrin remained adamant.

'But... ... How could you possibly think I would do anything like this?'

'You've lied to us already,' Warlow said. 'Who's to say you aren't lying now?'

'I'm not...' Realisation of just what his predicament was thudded home. The tremble became a shake. 'You can't ask me anything else. I want to leave.'

'Your choice,' Catrin said. 'But please do nothing silly. We will need a full statement from you regarding your movements. You can either do it now or come back with a solicitor for further questioning.'

Ralph dropped his head into his hands. 'Oh, God.'

———

RHYS GOT BACK from the Magistrate's Court in Llanelli a little after half ten. He knew from practice to get there before court kicked off was the quickest way to get the warrant signed.

'In the good old days, we could nip into town, to the magistrate's court there. Now everything happens in Llanelli.' Gil delivered the observation as Rhys settled himself at his desk.

'That would have saved a bit of time, sarge.'

'If you were a negative sort of person, instead of being blessed with sunny outlooks like you and I, Detective Constable, you might even start thinking how all these cuts and consolidations were concocted to make our job that much more difficult, *mynuffernu*.'

Rhys powered up his computer and logged on.

'How's your father?' Gil asked. 'And I mean that literally and not as a euphemism for sexual activity?'

'Pardon?' Rhys asked.

Gil settled back, hands interlaced on his chest. 'It's a term that has fallen out of favour. So much so that a man of your years might not even have come across it. A bit of "how's your father"?'

Rhys came back with one of his vacant looks.

Gil expounded, 'A reference to Victorian times when a young man with hormonally driven aspirations might ask after a young lady's male parent in order to establish his whereabouts before daring to sneak a quick… anything. Though even a surreptitious licking of the lips was considered scurrilous in those days. I suppose "where's your father" would be better, but there is no accounting for verbal slippage.'

Rhys blinked.

'Your dad,' Gil repeated, putting him out of his misery. 'Is he still in hospital?'

'Ah, yes, sarge. Still there. They think by mid-week he'll get down to Morriston to the cardiac unit.'

'Mum holding up?'

'Worried, obviously, but what can you do?'

'Keep yourself busy,' Gil suggested.

'Yeah, exactly what I thought. I read a report about a church roof theft on the night of Ronnie Probert's burglary.'

'Might be a link?'

Rhys shrugged. 'It's one way to keep busy.'

'Right, I shall leave you to it.' Gil got up. 'I have somewhere to be.'

'Anywhere interesting?'

'The big conference room. Superintendent Drinkwater is holding court with the press. Said I'd meet DCI Warlow there. We're going to sneak into the back and make faces at him.'

'Really?'

'No, not really. But the sneaking into the back bit is true. I will text you when we're done. Kettle on pronto at that point.'

Rhys gave a thumbs up and turned back to his screen.

CHAPTER TWENTY-THREE

IT WAS A ROGUES' gallery of top brass. The Assistant Chief Constable sat on one side of Chief Superintendent Drinkwater with Sion Buchannan on the other side. The police press officer sat on the end.

Normally, they'd have set something up outside of reception or in front of the Police HQ sign at the gates, but the weather was too miserable even to make the press suffer. At least half a dozen microphones were fixed in front of a long desk, behind which the officers sat as cameras clicked and videos ran.

The ACC kicked things off.

'In view of the press speculation surrounding the death of Ronnie Probert, we've decided to hold this press conference to clarify any misconceptions about this case. We can field questions you have once we're done.' The ACC continued to read from a prepared statement. 'As you will know, thieves broke into Mr Probert's house in the early hours of the 24th of January. They ransacked the house and demanded money. The attack was prolonged and brutal and left the victim with severe and life-threatening injuries. Initially, Mr Probert was able to tell us some details about the attack. However, five days after the event, Mr Probert succumbed to his injuries, and we are now pursuing a murder investigation.

'Ronnie's family has been kept informed and all our sympathies are with them. We recognise the special place Ronnie had in the nation's hearts, and I can assure everyone that we are pursuing this investigation with the same vigour that we do with every case of wrongful killing. As always, this is a complex operation involving many police officers. Some of you are aware we have established a staging outpost at Five Roads where we are examining the contents of Ronnie Probert's house and allowing our forensic colleagues to further examine the property.

'The family is humbled by the response of the public, and we, as law enforcement officers, are also grateful for their cooperation. Details of the investigation cannot be divulged, and I'm sure you will respect and appreciate that if you have questions.' He put down his speech. 'Are there any questions?'

Hands shot up. The ACC pointed to one.

'Katie Morley, ITV News. Can you reassure members of the public, who are rightly concerned about their safety, that this was an isolated attack?'

The ACC turned to his right. 'I will let Chief Superintendent Drinkwater answer that.'

'We believe that this was a targeted attack on Mr Probert. The burglar, or burglars, were demanding money. It will be no comfort, but we do not think there is any need for anyone else to be anxious.'

The ACC pointed to a second raised hand.

'Kabir Rani, BBC. You mention that there is no need for people to be concerned, but incidence of serious crime and violent crime has been on the rise, has it not?'

Drinkwater nodded. 'It has. But the devil is in the detail, as it were. Crimes against the person and theft have risen in urban areas. Not in rural areas. There is a difference.'

The third hand to be chosen belonged, to Gil's tutting disgust, to someone they all knew. A man with a hooked nose and small eyes, chubby from bad food and alcohol, wearing a trademark waxed jacket.

'Geraint Lane. Thank you for clarifying the urban-rural split. But isn't it the case that nationally, serious acquisitive crime, including domestic burglary, has poor clearance rates and justice for victims? Charge rates for robbery and burglary are at an all-time low. Surely allocating officers to sort through Ronnie Probert's effects in a community hall isn't exactly groundbreaking policing, am I right?'

'*Pwdryn yr uffern*,' Gil muttered.

Warlow couldn't agree more. He was a miserable sod. To be fair to Drinkwater, he seemed up to the task, armed as he was with the correct amount of bureaucratic vocabulary to parry Lane's thrust.

'To answer your question, Mr Lane, we've taken on board last year's report into the police response to acquisitive crime and have adopted the recommendation for both good and innovative practice regarding the PEEL inspections; that is police effectiveness, efficiency and legitimacy. The work we are doing in this case will, I am certain, lead us to the perpetrators.'

Lane looked anything but satisfied. Gil, however, nodded his approval. 'As good a stuff-that-in-your-pipe answer as you could get.'

'Much better than the one I'd have given,' Warlow muttered. Sometimes you needed a pen pusher in the van to shut a whining hyena up.

There were more questions, but with nothing concrete to report, it fizzled out. The ACC had delivered enough by way of soundbites to satisfy the crowd.

Gil and Warlow slipped out while they had the chance.

———

'So, NOTHING SIGNIFICANT, THEN?' Jess asked as they huddled for a quick catch up.

'Nah. Lane being a pest with thinly veiled criticism, but otherwise, no,' Gil replied.

'Catrin and I filled Rhys in over Ralph Probert.'

Warlow had done the same with Gil and the DCI responded now, 'He didn't like being caught out, that's for certain.'

'If it was Ralph, was he alone?' Rhys asked. 'And wouldn't he have taken other stuff to sell?'

'It doesn't quite add up,' Jess said. 'I mean, he could have been hoping for another handout from Ronnie. Why kill the golden goose?'

'Frustration? Anger? That's two reasons off the top of my head,' Gil said.

'The trouble with you is that you always think the worst of people,' Catrin said.

'Healthy scepticism, I call it.'

Warlow glanced at the clock. It was well before eleven. 'Okay. How do we stand with the NPT and the warrant?'

The neighbourhood policing team for Carway had been alerted, as had CID. 'All set up for today, sir. 1pm.'

'Excellent. Catrin, you're off back down to Five Roads with Gil?'

Catrin nodded.

'That leaves Jess and I to execute the warrant. Rhys, you stay here and man the office.'

The forced smile on Rhys's face said it all. But Warlow added the little qualifier. 'Just in case. You never know; they might get a slot in Morriston for your dad out of the blue.'

'I don't want this to be a hindrance, sir.'

'It isn't a hindrance. DI Allanby expressed her burning desire to visit a windblown scaffolder's depot only this morning. Isn't that right, DI Allanby?'

'Nothing I'd rather do.' Jess said. 'You carry on digging into Ralph Probert.'

'Yes, ma'am. There is one thing you should know about the scaffolder, Barry Kirkland, sir.'

'I've seen his record,' Warlow said.

'Not that, sir. He said he'd been playing darts at the Wheatsheaf in Hendy on the night of the burglary. And it is darts night. Only that night, the darts were called off because two of the opposition team had Covid.'

'Well, well.' Warlow grinned. 'Good work, Rhys Harries.'

'As Sergeant Jones always says, sir, not just a pretty face.'

'What I say is, not even a pretty face,' Gil corrected him. 'But well done, nevertheless. One day you'll make a fine…'

'Copper, sarge?' Rhys prompted.

'Soufflé. They're a bugger. Oh, and by the way, since DS Richards and I are down that way, why don't we call in on the Nicholases. Do a Swan Lake?'

'Swan Lake, sarge?'

'Keep them on their toes,' Jess explained.

———

JORDAN WAS on his phone in his room when he heard the knock on the front door.

The filth.

It was that kind of knock. Three loud raps. All business. Jordan could tell it wasn't the Amazon man bringing Linda's Buckfast. It took him twenty seconds to shimmy down the ladder and into the shrubbery at the rear. The great thing about the terrace he lived on was that getting around to the rear was an expedition. You had to cross other people's gardens to get to the Nicholas's. And once through the hedge at the back, it was open country.

Now he crouched and watched the back door. It opened and Linda came out, lighting up a fag as she did. The female cop, the redhead, followed and stood chatting with Linda for a while. What they were chatting about, he had no idea. But then he realised it gave the big guy, who he didn't know, the chance to sniff around.

Let them.

They wouldn't find anything in the bedroom. There was fuck all to find. He was living out of a couple of carrier bags. So long as he had his phone, he'd survive. He waited fifteen minutes after the cops had gone and then crept up to the back door, opened it a crack to hear Linda and Troy arguing in the kitchen.

'Is he here, Mam?' Troy's voice.

'I don't know. Honest.' Linda, pleading.

Jordan pushed the door open. 'Yo, s'up?'

Troy pivoted, eyes wide. 'Shit, were you here?'

'Course I was here. Saw them come and shimmied out the back garden. What are you doing here, anyway?'

'Half day at college. They're looking for you, man.'

'Relax, they've gone.'

'Shit.' Troy got up. 'They could still be watching.' He hurried through to the hall and peered through the glass of the front door, then opened it and looked up and down the street.

'See,' Jordan said from the kitchen. 'What did I say?'

'Jordan, what have you done?' Linda asked, her eyes dragging down at the edges, tired from asking the same question a hundred times over the years.

'Nothin'. I done nothin'.'

Troy came back to the kitchen. 'I can't be having this. You said you'd be straight. You said—'

'Relax, man. I ain't done nothin'. It's just the filth wantin' to drop shit on me.'

Troy shook his head.

'Come on, Troy man.' Jordan turned on his winning smile. 'I swear. They'll give up after a while.'

'They're asking about that Probert bloke,' Troy said.

'Not me, man.'

Linda, arms folded, leaned against the sink, her words slurred but heartfelt. 'Troy says he'll go if they keep coming back, Jordan.'

'Jesus. I haven't done anythin'.' He turned to Troy. 'You said you'd help me, Troy man.'

'I will. I want to, but you've got to get straight, Jord. This sort of crap, it does my head in.'

'Please, Troy, don't go,' Linda pleaded.

'Mam, I—'

'Look, Jesus, I'll be a ghost, okay? You won't see me until all this shit is sorted,' Jordan said. 'They won't find me because I won't be here except to kip and a quick shower an' that. Come on, Troy. I got a laptop comin'. A good one. I can start the codin' stuff. Why don't we play a bit of C.O.D? Or Ghost Reign.'

'Can't. I've got homework.'

'After that, then. It's early.'

'Said I'd go to Lola's. Her dad is picking me up at five. I'll stay at hers and go to college from there in the morning.'

'Half an hour, man.'

Troy's shoulders sank, and he nodded. 'Give me an hour.'

Jordan slapped him on the back. 'Mam, got any milk? I fancy some Cheerios.'

CHAPTER TWENTY-FOUR

'WHAT WE NEED IS A DOG,' Gil said as they pulled into the parking lot at the community hall. Geraint Lane's Renault was where it had been yesterday, smoke puffing out from the driver-side window.

'For what? Lane?' Catrin scrunched her face up.

'Lane? *Arglwydd mawr*, no. I wouldn't want to poison the dog with vampire flesh. No, I meant for that little scrote, Nicholas, in Carway. He has a ladder permanently attached to his bedroom window. I reckon he can slide down it like a fireman with the runs. But if we sent a K9 right around the back…'

'You ought to run that past the Wolf.'

'DCI Warlow is not a dog, though, is he?'

'I didn't mean for him to do the chasing—' She caught herself. 'You know what I mean.'

'One of those Belgian Malinois. Christ, they're agile. They'd make short shrift of boyo up the ladder. Shake him like a stick.'

Catrin's hand strayed to her safety belt clip. 'Are we going in or what?'

'We are. I am up to 1978 in memorabilia years. You?'

'Today is attic day.'

Still, Gil made no effort to move. All he did was sit and stare across at Geraint Lane, smoking in his vehicle.

Catrin waited.

Another grey February day had dawned, but today the temperature, according to the forecast, would struggle to reach a couple of degrees above freezing. There'd been snow overnight in the north and on the tops of the Beacons.

Gil had stopped on his way in to work that morning near a house that had once been a pub called the Halfway. He'd got out and stood to look back up the valley. The brooding remains of Dryslwyn Castle guarded the middle of that valley, and to the east, the ridge on the Black Mountains above Llyn y Fan stood white-topped with sugar icing. An affirmation of why he loved living where he did. With a bit of luck, if it stayed cold, he could take the girls up on the weekend and let them play in some white stuff. Anticipating that moment somehow made the reporter's presence even more irksome.

'See that smoke?' Gil nodded at Lane's car. 'Maybe the bugger's on fire. I mean, what the hell is he hoping to see, sitting there like that?'

'He's seen it once already, remember?' Catrin still smarted from the grainy photographs taken through the hall window of its interior. 'He's like a big toad waiting for a fly to drift past. Like he waited for us to be not there when he took his snaps.'

'Nice analogy, sergeant.' Gil nodded. 'No doubt he'll have concocted some bloody fiction around the press conference today, too. Come to think of it, it's a wonder he hasn't gone in that direction. Fiction, I mean. He could write some vampire diary books being as he is one. A blood sucker, not a diary.'

'Been done to death,' Catrin said.

Gil threw her a glance. 'Don't think I've read that one. Any good?'

'Hilarious.'

'Right, well, remember, no smiling as we cross the car park. Straight back, like you mean business, dour expression, bordering on the miserable.' He paused. 'Sorry, I forgot that's your default look.'

Catrin sighed. 'Can we just get on with it, please?'

'Tidy. Thought you'd never ask.' Gil unclipped his seat belt and swung the door open before Catrin could react. 'Why you insist on sitting here staring into space I'll never know,' he added before topping it off with the little groan that always accompanied him levering himself out of a car these days. 'You need to watch your motivation, sergeant,' he muttered as the cold air permeated the vehicle.

Catrin got out, silently seething, but quite unable to halt the resigned smile that came unbidden to her lips.

———

Jess, Warlow, and the designated officers from the NPT gathered in the empty car park at Ffos Las racecourse. Warlow had informed the inspector in charge of the chain lock on the Castell Scaffolding container office door, and so bolt cutters were to hand.

They went in convoy down the rutted lane and through the open gates of the compound. Jess and Warlow, flanked by two Uniforms, both in helmets and one brandishing the bolt cutter, walked up the wooden steps to the "office" door and knocked.

'This is the police. Open the door.'

The office window had blinds. They slid shut a second after Jess's knock.

'I can't let you in,' said a voice. Lorna's probably.

'We are in possession of a warrant to search the property,' Jess said. 'Open the door or we will break it down.'

'Wait... I've rung my boss. He's on the way.'

Warlow stepped up to the door. 'Lorna, this is DCI Warlow. We met the other day. Please, open the door or we will break it down.'

The door opened again on the chain. Lorna's face appeared, her eyes hooded with fear. 'I can't... ... He said never...'

'Lorna,' Warlow kept his voice even. 'Just open the door. No one is going to blame you. We have a warrant.'

Jess held up the papers close to the crack.

Lorna shook her unhappy head. 'No. He said.'

Warlow stepped back and motioned to the officer at his side. 'Constable?'

The Uniform slid the open jaws of the cutters into the gap, engaged the chain and it gave with one compression. Lorna stepped back, ripped jeans and a woolly jumper barely containing the flesh beneath.

'There,' Warlow said, and not unkindly. 'No one can blame you now.'

The office had a desk, a computer, a filing cabinet, and a corkboard stuck with cards from other businesses. A list of phone numbers and invoices waiting to be paid ran across the top.

On the table next to the computer sat a mug with a big red heart on it and "Lorna" in a handwritten font. On top of the filing cabinet was a tray with a silver kettle, a half pint of milk in a carton, tea bags still in their box, and a packet of Hobnobs, uncoated.

'Pop your coat on, Lorna,' Jess said. 'This room isn't big enough for you and the officers who'll be doing the search.'

'Search?' Lorna asked. 'What for?'

'Have you seen, or do you have knowledge of, Jordan Nicholas since we were last here?' Warlow asked.

'No. Jordan doesn't work here. Well, he does occasionally, but only when there's a big job on, and we're stretched. Didn't Barry tell you that?'

'He did. But no harm in asking, right?'

They ushered Lorna out to one of the police vehicles so that she could stay warm. Jess stayed in the office to go through the paperwork. Warlow zipped up his coat and went outside. Once again, the garaged area stood empty. The lorries, two of them, if he remembered correctly, were out on jobs.

As instructed, they had three Uniforms, one at the end of the compound inspecting the storage shed where the scaffolding boards and poles were kept and two at the garaging area. Warlow walked around the perimeter inside the fence.

He'd brought wellies and just as well. Stagnant pools of water covered in films of oil sat in the gouged-out potholes and next to an array of oil drums near the garage end. Old boards and palettes lay piled up in one corner, ready for burning, he assumed.

He walked through the gates of the chain-link fencing and took a narrow path that led to the right of the entrance. It ended where the fencing took a right angle. Beyond, through sparse bushes, were fields. But he could also make out some footprints in the mud leading off along the side of the fence towards the rear of the compound.

From behind, he heard the noise of a lorry approaching, the squeal of brakes, the high revs as it approached the entrance. Warlow ignored it and pushed on. In summer, this way would have been a challenge, but on a chilly February day with the foliage at its lowest, he had only to avoid the worst of the brambles. Trees grew close to the fence here, and he noticed a trickling stream separating the area from the field next door.

But there was a path of sorts. Narrow, and not well trodden. Like trails you often came across on mountainsides made by sheep. But there were no sheep here. Through the fence, he watched the Uniforms looking in and under equipment, searching for... what, exactly?

They'd know it when they saw it, had been what he'd said. A stashed tent or a sleeping bag, perhaps. Or something else?

The sound of the lorry's engine died. Shouts. Barry's voice, angry and vehement. Other voices, calming, but insistent.

Warlow got to the edge of the fencing, tearing away the clinging weeds. Once more, the path took a right angle here at the back of the compound, behind the area inside where the poles and boards were stacked. No reason for there to be anything other than a straight line of chain link here to the other side.

Except there was something.

Two-thirds of the way along, a small hut made up of scaffolding and corrugated tin sheets had been set up adjoining the rear fencing, steel poles acting as anchoring posts at the east corner, jutting out of the roof. The base appeared to comprise sturdy wooden boards with the edges reinforced with metal.

Warlow approached.

More voices came to him from the compound. Raised again.

'You can't do this. Jesus!' Barry, irate.

Warlow pushed his way through to the building. It lacked finesse. Three vertical corrugated sheets as walls on three sides, three tapering down front to back as a roof. There were gaps at the corners. Enough for Warlow to peer through.

He saw no sleeping bag or stoves.

What he saw was a room stuffed to the roof with curved, folded, and misshapen chunks of greying metal.

Warlow retraced his steps and walked into the compound to be met by a red-faced Barry and his sullen-looking partner, Lewis, today wearing a padded overshirt and a woolly hat pulled down over his ears.

'You,' Barry sneered.

'Me. But I brought some friends,' Warlow said.

'What the hell is this? Why are you harassing me?'

'I don't like liars, Barry.'

'What lies have I said?'

'First off, there were no darts the night of Ronnie Probert's murder like you said there was. Called off because of a Covid outbreak.'

Lewis, leaning against the cab of the lorry, said, 'Shit.'

'Therefore, I am wondering what else you've lied about.'

'Is this about Jordan? We haven't seen him.'

'Sure? Not had him in to shift some of that nicked lead you have in the little storage area behind the scaffolding there.?' Warlow nodded towards the area.

'I told you we should have shifted that, Bar. Fuck's sake.'

'Shut up, Lewis.'

'We'll need you to account for that. And perhaps, while we're at it, you can think again about the last time you saw Jordan.'

'I keep telling you—'

Barry got no further as a shout came up from the garaging area. A Uniform in Hi-Viz was squatting next to some big drums next to a diesel storage tank.

Warlow walked over. The Uniform had the oil drum tilted at an angle.

'Heavy?' Warlow asked as he approached.

'Quarter full, sir,' said the Uniform, his voice strained with effort. Warlow joined him and they swivelled the barrel away. Underneath it sat a crushed plastic bag with a FreshFood logo. Jess came over from the office, blue gloves on.

'What do you reckon?' she asked. The bag looked flat and unpromising.

'Can but try.' Warlow peeled open the bag so they could look inside. He heard Jess gasp as something flesh-coloured appeared, flesh-coloured because it was… faux flesh. A flat nose and a distorted, empty eye socket looked back at them.

Warlow felt a surge of adrenaline mingled with nausea crinkle the skin on his nape. This was something from a flayed Lecterian nightmare. He dragged his eyes down to the skin below the chin and felt the breath he'd been holding hiss out.

'It's a mask,' he said.

At the neck, the skin ended in a smooth, formed edge.

'Like one of those you slip right over your hea—' Jess paused and looked at Warlow.

'Just like Ronnie Probert described.' He stared across at the scaffolders and muttered, 'Let's get these two into an interview room pdq.'

CHAPTER TWENTY-FIVE

Jordan and Troy played Call of Duty until 4:30, at which point Troy called a halt.

'Lola's dad is swinging by at five, Jord. You can't be here.'

Jordan, heavily into the game, sat back in his chair, east his eyes on the ceiling, and whined, 'Can't you cry off, Troy?'

'I've already told you, I'm in college tomorrow. I'm staying at Lola's. Her mum is cooking supper for eight and—'

Jordan narrowed his eyes. 'You stay in her bedroom?'

'Yeah. We're both sixteen, man.' Troy dismissed the question with contempt.

Jordan shrugged. 'Okay, I'll make like a ghost.' He ran upstairs and returned in two hoodies and an anorak. In his hand was a small box. 'Nicked this from Halfords yesterday.' He took out a cycle lamp. 'I'm tooled up now, no worries. I'm craving a Big Mac from Cross Hands, so I'll cycle up there with this baby.'

'Okay,' Troy said, glancing at his phone. 'But Lola's dad will go ape if he sees you. Lola said the cops have been looking all over and… he's just funny like that.' They fist-bumped. 'Soon as you get that laptop, yeah?'

'On it.' Jordan slid out of the back door into the oncoming darkness and headed off through the fields towards his bike.

———

BACK AT HQ, Jess, Rhys, and Warlow stood hunched around Rhys's computer. The DC had a report of the church roof theft up on the screen. 'Saint Thomas's, over in Pontardawe.'

'Off our patch, then?'

'Yep.' Rhys pulled up a photograph of the ripped-up roof with slates missing and the exposed felt also ripped underneath.

'How much is lead worth now?' Jess asked.

Rhys had the answer. 'A pound a kilo.'

'Is there a way we can get what was at the scaffolder's matched to what's left on that roof?' Warlow asked.

'I'll run it past Povey,' Rhys said.

Warlow straightened up. 'We'll tell Messrs Drew and Kirkland we're doing exactly that, even if we can't it'll make them sweat. What do we know about them?'

Rhys moved the mouse and clicked.

'Barry Kirkland, forty-two, co-owner of Castell Scaffolding. They don't have a website, but there is a Facebook page.'

'Run by Lorna, I expect,' Jess said.

'They're not just scaffolders, sir, they're roofers. The Facebook site says they can do guttering, re-lay valleys, rebuild chimneys, the works.'

'What about Barry's record?'

'Nothing much, sir. No arrests. A couple of warnings: illegal parking, verbal abuse of traffic wardens. Not married but has a partner and two kids. He was in the army for twelve years.'

'And Lewis?'

'Lewis Drew, aged twenty-nine. No arrest record.'

'Right, enough to be getting on with, I'd say,' Jess said.

'Solicitors here yet?' Warlow asked. They were going to interview these two separately, and that meant two solicitors.

'Duty sergeant says they've just arrived.'

'What about your dad, Rhys?' Jess brought things down to earth.

Rhys looked at her with what Warlow suspected was his brave smile. 'He's being transferred tonight, ma'am. They've got a bed in Morriston.'

'How is he?'

'Bored stiff, according to my mother. I'm supposed to take some crosswords in to him later. And no, sir, I don't need to visit now. I'm about to contact the vicar of Saint Thomas's to get a better idea of the timeline on the theft.'

'Good, right.' Warlow rubbed his hands together. 'My turn to make tea while we wait for the solicitors to chat with Barry and Lewis.'

'You, sir?' Rhys's brave attempt at reeling in his surprise ended with a fizzling out of the sentence.

'Me. And we are cracking open the Human Tissue For Transplant box. What Sergeant Jones doesn't know will not hurt him.'

————

GERAINT LANE SAT in his Renault Captur or, as his ex-partner called it, his ashtray on wheels. He never counted how many he smoked in a day.

Lighting up helped him concentrate. At one time, in the past admittedly, his ex had commented in a moment of weakness that his rough voice, exacerbated by his phlegmy morning cough, gave him a sexy edge. An edge long ago blunted by too much wine and terrible food.

But his car was his office. And from that office, he saw the looks the cops gave him as they came and went and lapped it up. What they failed to realise was that he could work from his driver's seat, pushed back to the max, just as easily as from home; a small flat in St Clears, he shared with his current partner. A hospital doctor whose busy shifts meant he and Lane could go a week without seeing one another. But that was okay because Lane was happy to travel to glamorous places like a car park in the back of sodding beyond. But at least here he could be at the sharp end of things. Getting snaps of what they were doing in the hall had been bloody magic. He'd made a few bob from that.

He was no paparazzi, but he had a camera in a top-of-the-range phone with God knows how many pixels. That helped. He checked his pack of fags and grimaced. One left. How the hell did that happen? That meant a trip to the nearest garage or shop. He'd Google that. Might as well grab a tea and a sausage roll, too. He'd missed lunch after that sham of a press conference. Never mind. He managed a couple of snaps of the fat sergeant and the carrot top when they arrived. He'd do something with that. They'd both walked past with tight-arsed expressions, avoiding any eye contact as they crossed to the community hall door. He'd work up something around town council tax pounds being wasted by two senior officers sorting through jumble sale donations. And no way was it the best use of resources, no matter what Drinkwater said.

Not much of a story, but who cared? The Echo would buy it, especially with the snaps.

He was at the point of sliding in his seatbelt on the fag and sausage roll run when the cyclist rode past. A thin guy on an S-Works bike wearing a black and yellow helmet, goggles, gloves, leggings, and a windproof tight-fitting coat. Only his beard was visible beneath the line of his goggles, and that was grey. The man rode past slowly, looking over at the cop car, at the Hi-Viz jacketed officer on the door and the response vehicle the officer probably wished he was sitting in. But he paid most attention to the female sergeant's Ford Focus. He slowed down to stare at it, making Lane wonder if he was a Focus freak.

Lane's Renault had tinted windows that made it diffi-cult sometimes to see if anybody was in the car. Probably why the cyclist paid no attention as he rode by. But then he turned around and came back. He hesitated at the Ford before stopping and sipping from a bottle. Lane trusted his instincts. And, though the likelihood was that this was just another middle-aged idiot pretending to be twenty years younger, perhaps this was something else.

Lane didn't like taking photographs through the wind-screen. They never looked good. He leaned across, opened the passenger-side window and held the phone forward at arm's length to see if he could get a clear shot.

The afternoon had settled into still and silent under the dense grey canopy of clouds. Lane wondered if it might snow. Perhaps the lack of noise gave things away as the windscreen powered down. The cyclist turned and looked at the car and the camera phone in the window. Lane pulled back, but the cyclist had already stashed his bottle, turned his back, and set off.

Oh well, Lane thought. Tough. Now he definitely needed another fag. He closed the windows, started up the Renault, and drove out, too preoccupied to see the cyclist waiting behind a stationary car on the street and not noticing when the bike pulled out to follow a van going in the same direction as he was. He remained oblivious to the fact that the bike stayed one car behind him all the way to Kidwelly.

———

THE MAN on the cycle had a great deal of experience in stalking. Animals mainly, but sometimes people. He did it patiently, carefully, and thoroughly, and he'd done it for years. Made a living out of it. Not to hunt and kill the animals he followed, but to photograph them.

Still, it was a transferable skill for following people. And Roger Hunt, ex-TV presenter, wildlife photographer and wanted murderer, had a very different agenda these days. And his presence in the community hall car park was tied to Lane in a roundabout way.

His story of the team's involvement, and his snap of Gil Jones, had triggered Hunt. Having so far evaded a manhunt following the death of one person and the attempted murder of two others in Gil's hometown of Llandeilo just before Christmas, Hunt's reappearance in the world had everything to do with unfinished business.

One of his victims, Daniel Hughes, remained in hospital, in a coma, with life-threatening head injuries after Hunt threw him off some stairs onto a railway platform. A second victim narrowly escaped a horrible death entombed in a stone coffin and left to roast to death from a bonfire lit above. But he survived and was now in hiding.

Thanks to Dyfed Powys Police.

Hunt needed to finish what he'd started. Fear of not doing that outweighed the fear of being caught, though he'd gone to elaborate lengths to remain hidden, holed up in an abandoned Royal Observer Corps underground observation post at the edge of a forest between Abergewsyn and Tregaron.

The post was listed as having been decommissioned

and "filled in". Few people cared either way. Few people ever went near. But his target, a solicitor called John Napier, whom Hunt was convinced was complicit in covertly filming him at an Airbnb, remained unpunished.

The primary culprit, the one who'd admitted under duress to organising it all, setting up the cameras, collecting the images, posting them on certain websites, died a horrible death at Hunt's hands. But there was no moving on for Hunt. Not until he'd finished the job he'd started. Even then, what life he'd have would never be the same as the one he'd left behind.

But finding Napier, wherever they'd hidden him, was now his priority.

His obsession. His ultimate goal.

And the man who only minutes ago tried taking a photograph of him might be the first stepping stone to achieving that.

CHAPTER TWENTY-SIX

GIL AND CATRIN did not see Lane leave. Nor did they notice the cyclist who'd shown so much interest in DC Richard's car.

'One day,' Gil said, thumbing through a programme for the 1979 international rugby match between Wales and France, 'robots will do all of this.'

'You think so?' Catrin asked.

'I do. The digital age and all that. Look at how things have changed in the last few decades.'

Catrin rolled her eyes out of Gil's view. 'Please tell me this isn't another good old days' rant, is it?'

'Not at all. But I remember DWM. Days without mobiles. And now look at us. Might as well get the buggers implanted at birth.'

Catrin, wading through the contents of Probert's attic at last, but so far only getting past the first three suitcases full of more old training kit, raised an eyebrow. 'Modern policing totally depends on information technology, you have to admit that. We can't function without it.'

'Good point. But with all that endless technological

possibility comes the endless probability something will go the way of the gremlin, too.'

Catrin sent him a wry smile.

'I mean,' Gil continued, putting the programme down and picking up another, 'just this morning, I got a call from a nice girl from cyber security,' he dropped his chin to throw Catrin a glance, 'with a Kolkata accent, who assured me she was phoning on behalf of ST—'

'Is that who you're with? Sat Telecom?'

'Fibre fast deal, I'll have you know. It is important in the Jones' household for the Lady Anwen to be able to purchase whatever she requires at the touch of a button. Only last week, we almost ran out of pink Himalayan salt, and you can imagine what would happen if that apocalyptic event ever materialised.'

Catrin stuffed an old Cardiff RFC tracksuit back into a bag.

'Apparently,' Gil continued, 'they'd had reports, these cyber security honchos, from my area, would you believe, of people logging onto the internet after midnight hours and very possibly using my IP address to upload, and perhaps download, all kinds of things that would not only make me unhappy but are also against the law.'

'I bet. I hate scam calls,' Catrin said. 'What did you do?'

'What I always do. Followed every word they said, gave them access to my computer, and waited as they copied every piece of personal and financial information I had the misfortune to save, safe in the knowledge that at least the post-midnight internet thieves now could not get to me.'

'And what did you really do?'

'Put the phone down and let her go on at me for seven minutes, grunting now and again in the most un-computer savvy way as possible, while I searched for and then put on, a very loud live edition of the Trogs singing Wild Thing. I let it play for five minutes, phone next to the speaker, without ending the call.'

Catrin shook her head.

'She didn't ring back.' Gil's phone rang, and he swiped to accept. 'That might be her now.'

Catrin wheezed out a laugh while Gil took the call.

'DI Allanby,' he said when the conversation ended. 'DCI Warlow would like us to call in with Jordan Nicholas's grandmother on the way back. They have the scaffolders in for questioning after some interesting finds at the depot.'

Catrin arched her back. 'Okay. Glad to get a change from this. One more day, and I should at least have gone through most of the paperwork.' She eyed the still unopened boxes.

Gil followed her gaze. 'I doubt you'll need me for that.'

'No, I can manage tomorrow. One last effort. But I appreciate your help.'

'I've bloody loved it. Nostalgia central. Christ, I was at half of these games.' He held up another programme. 'Those were the days of the old Arm's Park. Before they built the new stadium. Standing room only on the East Terrace there behind the posts. From there, I watched Ronnie Probert bamboozle the Scots, taunt the Irish, and bewitch the English. You couldn't bloody move once you were sardined in, but someone always fainted. And don't ask what you did if you wanted to pee.'

'Sounds horrific.'

'I'll tell you, anyway. You peed in a bottle and did your best to remember you'd done that when you got thirsty later and forgot that was why you were holding that bottle. We all suffered together. But when they played the anthem….' Gil shook his head. 'Raw emotion. You had to be there. *Byth cofiadwy.*'

Unforgettable.

'My dad says much the same.'

They packed up and signed out. Lane's car had gone.

'Perhaps he's seen the light. Or a crucifix?'

'Run out of fags, more like. Shall I send out a search party?'

Soon, Gil would remember that quip and wonder at the irony of it.

———

WARLOW DIVVIED UP THE INTERVIEWS. He and Rhys would talk to Kirkland, with Jess observing. She and Rhys would talk to Drew, with Warlow analysing from the observation room.

Barry Kirkland's solicitor sat quietly while Rhys read the caution. Warlow knew him as someone who had no agenda. Barry sat with his arms folded, his thousand-yard stare under the bushy eyebrows so at odds with the shaved head. The little stubble that remained on that dome told Warlow that, had he let it grow, Barry would have had a circlet of hair three inches below the crown in a kind of monkish look. But without the humility.

'We all know why we're here, Barry,' Warlow said. 'Why don't you save us all some time and tell us what happened the night you broke into Ronnie Probert's property?'

'I never broke into anyone's property.'

'You're not a burglar, then?'

'I don't do that sort of stuff.'

Warlow nodded. 'That's good to hear. But you steal lead from the roofs of churches, is that right?'

'No comment.'

'Would you like to account for that lead, Mr Kirkland?' Rhys asked.

'We're often up on old buildings, changing lead valleys and that. It builds up.'

'The lead that we found in that little hidey-hole at the back of your compound is the old lead that you've stripped from houses?'

'Replaced,' Kirkland said.

'So, you weren't on the roof of St Thomas's church in the early hours of 24th January?'

'No comment.'

Rhys pushed a photograph of the latex mask they'd found under the oil drum, taken with the mask removed from the bag and placed flat, across the desk. It looked eerily lifelike, its exaggerated nose and big ears notwithstanding. 'And can you account for this being found in your place of work, Mr Kirkland?'

'No comment.'

'That's the trouble with the horns of a dilemma. No matter which way you wriggle, they keep on digging in, right?' Warlow said. 'Because as of this moment, we have a mask which, according to witness statements from Ronnie Probert, from the victim himself before he died, matches that worn by his assailant or assailants. We have you lying about a darts competition the night Ronnie Probert was attacked. Putting all that together does not paint a good picture, Mr Kirkland. If you admit to the church roof theft, we'd know where you were, and you would be off the hook for the burglary.'

'No comment.'

Warlow slid over another printed image. This one of the denuded church roof. 'St Thomas's Church. Out on its own halfway up a mountain. Easy pickings. A place of worship. You a religious man, Barry?'

'I don't believe in that stuff. You're only here once.'

Warlow sat back. 'Is your mate Lewis likely to say the same thing, you reckon? He has no record. He's young.

Make no mistake, Ronnie Probert's attackers face a murder charge. I have it on good authority from the CPS that this is the line they want to take. People demand it. National treasure and all that.'

'No comment,' Kirkland said.

'Fine. I'll let you have a comfort break while we go and have a little chat with young Lewis.'

———

KIDWELLY HAD A CASTLE. Sylvia Reeves did not. Her address turned out to be a ground-floor flat in a grey-rendered terrace at the southern edge of the town. Gil and Catrin declined the offer of tea, though the little kitchen they sat in looked decent enough. Through the window, a garden the size of a large postage stamp sported some pots with the sad remains of dead flowers drooping over their rims.

Sylvia herself had long since given up any semblance of a fight against the toxic environment of fast food, so endemic in the country. As a result, and in stark contrast to her almost cachexic daughter, Sylvia was round of face and round of everywhere else. That she was only five feet tall added to that circular theme.

'We're here about Jordan, Sylvia.' Catrin took the lead.

'I don't know where he is before you ask. He's wild, that one.'

'Are you in contact?'

'Sometimes. Not regular, like. Before, when he was younger, if his mother kicked him out, he'd turn up, sleep on the couch. That hasn't happened for a while.'

The kitchen smelled of burnt cooking oil, and Catrin noticed the deep-fat fryer on the stovetop. 'But you've looked after Troy, his brother?'

'I did. Made sure he went to school every day.'

'But he's moved out now, right? We met him at his mother's house in Carway.'

Sylvia nodded, but her eyes betrayed the fact that this was not an idea she was overjoyed by. 'Said he needed more room for his games and such like.'

'You don't agree?'

Sylvia's mouth tightened. 'He's sixteen. He can do what he likes. But no, I don't agree. He's still a child and my daughter…' She considered her words. 'My daughter isn't capable.'

'Troy seems quite capable, though,' Catrin said.

'Thinks he is. But as I say, he's still a kid. He'd have been better off staying here. But I wasn't having Lola here.'

'His girlfriend?' Gil asked.

'Sure you don't want that tea?' Sylvia deflected the question.

'No, thank you,' Gil said. 'Didn't you get on with his girlfriend?'

'Bright girl, but…' Sylvia wrinkled her nose.

'What?' Gil asked.

'I don't know. Probably just me, but since he started seeing her, I noticed a change in him.'

'He's sixteen, Mrs Reeves.' Catrin offered this up as if it explained most of everything. Which it did.

'I speak my mind,' Sylvia said, but not without a twinge of regret. 'We had an argument, Troy and me. He moved out. Trouble is, I know him too well.'

'And Jordan? When was the last time you saw him?'

Sylvia put a hand on her hip and sat down with an added explanation by way of apology 'Arthritis in my back. Doctor says I'm to lose weight. Easier said than done.'

'Jordan, Mrs Reeves' Catrin refocused the conversation.

'I haven't seen Jordan for two months. He'd come for

the odd meal. Fish fingers and chips. His favourite even when he was small. He was a lovely kid when he was little. Full of it. He lost his way. And badly. But they get on as brothers now. Jordan…' she shook her head, 'can't help himself when it comes to trouble. That's why I don't like the thought of Troy there with him and no… guidance.'

'His mother—' Gil began.

'Linda is a lost cause. She's had all the help it's possible to get. From me, from doctors, from social services. When Jordan's dad went to jail, it broke her. She's still broken. We don't speak unless we have to.'

Catrin put her cards on the table. 'Jordan might be in real trouble, Sylvia. It's important he gets in touch with us. Please contact me anytime if you know anything or find anything out.'

Sylvia looked at the card but didn't pick it up. 'The people at college say Troy's talented. Around computers and the like. We got grants for him to get a laptop. Lola is big into games. Bought him that new one for Christmas. When she isn't here, they're online together. They have a bit of money, does her family.'

'Is that why—'

'We fell out? No, we fell out because I wouldn't bring him his tea one day while he was playing on the computer. Said he couldn't spare the time to come to the table.' She tutted. 'I'm not havin' that. I never let him sit in front of the telly at mealtimes, not going to start now because of bloody games.' Realising she'd gone on a rant, she took a breath. 'I get that Troy's still young, and he's fallen for Lola, but she's not like… us.' She looked at Gil.

'Kids change, Sylvia,' Gil said. 'Not much you can do about it.'

Later, in the car, Gil remained unusually silent.

'What do you think?' Catrin asked.

'I'm thinking that no matter how much trouble my lot

are, it's nothing, is it? Not compared to some people's. The Nicholases are broken. What bloody chance did a kid like Jordan have?'

'At least Troy seems to have his head screwed on.'

'By his grandmother, yes. But that house in Carway isn't a good option. He's on his own there.'

'He has Lola,' Catrin said.

'Sylvia wasn't impressed by her. But then, first boyfriends and girlfriends are always a challenge. I remember the cocky little bugger my youngest brought home.'

'Did you get rid of him with Gil glares?'

'No, she married him. He's a smashing bloke. But I wasn't having any of that the first time I saw him.'

'Lola's stealing Troy's affection; that's why Sylvia dislikes her. Green-eyed monster and all that.' Catrin screwed her mouth down tight. 'I don't like this case,' she said. 'There's something about it.'

'*Drewdod*,' Gil said.

Catrin nodded. Stink indeed.

CHAPTER TWENTY-SEVEN

JESS PLAYED NICE. Lewis Drew looked like someone just awarded the prize for the man most desperate to be anywhere but where he was. He sat stock still, allowing only his eyes to follow the DI as she settled in her seat.

'Can we get you anything, Lewis?' Jess asked.

'No,' Lewis said.

As with Kirkland, Rhys did the needful, reading out the caution, explaining why Lewis was here, ticking all the correct PACE boxes.

The solicitor allocated to Lewis was almost as young as he was but wore a crumpled suit and, from Jess's previous experience, liked things by the book and was keen to point out when they weren't.

Jess gave Rhys a nod. He slid over the photograph of the church roof.

'Recognise this, Lewis?'

Lewis kept his head still but allowed his eyes to flick down. 'Looks like a roof.'

'It does.' Jess smiled. 'And the spire is a giveaway. So, try again.'

'A church roof.'

'Exactly,' Jess said. 'And a specific church roof at that. One relieved of much of its lead.'

'I can see that.'

'Any idea how that might have happened?'

Lewis shook his head.

'You're certain about that, are you? Because, as you know, we found a large amount of lead at Castell Scaffolding. And the ironic thing is that the church roof in that photograph got stripped the same night as Ronnie Probert was attacked.'

'So?' Lewis's shrug was fuelled by bravado and no doubt warnings from Barry Kirkland. But it was also a shrug that oozed fear.

'Well, if it was you and your friend Barry up on the roof of the church, and by the way, we are testing the lead to see if it matches that of Saint Thomas's, we will find out. Only that will take a bit of time. If the lead matches, then game over. But I'll be honest with you, time is one thing that is in short supply. And if you can save us some, it would help. So, if you weren't on the church roof, it means that you could have been somewhere else.'

'I told you I was at my girlfriend's place.'

'You did, but that will be difficult to corroborate. It's called a Swiss cheese alibi because it's full of holes. Especially since we also found this mask at your place of work. And this mask is like the one worn by the thieves who burgled Ronnie Probert the night he was attacked.'

Rhys slid the photograph of the mask across, once more announcing that he'd done it by linking it to a number in the evidence file.

'I've never seen that before,' Lewis said. His Adam's apple bobbed as he tried, with difficulty, to swallow.

'Let me explain this to you, Lewis,' Jess said, calmly. 'Being on that church roof drops you in the doodoo. Not being on it drops you in different doodoo and from a much greater height.'

'What did Barry say?'

Jess's face fell in disappointment. 'Really? You know we can't tell you that. Let's just say his voice is getting hoarse from all the talking he's doing.'

Lewis muttered, 'Shit.' He leaned over to the solicitor, cupped his hand over his mouth, and whispered something.

The solicitor looked across at the officers. 'Mr Lewis would like to make a statement.'

'A written statement?'

The solicitor nodded.

Jess got up. 'You have pen and paper. We'll give you an hour.'

Warlow was all smiles when Jess came back to the interview room. 'Good job, DI Allanby.'

'Let's hope he comes up with the goods.'

'You get off home to that daughter of yours. I'll hang about for a while. Rhys, are you going down to Morriston tonight?'

'No, sir. No point. Dad hasn't left Glangwili yet. My mother's gone home. We'll find out what the plan is tomorrow.'

'Okay. Let me know when that statement is ready.'

'Where are you off, sir?'

'I have an errand to run.'

Warlow grabbed his coat and walked out to the Jeep. He had his wellies in the car and a couple of flashlights. He arrived at Horeb and Ronnie Probert's house in twenty minutes. He parked outside but didn't go in. Instead, he walked the two hundred yards along the road to the old, abandoned chapel the village got its name from.

A certain Stephen King might have felt he'd died and gone to heaven at this point. The boarded-up chapel, surrounded by the denuded branches of old trees and lit only by a streetlight on the road thirty yards back, cast its shadow over the access point to the cycle path. Beyond the brooding building, a graveyard with its stones canted at odd angles whispered dead memories in the breeze. Warlow turned gladly away from that and headed north.

After two hundred yards, lights from the villages of Five Roads and Horeb faded, and he found himself alone. The B4309 ran only fifty yards to his left, but it was invisible and only the sound of the odd car hinted at its proximity. Ahead and behind, the path stretched away, empty.

He'd wanted to experience this for himself. Though he was on foot, he covered a mile at an easy walking pace in twenty minutes. Another twenty, and he'd be in Cynheidre. On a cycle, it would have taken him five minutes to get to this point. But here, halfway between the two villages, all he could hear were his own footfalls. The point of the exercise had been to understand how accessible the path was, and how easy the walking, or cycling.

Ten out of ten for both.

He turned off his torch and let his eyes adjust to the darkness. The sky had been blanketed in clouds all afternoon after the early frost. No starlight or moonlight filtered down through the dense canopy. Around him, the night was like a thick cape, enveloping all his senses. Vague shapes took form. The bushes and the trees. But it was too dark to navigate without the help of a light. He'd need to tell the team that.

He was at the point of turning back when he saw it. Ahead of him in the darkness. A light, moving slowly back and forth. Red, hazy in the distance, but there, waving to him. A siren call.

A signal.

Warlow had a red filter on his torch to help with dark adaptation. He'd learned that a while ago whilst following a dog napper at a lake in the Gwendraeth Valley. He flipped it on now and used the illumination to move swiftly along the path toward the red light ahead. Five minutes of rapid walking brought him to an open stretch of the path where the bordering foliage fell away. The light was closer, still waving, at times brighter than others. Warlow lifted his torch and waved it back.

The light ahead disappeared.

He walked on, but something told him that whatever or whoever it had been behind that signal had gone. Was this the Signalman that everyone seemed so animated about? All he knew was that the light had been real. At least as real as seeing it alone on a path with no other living being within shouting distance and only the dead silence of an old railway line would allow. He turned and retraced his steps, glad when the lights of Five Roads glowed ahead of him.

He got back to the Jeep and checked the time. He'd been on the path for a good half hour.

He found Gil's number and pressed the button that would dial it.

'Evan, aren't you home yet?'

'Decided I needed some air. I'm just leaving Five Roads.'

'Oh,' Gil said. 'What's the attraction?'

Warlow told him where he'd been and what he'd seen.

'For God's sake, man. Didn't you get the memo about a vicious murderer in the area? If you needed company, you should have given me a shout.'

'It wasn't… … It didn't feel like that. And tell me why a murderous thief would wave a red light on a cycle path.'

'So, you've seen our Signalman, you reckon?'

'Not sure what I saw. But we'll come back, you and I, and scout around.'

'Can't wait,' Gil said. 'That neck of the woods has its own violent history.'

'The Rebecca Riots?'

'Very biblical, the Rebecca crowd. The hand of God and all who sail in her. Admittedly, two hundred years ago, but I reckon there is something in the water. And before all of that, if you look hard enough, witchcraft was rife in rural areas. And you could not get more rural before they discovered coal where you are now. Bloody hotbed it was. You couldn't go for a walk without risking being turned into a toad.'

'Have you been on the Laphroaig already?'

Gil sighed. 'All I'm saying is that perhaps you should not be walking on an unlit path alone. Or at least without a crucifix. Catrin and I are already convinced there are vampires about.'

'Vampires?'

'Geraint Lane.'

Warlow chuckled. 'How is he?'

'Wasn't outside the hall when we left. Perhaps he's seen the light, too.'

'Like me, you mean?'

'Not a wavy red one, no. How goes it with the scaf-folders?'

'I'm about to find out.'

'Right, well, if you fancy more Signalman jaunts, give me a ring. I'll bring the garlic and something made of iron. That should cover all bases.'

Rhys was waiting for him in the Incident Room when Warlow got back. It was knocking on seven by now.

'Well?' Warlow greeted the DC.

'Drew has coughed to the church roof theft, sir. They got there around 1am and left around at half three. I haven't charged him yet.'

'Nothing from Kirkland?'

Rhys shook his head.

'Okay, we'll keep them overnight up at Ammanford in the custody suite. Let them sweat a bit.'

'This is good, though, sir, isn't it?' Rhys seemed a little deflated by Warlow's lack of enthusiasm.

'Good that we've nabbed them for theft from a church roof, but not so helpful in our murder case.'

'I suppose.'

'And I'm staying sceptical until we have some proof.'

'Proof, sir?'

'They're roofers. We've just given them an alibi for being somewhere else when the burglary took place. Now I want proof that's where they were.'

'And how are we going to get that, sir?'

'We'll get CID onto it overnight. See what they can come up with. And then you go home. Gina will think I've abducted you.' He issued some instructions, and Rhys made the calls.

By 8pm, Warlow was heading home to pick up his patient and understanding dog from the sitters.

CHAPTER TWENTY-EIGHT

AT ABOUT THE same time Warlow finally drove out of the gates of Dyfed Powys Police HQ, the front doorbell rang at Jess and Molly's house in Cold Blow.

Jess had installed a video camera. She flicked on the app and saw two people standing there, a man and a woman. The man in a suit and tie, the woman in a zipped-up, full-length puffer coat. Jess used the app to communicate.

'Can I help you?'

Her voice caught them both by surprise. The man recovered first. 'Hello, DI Allanby? Sorry to bother you.' The man pulled out a small wallet and held it up to the camera. Jess recognised the silver metal crest before she looked at the photograph and the name. She'd had a wallet exactly like it for several years. The plastic card on the left read, DI Simon Taube, Greater Manchester Police. The woman held a similar wallet out with an identical crest, but her ID card read DS Paula Bolaji.

'Apologies for turning up late and unannounced. Can we have a quick word?'

Molly ran down the stairs. 'Who is it, Mum?'

'Colleagues,' Jess said. 'Go upstairs, and no listening.'

Molly sighed and rolled her eyes. 'I'll put my earphones on.'

Jess opened the door. Taube was tall and spare of frame. Bolaji was more difficult to assess under the shapeless coat.

'Come in.' Jess noticed a dark Jaguar in the drive. 'You're a bit off your patch, aren't you?'

Taube answered, 'We are. But we, that is me and my boss, felt this ought to be done face-to-face.'

A flutter rippled through Jess's viscera. 'That sounds ominous. Come through to the kitchen.' She led the way, offered them seats, put the kettle on and, as the element rumbled, said, 'My daughter is upstairs. She has big ears. I take it this needs to be a confidential conversation?'

Taube nodded. He hadn't smiled yet. Jess walked to the radio and put some music on low before turning back to the officers.

'To what do I owe the pleasure?'

'We're here about DS Rick Allanby, your ex, ma'am,' Bolaji said.

'Well, since neither of you have asked me to sit down to hear the news, I assume he isn't dead.'

'Nothing like that,' Taube said. Both he and Bolaji spoke with Manchester accents, the latter's a little broader. 'You're aware that Sergeant Allanby went undercover?'

'I am.'

'We're here because DS Allanby's identity became compromised, and we had to extract him from a dangerous situation. He's on leave, but it is expected that he will be seconded to the Northwest Regional Crime Unit out of Carlisle.'

Jess's laugh was as dry as baked sand. 'I still have friends in Manchester. So, I already knew he'd been extracted, but…Shit, he's going to love that.'

'It's the safest option for now.'

The kettle stopped boiling. Tea was offered, preferences given. As she spooned in some sugar for Taube and with her back to the officers, Jess put them out of their misery. 'But you haven't come here to confirm something I already knew, have you?'

'Not entirely, no,' Taube answered.

Bolaji elaborated, 'The situation was complex. Rick was recognised by someone he'd interacted with before. Just bad luck. We were able to intercept and extract. However, we've received intel from the group he was involved with. They've threatened reprisals against DS Allanby and… his family.'

Jess pivoted, spoon in hand, mouth open.

'I'm sorry, Jess,' Taube said.

'We don't think they have any actual intelligence. It's their way of lashing out,' Bolaji said.

'But it's tangible enough to have come down here to tell me, correct?' She slid the mugs across the table.

'Hyper-vigilance is what we recommend.' Bolaji kept up the buzzwords. 'And, since this is a rented property, it might be an idea to consider moving.'

Jess dropped her head. 'Are you serious?'

'I realise it's not always easy. Especially where property is owned, but in your case—'

'Is he okay? Rick, I mean?' Jess interjected.

'Yes, ma'am. The group he was trying to infiltrate are known for being brutal. He was not the only officer we needed to get out.'

'My daughter's doing her A levels.' Jess couldn't quite hide the note of petulance in her voice and grimaced at hearing it.

Bolaji nodded. 'We don't recommend moving completely, ma'am. Not out of the area, but a change of address might be—'

'The safest thing?' Jess jumped in a second time. 'Jesus.'

'We're monitoring the activity of known members of this criminal group,' Taube said as if that helped. 'Obviously, if we thought there was any direct threat, we'd let you know.'

'Very kind.' Jess nodded, hating herself for letting the sarcasm bite. She had a glass of wine, not tea, and enough insight to realise none of this was these two officers' fault. She drew a breath and let it out slowly. 'You staying down overnight?'

'No, we're going back right after this.'

'It's a four-and-a-half-hour drive.'

'We know, ma'am.'

'Can I make you a sandwich?' She paused before adding, 'For turning up and torpedoing my life.'

'Will it have ground glass in it, ma'am?' Bolaji asked.

It broke the tension. 'Only a bit.'

Taube smiled. 'You don't have to make us food, Jess—'

'Yes, I do. There isn't anything around here. McDonalds and KFC in Carmarthen, if you're lucky. I've got some decent bread and ham and cheese with pickle. That do you? You can eat it as you go.'

Bolaji and Taube exchanged glances. 'That would be really nice,' Bolaji said.

'Right. Drink your tea and tell me who or what I should look out for while I make your supper.' The flutter inside had grown into a palpable grinding. The tips of her fingers had gone cold, too. But making the sandwiches helped.

However, there were no sandwiches to make later in her bed after the GMP detectives had left. Not when her thoughts went round and around like a pair of trainers in a washing machine, thumping in accompaniment to her pounding heart.

Bloody Ricky. Top marks for buggering everything up.

She hadn't told Molly yet, fobbing off her questions with the plausible lies of an old case needing her input. An old case that merited two officers travelling all the way from Manchester.

But she was going to have to tell her the truth, and soon.

Jess finally fell asleep at around two and was wide awake again at six.

Happy days.

———

WARLOW CALLED a team meeting first thing the next morning.

He noticed Jess looking a bit tired but said nothing. He suspected the same could be said of them all when a case took hold.

'Rhys, I believe CID had something for you this morning?'

'They did, sir. We had someone do an ANPR search for vehicles owned by Lewis Drew and Barry Kirkland on the night of Ronnie Probert's attack. They came up positive on a panel van owned by Kirkland that he drives to and from work. A Vauxhall Vivaro.'

'Great,' Catrin said.

But Rhys wasn't smiling. 'The vehicle was picked up on the M4 and A4067 on two occasions several hours apart. The first time, heading east on the M4 just after junction 47, spotted on a speed camera and then again at a round-about in Pontardawe. That was just after midnight. The same camera picked up the van travelling in the opposite direction a little after 3.35am.'

'That's nowhere near Five Roads,' Gil said.

'Exactly,' Rhys agreed.

Warlow stood up. 'I'm sure you will have noticed DC

Harries's subdued enthusiasm regarding this bit of detective work. Bottom line, we have Barry Kirkland's van near a church roof lead theft on the night of Ronnie Probert's burglary. Lewis Drew has confessed to the same, implicating Kirkland. A situation I remained sceptical about until this.' He pointed to a posted-up image of Kirkland's van as taken from the cameras. 'Much as I hate to admit it, this rules out the scaffolders as our burglars.'

'So, how do we account for the mask found on site, sir?' Catrin asked.

'That, sergeant, is an excellent question.'

'It's no mystery who else had access to the depot, sir,' Rhys said. 'That could have been Jordan Nicholas, surely?'

'Don't call me surely,' Warlow muttered, slurring the surely into Shirley.

Rhys blinked.

'Old joke from an old film,' Gil explained.

'First things first.' Warlow turned back to the team. 'Gil, how did you get on with Jordan Nicholas's grandmother yesterday?'

The team listened as Gil gave them a summary of the meeting with Grandma Reeves. And all the while, Warlow had one eye on Jess, who seemed to be staring off into space and seeing a different scene to the one Gil was conjuring up.

'I wouldn't say she has a soft spot for the Jordan Nicholas of today,' Gil said. 'But there is no doubting she did her share of parenting when he was a kid. Her relationship with her addict daughter, Jordan's mother, is… fragile.'

'What about the brother?'

'Troy? She isn't happy about him moving out, but then again, he is sixteen and has a mind of his own, as well as a girlfriend and a PlayStation. He wanted the extra space for his gaming room, apparently.'

'I've seen that,' Rhys said. 'He did a good job there.'

'The girlfriend, Lola, seems to have been a bit of a disruptive influence when it comes to Grandmother and Troy,' Catrin added.

Nods all around. No one said it, but Warlow suspected they were all thinking 'hormones.'

'But you don't think the grandmother is hiding Jordan?'

'I doubt it, sir,' Catrin said. 'The flat she lives in isn't big. Nowhere to hide—'

Jess got up suddenly and excused herself, cutting Catrin off before striding from the room, all eyes following her.

'Ma'am?' Catrin asked, but Jess waved her away.

Warlow, however, got up and followed her out. He turned at the door. 'Chase up forensics. See if they've found anything on that mask from the scaffolder's place.'

Rhys nodded, but just then, his phone rang. He looked down and back up again, doing a wonderful impression of a cornered mouse. 'It's my mother, sir.'

'Take it in my office. Go.'

Warlow hadn't seen where Jess had gone, but he had a rough idea. And so, when she emerged from the ladies, he was leaning against the wall, waiting for her.

'Care to talk about it?' Warlow asked.

'Upset stomach,' Jess said with the briefest of smiles.

'I bet. But what's brought it on?'

'I let Molly cook last night.'

Warlow shook his head. 'Shame on you for using your daughter's culinary shortcomings in a blatant lie.'

Jess shut her eyes for a three-second beat and then opened them again. 'I got a visit from two GMP OC detectives last night,' she paused before adding, 'they think that me and Molly might be at risk.'

'From Rick's undercover cock-up? Shit,' Warlow said.

'On toast, as well as the bed,' Jess said.

OC did not stand for Orange County as much of the Netflix generation might assume. Here it was an acronym for organised crime.

'Is Rick okay?'

Jess smiled. 'You're a better man than me, Evan. I didn't ask about him until three sentences in.'

'Are they offering protection?'

'No need, they said. The risk is low, but they're suggesting a change of address, just to be safe.'

Warlow nodded. 'Probably sensible. What did Molly say?'

'I haven't told her yet. She is going to go ballistoid.'

'That must be one of Rhys's words.'

'It is. And it can't have come at a worse time with her A levels looming. But she's going to be upset, I know that.'

'Right, well, let me tell her.'

'No, that's my job.'

'Your job is to make her feel safe.'

'I'm still going to tell her. This is Allanby dirty laundry.'

Warlow wasn't to be put off. 'Okay, but at least let me help get you out of there pronto. You can come to mine until you find somewhere decent. And she will not turn that down because of the added attraction.'

'You mean Cadi?'

'I meant me, but Cadi will do.'

That brought Jess's first smile of the morning. 'Thanks, Evan, but we both know there isn't room. You've only got the two bedrooms.'

'True, but I have been working on my garden room over the winter. It's almost finished. Only needs a lick of paint. I wasn't going to do that until the spring, and that can wait. I've had the Davies boys working on it. It's insulated, double-glazed, and I've just moved a sofa bed into it. I can stick an oil heater in there for now.'

'No, Evan, that's—'

'An easy answer to a tricky problem. You know it makes sense. It'll give you time to find somewhere reasonable.' He was glad to see her resistance faltering.

'They said all we needed to do was be vigilant.'

'Then be vigilant from Ffau'r Blaidd. And believe me, they'll never find you there. They're still searching for two Amazon drivers.'

She looked into his face, the strain of earlier already easing. 'You're a good man, Evan Warlow.'

'Please don't. Rumours like that can get a DCI into all kinds of trouble.'

CHAPTER TWENTY-NINE

WARLOW AND JESS got back to the Incident Room as Rhys emerged from the SIO cupboard, phone in hand.

'Well?' Warlow asked.

Rhys shrugged. 'It's nothing, sir. Just my mother telling me that my dad's going down for a CT angiogram this morning. She was only keeping me informed. I suppose I'm a bit jumpy.'

'I'd be crawling up the wall,' Jess said and put her hand on his arm.

Rhys gave her a grateful smile. 'And one of the dispatchers contacted CID because they took a call from Geraint Lane's partner who said he didn't come home last night.'

Gil looked up from his desk. '*Iesu post*, he has a partner?'

'Apparently.'

Gil shook his head. 'Please don't tell me they've found two corpses completely drained of blood.'

'No, sarge,' Rhys said, nonplussed.

'Take no notice, Rhys,' Catrin said.

'Please don't tell me you buried Lane,' Warlow said to Gil.

'I'd be lying if I said it hadn't crossed my mind, but no.'

Warlow nodded. 'When was the last time either of you saw him?'

Catrin answered, 'Outside the community hall when we went back yesterday but he'd gone when we came out just before five.'

'I can't see how any of it is related, but let's get his registration out to the Uniforms and see if he's parked up somewhere. And ask CID to give the partner a ring. Make sure Lane's not diabetic or something odd like that. Stranger things.'

'Maybe he's had a stroke, sir,' Rhys said.

'Or an illicit liaison,' Catrin suggested.

'Or a stroke after an illicit liaison,' Gil said. 'That would—'

'Right.' Warlow put a stop to the thread. 'Let's not waste any more time on Lane for now. I need to speak to Buchannan with DI Allanby. By the time I'm back, it'll be coffee, or other warm brown liquids are available, time. Rhys?'

'Got you, sir. I'll get the kettle on.'

Buchannan proved to be even more insistent for Jess to move out once she'd outlined her visit from GMP colleagues. He arranged for some Uniforms to be at hand and suggested Jess go back immediately, with them as escorts, to pack up some essentials. When she objected, citing a busy workload, Warlow shut her down. 'We'll survive for half a day, Jess.'

She looked from Buchanan to Warlow. 'I'm so sorry about this.'

'Goes with the territory, Jess,' Buchannan said.

'Now I have to ring my daughter and tell her the news.'

'Stab vest?' Warlow asked.

'Don't joke. I can already see that look.'

'The one that can penetrate steel?' Warlow asked.

That got him a rueful smile.

Warlow went back to the Incident Room alone. 'DI Allanby has had to attend to some personal business. She'll be back when she's done.' Warlow eyed a mug of steaming tea. 'Mine?'

Rhys nodded.

Warlow took a sip. 'Right, where were we? The scaffolders are out of it. So, that leaves us with Jordan Nicholas unaccounted for and looking more than ever likely, since he has knowledge of the scaffolder's yard where he may have tried to hide the mask.' He turned to Catrin. 'I take it you've learned nothing from Probert's effects that might surprise us?'

'Just a few boxes to go, sir. But nothing yet.'

'Ralph Probert is still on our radar, though,' Gil said.

Warlow nodded. 'Let's see if he has any connection with Castell Scaffolding. Has he used them in the past? Does he know Kirkland, or Drew, or Lorna, the secretary?'

The team wrote notes in their pocketbooks.

'But that brings us back again to Jordan Nicholas.' Warlow walked to the Gallery, eyeing the image of the man, really only a boy, posted on the board.

'Would it be worth another chat with his brother?' Gil asked. 'Their grandmother suggested Troy had promised to help Jordan change direction.'

'Brotherly love?' Warlow tried not to sound too sceptical.

Gil shrugged.

'But it is a thought. While Catrin finishes at the hall, why don't you and I visit him at his college? Which one is it?'

'Gorseinon, sir,' Catrin said,

'Yes. Wouldn't do any harm to catch him a bit off guard.'

'Good idea, sir.'

'Should I stay here, then, sir?' Rhys asked, ever hopeful for a jaunt in the car.

'You should. We have access to Castell Scaffolders records. Find out who else they employed on an ad hoc basis. They might be a link to Jordan Nicholas.'

Rhys nodded.

What remained unsaid, but at the front of everyone's minds, was that Rhys needed to stay put in case his mother rang.

———

GOWER COLLEGE'S Gorseinon campus sat on the other side of the River Loughor. The other side denoting a different county, police force, and local education authority from Dyfed Powys. But the range of courses it offered pulled students in from all over. Access was via the rather grandly named Belgrave Road, a residential street. Though any resemblance to its more renowned SW1 London counterpart began and ended with the name.

Warlow spoke briefly to the principal, explained he did not need permission from any parent to talk to Troy, nor that he was under any direct suspicion, and was introduced to Tina Bridge, a student support officer. Warlow took up her offer of a room to use and suggested she sat in on the discussion.

The room was light, painted white with grey and maroon padded seating, a round table, and blinds. Tina texted Troy, who turned up looking slightly bemused. A look that evaporated on seeing Warlow again, to be replaced by anxiety.

'What's this about?'

'Troy,' Tina began, 'these gentlemen are police officers.'

'We've already met,' Warlow said. 'Sorry to interrupt your studies.'

'I've got some free time. My next lecture isn't until after lunch.'

'Good timing,' Gil said. 'We need to run a couple of questions past you again.'

Troy shrugged but sat down, sliding a backpack off his shoulder.

'I spoke to your grandmother yesterday,' Gil said. 'She told me that you and Jordan didn't get on, but that things are better now.'

'Jordan didn't like that I was the one who got to stay with Gran, while he had to stay with my mother. My gran doesn't have room for both of us. He took it out on me when he was younger. Not bad, like. Ignored me more than anything.'

'But that's better now?'

'I'm older.' Troy shrugged. 'We chill, play games sometimes. Now we have that in common.'

Gil nodded. 'Have you spoken to Jordan lately?'

Troy didn't answer.

Warlow spoke into the void. 'If you have, if you or your mother have seen Jordan since we spoke and you don't tell us, you could both be charged with obstructing our enquiries. That would not look good on the CV, Troy.'

Tina sent Warlow a disapproving stare. The DCI ignored her.

'The longer this drags on, the longer it is that we can't talk to Jordan, the worse it will be for him in the end.' Warlow pulled a chair up opposite the boy. 'If you can tell us anything, you'll be doing him and your mother a huge favour.'

Troy stared at Warlow before arching his neck backwards over the back of the chair. Warlow thought he heard him whisper, 'Shit.'

'Troy?' Gil prompted.

The boy's head came forward, his expression set. 'Yesterday. We spoke yesterday. He came back to the house, and we played some games.'

'Where is he now?'

'I don't know. He has a bike. He uses the cycle path a lot to avoid the roads.'

'Where does he go at night, Troy?'

Troy shook his head, a tiny smile curling the corner of his mouth.

'If you know—'

'He doesn't go anywhere. You've been to my mother's house. The place next door is boarded up. All the noise and the shouting and Jordan being an arse, it drove the neighbours away. The council boarded up the house. It's like a cave inside. But there's a way across. From our upstairs bathroom. There's a hole in the wall that Jordan covered over with a panel. He leaves the ladder outside his bedroom to make it look like that's where he goes every time. But it isn't. Not every time. He keeps stuff in the other house. Tools and stuff.'

Gil exchanged a darted glance with Warlow before asking, 'Has he ever mentioned anything to you about the property that was burgled? The Probert property.'

'It was all he talked about when he was putting the scaffolding up. Ronnie Probert's house. The flashy furniture he saw through the windows. The photos on the wall. Not a big rugby fan, Jordan, but he knew who Ronnie Probert was. Who doesn't? He came home and kept on about how he bet there was cash there. Somewhere. I told him that was stupid. People don't keep cash these days. Not with phones and stuff. But…'

'But what?' Gil pressed the boy.

Troy sucked in a lungful of air. 'I don't know anything else.'

'We need you to come with us now, Troy. I'll make sure you're back here for your lecture. We need you to show us the bathroom.'

Troy, looking miserable, nodded.

Warlow thanked Tina. Ten minutes later, they were in the Jeep and on the way to Carway.

―――――

THE LAST BUT ONE BOX.

A 50-litre box, opaque plastic sides, a black lid on top. More modern than the old suitcases and cardboard boxes Catrin had been dealing with up to now.

Inside looked organised. Another smaller plastic box and a carefully arranged set of envelopes stacked upright.

She took out the envelopes first.

The letters contained within were all from the last five years. From after Probert had lost his wife.

A revamped will and more correspondence from his financial advisor showing that Ronnie Probert had been a wealthy man. And the "joke" of an advisor, at least according to his sister and niece, had done him proud. His investments had flourished over the years. ISA holdings in excess of £600,000, a SIPP valued at half a million. Ronnie could be drawing down from these investments, living high on the hog, and still seeing his investments grow.

Then she turned her attention to the box.

Inside were toys; a couple of small teddies, and more papers. But these were in buff envelopes that looked much older than the stacked reports from the financial advisor, thin from much handling and tri folded. Catrin took one out, read the contents, and felt a little thrill of horror run through her.

She photographed everything on her phone, turned back to the other papers, to take a photograph of the header that showed the financial advisor's name, address, and number. Then she wrote the name separately in her notebook.

William Clement Associates.

She spoke to the evidence officer briefly and explained that she wanted to take the box back to HQ. Then she phoned William Clement Associates. They had an office in Carmarthen.

She made an appointment for 3pm.

CHAPTER THIRTY

They didn't need a warrant.

They'd phoned ahead and got some Uniforms out to Carway, as well as an officer from the council. Between them, they took down the marine ply-boarding over the front door of the property next to the Nicholas's house. Gil was going to come in from that direction.

Warlow, meanwhile, after explaining why he was there to an already drunk and methadone-chilled Linda Nicholas, allowed Troy to lead the way up to the bathroom.

It was not the biggest bathroom Warlow had even been in.

Nor the most hygienic.

Something had left a dark stain above the water line in the toilet bowl. Soap had built up a crust on the sink and hair and dirt had formed a nice dark topping. The mirror above the sink had a misty sheen from years of not having been cleaned. Black mould grew around the shower-tray sealant. The bath, too, could do with a scrubbing. But Warlow wasn't here as a health inspector. He followed Troy in.

Above the bath, one entire wall was mocked up in blue-veined marble at odds with the grubby tiling else-where, but easy to clean if anyone in the household felt so inclined. Which, by the look of things, they did not.

Troy stood at the marbled wall over the bath. Marble that turned out to be a sheet of Respatex. A sheet that, on closer inspection, didn't quite extend to the edges of the wall.

Troy stepped over the bath rim into the tub and, facing the wall, slid his fingers under one side of the panel and inched it out. He repeated the same on the opposite side and, with one motion, lifted the panel up and away. Stale cold air washed in from the opposite room. Another bath-room, this one painted yellow, dark and dingy with no light from the boarded-up window.

From inside the house, Gil's voice echoed. 'Hello?'

Troy stepped out of the bath, and Warlow stepped in and over into the bath on the other side. One more step took him to a filthy, dust-covered floor. He stepped across to the closed door and opened it.

'Up here. We're inside.'

Waving beams of torchlight came up the stairs. 'Lucky Catrin isn't with us,' Gil said. 'She'd have hated this. Where's the mother?'

'Kitchen,' Warlow said. 'We'll need to talk to her, but first, let's give this place the once over.'

The council had gutted the property, though the kitchen still contained a fridge and washing machine and there were two cheap faux-leather chairs in the living room. But in the bedroom next to the bathroom, they found a tool bag with a Castell Scaffolding logo on the side. Whether stolen or a gift, Warlow cared less. Inside the bag, amongst a collection of other tools, they found a crowbar and a claw hammer.

'I'll ring Povey,' the sergeant said. 'Does she need to come here?'

'We need photos before she takes it to the lab.'

The crime scene crew arrived an hour later. While they did what they needed to do in the bathroom, Warlow spoke to Troy and his mother.

Her eyes showed that lag that came with intoxication, the lids moving in slow motion and returning to half-mast as if she was constantly fighting sleep.

'How are you holding up, Linda?' Warlow asked.

'Same old.' Her words were slurred.

Warlow glanced at his watch. It was now half-past twelve in the afternoon. A long day stretched ahead of Linda.

'Did you know about the bathroom?'

'Jordan... he fixed it.' She shook her head. 'He's handy like that.'

'You were aware there was a hole in the wall?'

'What hole? Tiles kept falling off... Jordan fixed that.'

Warlow didn't know whether to believe her or not. Nor did he see the point of taking her in for questioning. That would do no one any good. She'd been better the last time he came. He glanced across at the sink. Two empty wine bottles sat there. He didn't recognise the labels. 'Where is Jordan, Linda?'

She shrugged. 'You bastards keep chasing him. You tell me. But you don't... you don't know the half of it. You don't know... nothing.' Slowly, she tapped her nose with what passed for a gummy smile on her face.

Warlow turned to Troy. 'Thank you for this. It's for the best.'

'Is it?' Troy sat with his arms folded.

'We can arrange for your mum to go to the hospital.'

'Hospital?' The word dripped with derision. 'What's

the point of a hospital? She's upset, that's all. When she's upset, she ups the dose.'

'Of what?'

'Of whatever's here,' Troy said. 'Tesco brought some vodka and wine yesterday. Her lucky day.'

'What about you?'

'You said you'd take me back to college.'

'I mean afterwards. Tonight?'

'I'll stay at my gran's or my girlfriend's place.'

Warlow nodded. 'Is Jordan likely to come back tonight?'

Troy snorted. 'You're kidding. Jungle drums are loud on this estate. Someone will have texted him.'

'Not you?'

Troy shook his head. 'I want this to be over.'

'We all do, Troy. We all do.'

Povey's team did a sweep of the empty house but found nothing. By six, a prelim exam of the hammer and the crowbar confirmed they were stained with blood. They'd have to await DNA. But the blood was enough. Finding Jordan Nicholas was now a manhunt.

They had officers posted at both ends of the cycle path at Tumble and the nearest access point to Carway. They were also watching the roads in and out of the villages. If Nicholas was using the cycle path, Warlow wanted as many bases covered as possible. Regular patrols drove past the racecourse at Ffos Las. But it was a waiting game. If Troy was right, Jordan wouldn't come near the house. Though it was not a crime scene, the abandoned property next door to the Nicholases attracted a lot of attention that afternoon.

By early evening, they'd boarded up the property once more. All evidence had been removed, and Linda Nicholas was left alone to find what peace she could in the contents of a bottle.

———

AT FFAU'R BLAIDD THAT EVENING, Warlow entertained his guests. He made some *cawl* from vegetables and lamb and served it up with some sourdough from a bakery in Narberth together with some sharp Welsh cheese. After Jess had thanked him for the fifth time, Warlow put up his hands in protest.

'Look, this will not happen every evening. Just so happens I had enough supplies in. I make this and it lasts me a week. Obviously, not this week.' Warlow flicked a glance Molly's way.

She was halfway through biting into a crust and her second bowl. 'I heard that,' she said. Cadi watched her warily from her basket, hoping, no doubt, for a crumb or two.

'We'll share the meal preparation,' Jess said.

'If you like. And I'll use the downstairs loo and shower; you two have the upstairs. Like we did when you were away and Molly stayed.'

'This is so disruptive,' Jess said.

'I have the room.' Warlow stated it in a way that brooked no argument.

'Fine,' Jess said. 'But first, I need to see where you are sleeping.'

Molly perked up. 'Yes, come on, I want to see your pad.'

'Now that's not a word you hear much of these days.' But he complied with a grin and led them out of the back door along a crushed-slate path the dozen yards to the garden room. He flicked on some LED ceiling lights to reveal a room with tongue-and-groove walls, his laptop on a small table, a foldaway chair and the made-up sofa bed and bedside lamp.

'Wow, this is so cosy,' Molly cooed. 'An Airbnb in the making, Evan.'

'No, I prefer a guest room for when people come to stay. And a useful workspace for me.'

'Oh.' Molly looked intrigued. 'What kind of work?'

'Don't know yet,' Warlow said. He had his ideas. Some kind of writing maybe. But that was not for public discussion. 'We put down a base when we were finishing the cottage because we had concrete left over. The frame and the roof are all from the conversion, too. All spare stuff. We only needed some walls. The guy who's done this is a genius.'

'Tidy,' Jess mimicked Gil.

Molly disappeared with Cadi to finish clearing the table and finish off that crust, no doubt. Jess lingered. 'This is great, but hardly luxurious. You're making a massive sacrifice here, Evan. Thank you.'

Warlow gave her an old-fashioned look. 'That's the last one now. Say it again and I'm kicking you out.'

'We might even share lifts to work,' Jess teased.

'Can you imagine that? The rumour mill would go into meltdown.'

'Let me at least pour you a glass of wine.'

'Now you're talking my kind of language. I don't usually mid-week, since Oz anyway, but finding the murder weapons deserves a mini celebration.'

He followed Jess out and back into the cottage.

JORDAN NICHOLAS HAD SET up house in the old brickworks three hundred yards south of Horeb. It sat just off the cycle path, a listed building. No true access existed from the cycle route, but Jordan knew the way. He'd been here as a kid, many times, to drink beer and mess about with girls. But the looped chambers of the Hofmann kiln were dry and sheltered. In the summer, the foliage made it difficult, but in February, thanks to all the dieback, he'd got in no trouble. He had his sleeping bag and a stove. Camping out, like he'd done as a kid. He'd put two and two together from texts he'd got telling him that the filth had been at his house again and at the house next door.

Bastards.

He needed a plan now. Needed to get further away. If he could get the bike on a train, he'd sod off up to mid-Wales. He'd done a job with Barry and Lewis up there once a few months back. An old place up near Llangammarch. A country house they were converting. Rumour was they were running out of money. But he'd scouted it out. If he could get up there, he could stay in the grounds and no one would find him.

However, he needed to get on the Heart of Wales line. Safest option was Pontarddulais. From there, the train would take him all the way up. That's what he'd do. First thing tomorrow. There was a train at half nine. He could make that. There'd be other people about, but that train wasn't busy.

He hadn't eaten, but he had bread and some ham.

It would have to do. Best he get his head down.

When he turned off the lamp, darkness filled the tunnel utterly. The place smelled of damp and something feral and unpleasant. He'd slept in worse gaffs, though. At least there were no junkies wandering around like zombies here.

Though the distance between where he lay and his mother's house in Carway, where she had already passed out on her bed, was only a couple of miles, in the darkness of his hideaway he could not see the smoke that began trickling out from his mother's bedroom window. Or see the orange flames that flickered behind the glass and rose like a hungry beast to consume the curtains.

Half asleep, the distant bleat of a fire engine and an ambulance, when someone eventually raised the alarm, drifted in and out of his consciousness.

But then, in Jordan Nicholas's dysfunctional mind, that was all someone else's problem, not his.

CHAPTER THIRTY-ONE

WARLOW GOT the call at 4am from Gil. He fumbled for his phone, disoriented by the smell of wood and resin in the garden room–aka shed–and the unfamiliar bed.

'Evan, apologies for the ungodly hour. I'm on the way to Carway. There's been a fire.'

Warlow went from groggy to awake in two seconds flat. 'The Nicholas house or next door?'

'The Nicholas house.'

'Shit. I'm on my way.' He sat up, discarding a duvet, and rubbed his face. The February chill caressed his legs as he switched on a lamp and fumbled for his clothes. He crossed the space to the house and found the kitchen light on. Jess had obviously had a call, too. She was up, in rumpled pyjamas and fluffy slippers, looking puffy-eyed.

'Jess, stay here. No point us both going.'

'I could say the same to you,' she said.

'You could, but I outrank you. You can't let Molly wake up to an empty house.'

Jess sighed. 'Who was at the house in Carway?'

'Troy said he was going to his grandmother's. I'm

hoping he did that.' Warlow cringed at the next sentence. 'That leaves only Linda Nicholas.'

'Possibly Jordan?' Jess noted.

Warlow already had jeans and a sweatshirt on. He grabbed a coat and threw it over the back of a chair. Cadi got up from her basket, reading the signals and hoping for a walk.

'Dim nawr, cariad.'

'You just said "not now, darling".'

'Wasn't that a Doris Day film?'

'Doris who?'

'Don't you start. But yes, you're right. Words to that effect, anyway. Your Welsh is improving.'

'I keep trying.' She ran a hand through sleep-tousled hair. 'Not sure I'll get back to sleep, though.'

'Try. And ask Molly to drop Cadi off at the Dawes when she leaves for college. She knows the drill.'

Jess gave Warlow a wry smile. 'She knows it better than me. But let me put the kettle on. By the time you're back from the bathroom, I'll have a cup of tea for you to take with the tea bag in.'

The roads were empty. Warlow pushed the Jeep over the limit and made it in fifty-five minutes. He spotted the blue lights washing the sky from two miles away. Gil was talking to a fire officer as he pulled up but joined Warlow once he'd exited the Jeep. Both men stared at the smoke still billowing out of a gaping hole in the Nicholas's roof.

'Tell me,' Warlow ordered, zipping his coat up to his neck against the February night.

'One casualty. She was in the bedroom where the fire started. Early days, but they think a cigarette fire.'

Warlow felt his heart sink. His mind filled with images of earlier. Linda Nicholas, half cut, slurring her speech, a cigarette lit and in her mouth. He shouldn't have left her alone. But was aware she would have accepted none of his help.

'Are you sure it's her?'

'One side of the torso and legs are very charred, but her rings and watch are the same as what I remember. Half of her face is intact. The hair is the right colour. Otherwise, I wouldn't say there's enough for a formal ID.'

Warlow's head sank forward.

'Let me say it for you,' Gil said. 'Foxtrot, foxtrot, sierra.'

Warlow spoke to the fire officer. They discussed cigarettes as a cause of bed fires and no, there was no fire alarm. They'd found no evidence of accelerant either. But if she was intoxicated, the chance of survival was significantly reduced. The most likely thing in a chain-smoker like Linda Nicholas was that she'd fallen asleep with a lit cigarette in her fingers. She probably didn't even wake up.

Warlow waited until seven before he and Gil travelled to Kidwelly and knocked on Sylvia Reeves's door. Dawn had yet to arrive as if the light seemed reluctant to illuminate this already difficult day. The door opened to reveal Troy standing there, puzzled.

'Me or Gran?' he asked.

'Both of you. And not on the doorstep,' Gil said. He did not wait to be invited in but led the way to the kitchen. Sylvia Reeves wailed when Warlow told her what had happened. Wailed and sobbed miserably. Troy said nothing. He sat, stony-faced, shaking his head.

When he looked up, he asked, 'How?'

'Probably a cigarette,' Gil said.

'I told her never to smoke in bed,' Troy muttered. 'I told her.'

Sylvia Reeves's own smoke-ravaged skin turned an ugly red from crying. 'Can I see her?'

Warlow's nostrils flared, and he shook his head. 'I

wouldn't advise that, Sylvia. You don't want to remember her that way. There will be a post-mortem, of course.'

'She was upset,' Troy said. 'After you left. She wanted to warn Jordan.'

'Did she?'

'You need to check her phone.'

'We will.' Warlow took a breath. 'I'm sorry this has happened.'

'It's not your fault, is it?' Troy blurted. 'It's fucking Jordan's fault.'

'It's nobody's fault,' Gil said.

'No.' Sylvia Reeves looked up, her face twisted with anger. 'It's *her* fault. It's all Linda's fault. All of this… mess.' She sniffed up a tear and ratcheted out another sob. 'A hundred times I tried to help. When they were babies. When they started school. She promised, every sodding time, she promised. But you know what? It was the love of her life. The drugs and the booze and the fags. She cared more about them than us.'

Warlow wanted to say that if that was so, then what Linda had was an illness. Blame or no blame. But this was not the time for platitudes like that. This was too raw.

'It isn't safe to go back to the house, Troy,' Gil said.

The boy shrugged. 'I've got what I need here and at Lola's. I never want to go back there now.'

Warlow left them to their grief, and he and Gil headed back to HQ.

They found Catrin and Jess in the Incident Room. No big smiles of greeting today. Only small, sombre ones of understanding.

'Bad?' Catrin asked.

'I didn't see her,' Warlow said.

'I did,' Gil muttered. 'We used her jewellery mainly. To confirm.'

'Where's Rhys?' Warlow asked.

'Morriston Hospital. It seems his dad needs some stents. They're doing that this morning.'

'This is turning out to be a real humdinger of a bloody day,' Warlow growled.

'Haven't heard that one from you before, Mr Warlow.' Gil said.

'Special circumstances.'

Jess nodded towards the SIO room. 'Quick word, Evan?'

He followed her through the room. She smelled wonderful. He reeked of smoke. She stood aside as he stepped in and then shut the door. 'I brought some fresh clothes for you.'

'Brilliant. I must honk like Guy Fawkes's waistcoat. I'll have a quick scrub down and change.' He stopped as an idea gelled. 'That means you had to go through my drawers and my wardrobe. Sorry about that.'

'At least I know that Christmas and birthdays will be underwear and socks for the foreseeable.'

Warlow considered something scathing but erred on the side of gratitude. 'Thanks for doing this. Very thoughtful. Molly, okay?'

'I left her and Cadi to it. That dog is the best psychological salve there is. Especially for the trials and tribulations of the Allanby family.' Jess loitered, more to say. 'Evan, I realise how much of an imposition we are. Having two people around, and female Allanbys at that, I mean—'

'I'll have to hoover a bit more often, I get it.'

'I, we, are both extremely—'

Warlow drew his fingers over his lips. 'Give me five minutes to get changed and we'll have a catch-up, agreed?'

Jess smiled. 'I'll get the tea on.' She turned and then pivoted back. 'I almost forgot, there's a breakfast roll in the plastic bag behind your chair for you and Gil. I know you don't indulge normally, but I thought—'

'You thought correctly.' He hadn't realised how hungry he was until she'd mentioned the roll. 'Gil is going to do a somersault.'

'That, I would pay to see.'

Five minutes later, refreshed and revived, he and Gil munched their way through their rolls while Catrin told them what she'd found yesterday in Probert's attic box.

'I have confirmed with his financial advisor that the statements I saw were genuine. Ronnie Probert was a well-off man.'

'And all that as an amateur,' Gil said. 'He played years before the game turned pro in Wales.'

'There are a couple of other letters in that box addressed to his brother and sister. I probably should open them, but they're sealed and, I don't know, I don't like to.'

'Why don't you get them in and let them open the letters in front of us,' Jess said.

'Good idea.' Warlow wiped a crumb away from the corner of his mouth.

'The other things are more difficult to explain. The mock death certificates. '

'Mock? You don't think they're genuine?' Gil asked.

'They're not standard issue, so no point contacting the registrar. No surnames for a start, and no birth date. Just a date of death. A Jac – one "c" – and a Betty.'

'But they're dated?' Gil asked.

'They are. I thought I'd ring the hospital, see if they might shed any light on things.'

'Again, good idea, Catrin,' Jess said.

'What about our scaffolders?' Gil asked. 'They're still here. We ought to charge them with something.'

'I know, but we have them for another few hours, don't we?'

Jess nodded. 'We have them for seventy-two hours on

the extension. Question is, do we charge them for the church theft or not?'

Warlow's silence drew quizzical looks all around. 'I know what they've said,' he explained after a while. 'I know the van is captured on camera in the right place at the right time, but we need Jordan Nicholas.'

'Why, sir?' Catrin asked.

'Maybe it's because I didn't get enough sleep last night. I don't know, but something isn't right.'

'Not enough sauce on the roll?' Gil asked.

Warlow ignored him. 'I read a story once. Science Fiction. About this man who had a parasite in his head. An alien parasite. When it woke up, it made him brilliant. But it only woke up when it felt like it. Not when he needed it.'

'Maybe you put *too* much sauce on it, ma'am,' Gil muttered.

Warlow pressed on. 'What if we've inadvertently handed our two scaffolders an alibi on a plate with the church roof lead theft?'

'But, sir, as you've already said, we have the van in the Pontardawe area on the night of the theft,' Catrin said.

'Right. But what if it wasn't either of them driving? What if it was Jordan Nicholas? What if he stole the lead, and the scaffolders were at Ronnie Probert's?'

'Hang on,' Gil said, and then added, 'Am I speaking to the parasite now or you?'

'One and the same.' Warlow sat back, arms folded.

'Then what about the tools in the house next door to Jordan's? The house he was using.'

'I haven't forgotten them. But they were in a Castell Scaffolding bag. What if they gave them to Jordan for safe-keeping? It was a closed bag, right?'

Gil nodded, his brow wrinkling. '*Diawl*, that parasite of yours is a devious bugger.'

'It all comes back to Nicholas, though, doesn't it?' Jess said. 'We need to get him in here.'

'We also need his phone records,' Catrin said. 'Let's see what his texts and calls can tell us about where he was that night.'

'Might as well do it for all the Nicholases. Let's find out if they were communicating behind our backs,' Gil suggested.

'Good. Now I'm going to have to talk to the Buccaneer and Drinkwater again.'

'Think you should take a blood pressure cuff for Drinkwater, Evan?' Jess asked.

'Nah. He'll be cucumber cool, I'm sure.'

The cackle of derisive laughter followed him down the corridor as he exited the Incident Room.

CHAPTER THIRTY-TWO

CATRIN SAT at her desk with the two mock death certificates in clear plastic folder wallets. Why would anyone want something like this? Could it have been from a game? A Murder Mystery supper event? But that didn't seem right.

She had some information about Sian Probert already. Ronnie's wife died of bowel cancer in 2018, aged sixty-eight. Young for this day and age. All that was common knowledge. What she needed now was not common knowledge. She'd rung Ronnie's sister, explaining how she was ticking boxes and, without giving too much away, asked if the names Jac and Betty meant anything to her. Her enquiry drew a blank.

She'd toyed with trying the hospital. The NHS held records after someone's death for twelve years. But that might be hit and miss. And it depended on who you spoke to. They might be helpful; they might play the information governance card. Would digging into Sian Probert's medical history be in the public interest? Or would protecting her confidentiality outweigh the police's curiosity?

Catrin had been in situations where vague requests like this were turned down. And, 'Who were Jac and Betty?' Didn't seem very specific to Catrin.

Instead, she rang the GP practice Ronnie Probert was registered with and spoke to a practice manager, fingers, and everything else she could scissor, crossed.

Catrin knew she'd lucked out within ten seconds. The secretary who answered was a Welsh speaker, and chatty. They shared a mutual sorrow over Ronnie's death. The secretary, an ex-nurse, probed about how far along the police were in finding the killers. That brought things around nicely to Sian Probert.

'Not much point you talking to anyone here. The whole surgery is new. Belinda Macefield is the senior partner, and she's only been here four years.'

'Ah.' Catrin didn't hide her disappointment.

'Shame Roy isn't here still. He'd have known.'

'Roy?'

'Banfield. He set up this practice. People still ask for him.'

'Oh, dear. When did he die?'

'Die? He's not dead. Lives in Kidwelly. Mad about the Scarlets.'

'You don't have his number, do you?'

Roy Banfield did not have a local accent. Even after living in the area for nigh on forty years, he'd kept his Hertfordshire received pronunciation. Catrin introduced herself and explained the nature of her call. For a moment, after she'd explained, the line went quiet. After a long beat, though, Banfield cleared his throat. 'Sorry, I… Ronnie was a good friend. We played a bit of golf at Machynys. In fact, we played on a bright day in December. Nine holes only, but I miss him.'

'I'm sorry.'

'It's fine. I spend more time at funerals than I do in Tesco these days.'

'You knew him and Sian, his wife, then?'

'Absolutely. Friends as well as patients. It broke him when Sian died. Never quite the same after that.'

'It was Sian Probert I wanted to talk to you about. As part of the investigation, I've been going through Mr and Mrs Probert's belongings. I came across something I hope you might help me with.'

'Anything I can do,' Roy Banfield said.

'Do you have a computer, Dr Banfield?'

'It's Roy. I'm not a doctor anymore. But yes. I do.'

'And an email?'

'That, too.'

'Can I send you some images, and I'll ring you back in five minutes?'

'By all means.'

Catrin scanned the certificates, sent them off, and got on with something else while she waited.

———

JORDAN GOT on the train at Pontarddulais with his bike. The train was a single-carriage diesel. A trundler that he'd used in the past on day trips to Swansea for a couple of summer gigs. He got on at the back and breathed a sigh of relief to see one of the cycle spaces empty, the other already taken up by a thick-tyred mountain bike.

The bright saloon had airline seats except for the four-seaters near the halfway partition. Jordan stayed at the back, his hood up. Never a busy train, this morning's passengers did not look as if they were in a hurry to get anywhere. Jordan hunkered down on the hard seat, turned his face to the window and quelled his grumbling stomach. He had fourteen stops to Llangammarch, but he'd eaten nothing since the night before. And Troy wasn't replying to his texts.

Little shit.

He'd come off the cycle route at the top of the Llieidi Reservoir and cut across along quiet lanes to Pontarddulais. It had taken him an hour to do that, but he'd set off early while it was still dark. He'd met no one in the morning and traffic had only picked up after he'd ridden under the M4. But he was here now, and it was good to sit in the warm. The conductor came, and Jordan handed over his ticket.

'Got a bike, too.'

'You're alright,' the conductor said. 'It's not busy. There's no charge for that.'

Jordan nodded. He hadn't given things much thought other than to get on the train. Now that he'd succeeded, other concerns seeped in.

Money for a start.

He had about forty quid in his wallet and a Monzo card that would not last more than a couple of days. Chances for stealing things would not be great at the place he was heading. What he would give now for a chicken bake and a sausage roll.

He thought of Troy and his mother. That he needed to get his act together. He would, but he couldn't be doing with the cops chasing him all the time. He needed somewhere to get his head on straight. Then he would talk to them… Jesus, why was life so fucking complicated? Work had dried up over the winter, his kind of work, the casual kind. Carrying scaffolding poles or lugging bricks for a builder mate. It would pick up again come April. But winter was crap.

He'd had offers of other work. Watching corners like those three who had chased him and cut him in Llanelli. He hated that crap. And Troy said he would help him with the computers. But that cheap laptop he was going to get would end up with someone else now. It all came down to cash in the end. And the easiest way to get cash was to nick it. That brought his mind back to Ronnie Probert. Didn't seem right, somehow, getting that big house and all that stuff inside it just by playing a game.

Troy said you could do the same with computer games these days. But Jordan wouldn't be playing any games in Llangammarch. What if there wasn't even any leccie?

He checked his phone. The battery was low. Too low for him to watch a film or listen to anything. The signal would be shit, anyway. Better he turned it off and kept what he had until he got to where he was going. Then maybe he'd try Troy again. See what things were like.

Jordan rested his head against the windows, folded his arms, and shut his eyes.

What he could not have been aware of was that Dyfed Powys Police, that morning, had issued a nationwide alert that had made the BBC and ITV News, informing the public that if anyone spotted Jordan Nicholas, they should report it immediately.

———

It was turning out to be a "phone call" morning in the Incident Room. While Catrin phoned the ex-GP back, Gil took a call from her partner Craig, a traffic officer.

'*Bachan*, how's it going?'

'Going well, Gil. You?'

'Tidy. Living the dream, Craig. As per. You want Catrin?'

'Her phone is either broken or constantly engaged.'

'Busy girl, as usual.'

'Yep. But you'll do. Geraint Lane ring any bells?'

'Certainly does. Catrin thinks he's a vampire. Did she tell you that?'

Craig chuckled. 'She says you think he's a vampire.'

'I keep telling her. Don't be s'oh negative.'

Static crackled over the line for four seconds. 'Was that a blood joke?' Craig eventually asked.

'Indeed. And I'll throw another one in for good measure, since we all need cheering up. What is Geraint Lane's favourite chocolate?'

'You mean, Geraint Lane as a vampire?'

'Oh, do you think he is one, too?'

'No, I—'

'Rhesus pieces.'

Two seconds of silence this time before Craig said, 'That's actually not bad.'

'Right, well, constable, let's stop wasting police time. What is it about Lane you wanted to tell me?'

'They've found him.'

'Not in a graveyard, I hope. Or in a blood bank, which would be worse.'

Craig chuckled over the phone. 'In the Kidwelly Quay car park. Someone was down there this morning and heard banging from the trunk of his car.'

'What?'

'Yeah. He's okay, but they took him to hospital. That's where he is now. I thought you'd want to know.'

'He got into the trunk to avoid the sunlight, you reckon?'

Another chuckle. 'He says he was mugged.'

'Glangwili, you say?'

'Yes.'

'I might just pop down there and have a word. Thanks, Craig. Now you have a rest. You need to preserve your strength.'

'Do I?' Craig sounded suddenly very wary.

Gil let the IVF implication simmer unsaid. 'I'll tell Catrin you called.'

———

WARLOW GOT BACK to the Incident Room to find Catrin on the phone and Jess looking startled, with her own phone to her ear.

'How did it go?' Gil asked.

'Only the Buccaneer was there. Drinkwater was elsewhere. I still have that pleasure to come.'

'And I've just had the most bizarre conversation with Craig.'

'Catrin's Craig?'

Gil nodded and filled Warlow in on Craig's call.

Warlow could tell his mouth had dropped open as he listened. He shut it with a snap and said, 'I have no idea what to make of that.'

'Thought I might slip down there and have a chat,' Gil said.

'Why not? Nothing to lose. He's a slippery bugger, mind.'

'I will talc up, don't you worry.'

Catrin ended her call and, her big eyes even bigger than normal, looked over at her two colleagues with a troubled expression. 'That was the Proberts' ex-GP.'

'Proberts plural?' Gil asked.

Catrin nodded. 'I had a long conversation with him about Sian and Ronnie.'

'Is this about those mock death certificates?' Warlow inquired.

'It is, sir—'

Jess's urgent voice cut across them. 'Sorry, Catrin, whatever it is, it'll have to wait. That was CID. They've taken a couple of calls from people who claim to have seen someone answering Jordan Nicholas's description.'

'Went out on the bulletin, did it?' Warlow wanted to know.

'It did,' Jess confirmed.

'So, where is he?' Catrin asked.

'On a train heading up towards mid-Wales.'

'Heart of Wales line?' Gil asked.

Jess nodded. 'I'm pulling up the stops now. The last call was from someone on the train who got on at Pantyffyn-non.' Jess clicked her mouse and a map appeared.

Warlow joined her at her desk. 'When did that come in?'

'Five minutes ago.'

'Get the timetable up.'

Catrin called across. 'Got it, sir. That train is in Llandybie now.'

Warlow glanced at his watch. One minute to ten. 'How long will it take us to drive to Llandovery?'

'Forty minutes,' Gil said.

'What time is the train due there?'

'Half ten.'

'Catrin, get on to British Transport Police. See if they can delay the train to give Jess and me and some Uniforms time to get to Llandovery.'

'On it, sir.'

'Right.' Warlow looked at Jess. 'Let's do this.'

CHAPTER THIRTY-THREE

THEY TOOK a job car driven by a Uniform qualified in pursuit. They travelled blue lights all the way, a second vehicle behind, and a response vehicle already on the way to Llandovery to meet them there.

'Why do you think he's on this train, Evan?' Jess asked, one hand on the handle above the rear window of the BMW X1 as they overtook another lorry.

'Who knows what his thought processes are at this point. He only knows we're after him. He's running.'

The A40 led east from Carmarthen to Brecon, skirting the Black Mountains. But no stretch from HQ to Llandovery was a dual carriageway. And though sometimes the speed limit dropped to forty, the main issue was finding safe places to pass slower traffic. Once past Llandeilo, those stretches became a little easier to find. Warlow watched the valley speed by, the river an almost constant companion on their right. As they negotiated the roundabout at Llangadog, Warlow spoke to the officers in the response vehicle who had already got to Llandovery station.

'Will he see your vehicle when the train pulls in?'

'Yes, sir.'

'Then move it. Get passengers off the platform and wait for us to turn up.'

British Transport Police got the train driver to announce signalling problems at Llangadog as the cause of the delay. They also confirmed that, as the train left Llangadog station, the man identified as Jordan Nicholas remained on board.

The convoy from HQ parked up. Two plain clothes CID officers stood on the platform, looking innocent but ready to block the doors. Two Uniformed officers stayed out of sight, as ordered, ready to get on at the rear. Warlow and Jess sat in the unmarked car, facing the track behind railings, waiting for the train to arrive.

Jess glanced at her watch. 'Rhys's dad should be out of whatever it is they did. I hope he's okay.'

Warlow nodded. 'It's one of those bloody days, isn't it?' he said. It was the best he could do.

———

FOR THE SECOND time in a week, Gil walked through the doors of A&E at Glangwili. At the rate he was going, he'd soon get a parking space with his name on it.

He spoke to the Uniforms who had brought Lane in, relieved them of their duty of care and walked to the reception desk. He flashed his badge and asked for a progress report on Geraint Lane, and how long he might be.

She checked her screen and said, 'Not long. He had a skull X-ray and is waiting for discharge.'

That came ten minutes later, just as Warlow and Jess were pelting around the roundabout in Llangadog. Lane emerged, remarkably unscathed apart from some butterfly sutures over a cut on his left temple.

'Mr Lane, DS Gil Jones.'

'I know who you are,' Lane muttered.

'Good. That saves time on small talk. My colleagues have had to leave, but I wondered if we might have a quick chat?'

'About what?'

'About the fact that you were attacked and locked in the boot of your own car. With the keys left conveniently on the back wheel, I may add.'

Lane shrugged. 'You meet a better class of mugger in Carmarthen, obviously.'

'Or I could take you home or back to your car and we could chat as we drive?'

'No, thanks, I'll get a taxi.'

'Really? I promise I won't charge you much.'

Lane wasn't amused. 'Save the jokes. My head hurts too much.'

'So, how did it happen? Did he hit you first?'

'I didn't see. He came from behind, struck me, and I fell forward. Might have hit my head on the boot of the car, too. All I know is that I was groggy. Next thing, I'm in the boot.'

'So, he attacks you, puts you in the boot of your car, and drives you to Kidwelly Quay. Then leaves with the keys on the rear wheel. This a new form of Uber mugging, is it?'

'No idea.' Lane grunted out the words.

'And why Kidwelly?'

'That's where I was. I came out of a shop and…' Lane shrugged.

'What did he take? Money?'

'I don't carry any cash. But he took my phone.'

'Just your phone? And attacked from behind, you say? No description, then?'

'No. I don't have eyes in the back of my head.'

'And vampires can't even see their own reflections, either can they?'

'What?' Lane spat out the question in irritation.

Gil stared at the man. He was obviously shaken, dishevelled, with bloodstains on his shirt collar. Time for a little milk of human kindness. 'Look, we may have had our run-ins over the years, and you may not like me, and I may not like you. But if a crime has been committed—'

'I'd rather forget about it.'

'It's not unusual to feel humiliated by something like this,' Gil said. 'But you were sucker-punched. Not much you could do.'

Lane snorted. 'I'm here, aren't I? Good enough for me.'

'So, you don't need a lift, and you aren't prepared to give a statement?'

'Are you deaf? I just did. I saw nothing.' Lane's brow clouded before he mumbled, 'But my phone is missing.'

'And there is no one you can think of who might want to do you harm?'

A humourless grin split Lane's cracked lips. 'You are kidding, right?'

'Maybe I am,' Gil conceded.

'Where were you last night at half-past five?'

Gil breathed out a wheezy laugh. 'Very good, Mr Lane.'

'If I think of anything, you'll be the first to know.'

'You need a card?'

'I know how to get a hold of you, sergeant.'

'Any time,' Gil said as Lane shuffled off. 'We're here to help.' As the door slid shut, Gil couldn't help but ease out the word '*Pwdryn*,' under his breath. As always, these days, he translated it in his head for Jess's sake, even though she wasn't there. Bloody waster came close. It would have to do.

———

THE TRAIN PULLED into Llandovery station just west of the A40. This line continued northeast at a level crossing. The station itself would not have looked out of place in an Ealing comedy. To all intents, this was a heritage line with heritage buildings and the bonus of a regular service. People came from miles around to travel over the viaduct at Cynghordy a little further on. Or even to walk to it and marvel at the engineering.

Platform Two was where Shrewsbury-bound passengers got on. There was no shelter from the elements. That made the two Uniforms' life a little difficult, so they stood off at the entrance near the road crossing. But as soon as the train braked to a halt, they walked swiftly along to the back door of the single carriage.

The doors opened, and the two CID officers entered just as the Uniforms stepped on board.

Four to one.

Still, Jordan Nicholas wasn't one to give up without a fight.

'Jordan Nicholas,' one of the CID officers said.

Jordan sat slumped in his seat. He turned his head, and with no warning, lunged upwards. Though they'd been expecting some kind of resistance, the rapidity of that lunge took the officers by surprise.

Jordan kicked out and caught the nearest CID in the chest and sent him sprawling. His attempt at steadying himself caught his partner and they fell back into the seat, one flailing over the other, their legs kicking out, effectively preventing the Uniforms from passing.

Jordan took his chance.

He leaped over and ran for the door.

'Stop. Stay where you are.' A yelled order from the detectives.

Jordan half fell but scrambled forward. The middle doors were wide open. He jumped out, looked around and turned for the entrance along a narrow walkway flanked by fencing.

A man stood where that walkway met the platform. Watching, unmoving.

Jordan gritted his teeth. 'Get out of the fucking way,' he bellowed.

The man stepped aside.

Well, half-stepped aside, leaving one leg trailing across the entrance to the walkway. A leg which Jordan ran into and tripped over to land flat on his face.

'Shit,' he groaned and tried to push himself up.

But a weight on his back pushed him back down.

'Stay there, Jordan,' said a voice. 'Better if you do.'

Jordan strained and pushed as the pressure on his back increased, pinning him. He turned his face to look at the man who had tripped him.

'Get off, you—'

The Uniforms arrived. It was over in seconds once they fell on him, twisting his arms around behind his back. They cuffed him and stood him up to face the man who'd caught him. Not a tall man, not a big man, but someone who looked capable and in command. A man who held out his warrant card and spoke his name in introduction.

'DCI Evan Warlow. Jordan Nicholas, I am arresting you on suspicion of the murder of Ronald Probert. You do not have to say anything. But it may harm your defence if you do not mention when questioned something which you later rely on in court. Anything you say may be given in evidence. Do you understand, Jordan?'

'Piss off.'

'We'll take that as a yes.'

CHAPTER THIRTY-FOUR

BECAUSE HE'D FALLEN, they waited two hours while a doctor was sourced to get Jordan Nicholas checked out. He'd been taken to the custody suite at Ammanford. A seven-million-pound new-build in Dafen on the edge of Llanelli would, eventually, provide a lot more cells. But for now, the absence of 24-hour custody at HQ remained a bloody nuisance.

Bruised, but nothing broken, said the doctor. At around 2pm, once all the boxes were ticked, Warlow and Jess headed out to their cars for the half-hour trip over to Ammanford nick. As they left the Incident Room, a flushed Rhys Harries sauntered down the corridor towards them.

'What did I miss?'

'What the hell are you doing here?' Warlow asked.

Rhys, grinning, did a Tigger bounce on the balls of his feet.

'They put two stents in, sir. One in the proximal right and one in the left anterior descending coronary artery.' It was clear he'd memorised the anatomical terms and practised them. He used his finger to demonstrate the arterial supply of the heart muscles, which in his mind worked well. But to everyone else looked more like an attempt at index-finger swordplay. 'He's fine. They say he'll be home in a couple of days. Nothing for me to do, so I thought I'd come in.'

'You didn't have to,' Jess said.

She was right, but Warlow recognised this as a need, on Rhys's part, to get rid of nervous energy. Some people might have damped it all down with a Leonard Cohen album and a bottle of Malbec. But Rhys was not made like that.

'Well, we're off over to Ammanford. You might as well come with us. Watch us have a go at Jordan Nicholas.'

'You've got him, then?' Rhys grinned.

'We found him on a train heading north.'

'What was he doing—'

Warlow held up a restraining hand. 'We're about to find out. But first, I need to break the news that his mother is dead.'

'That doesn't sound good.'

An understatement of epic proportions.

They made the half-hour journey without delays. After Jess did the needful and read Nicholas his rights again, Warlow got straight to it.

'You weren't anywhere near home last night, Jordan?'

'No.'

'Mind telling us where you were?'

'The old brickworks. Near Horeb.' Jordan's speech was rapid and blunt.

'And you've had your phone off?'

'Battery is down to 5%. I was saving it, wasn't I?'

Warlow sat forward. 'DI Allanby has explained you're here because we need to talk to you about Ronnie Probert, but it's only fair that we tell you about what happened last night first.'

They'd given the prisoner some clean clothes: joggers

and a sweatshirt. He sat, not fidgeting, an old hand at this little game, even at nineteen. Only the bunching of the muscles above his eyebrows indicated any interest on his part.

'There was a fire at your mother's house.'

'What fire?'

'We think a cigarette might have set some bed clothes alight. It started in your mother's bedroom. Jordan. I'm sorry to tell you, but Mrs Nicholas did not survive.'

'Fuck off,' Jordan said as an odd and unpleasant smile flickered over his lips. 'No way. Linda didn't smoke in bed. She always went outside.' He spat the words out as irrefutable facts.

'We visited Linda at your house last night. We found the Respatex panel above the bath, Jordan. It's clear that you've been using the other house as a hideout. We found your tools, too. Your mother had been drinking—'

Jordan shook his head. 'No, no, no, this isn't right. You bastards. You're trying to trick me. You total bastards.'

'This is no trick, Jordan. I'm sorry to have to tell you like this.'

'You liar.' Jordan's voice quivered like a plucked string. Both hands bunched into fists on top of the desk.

'It's true, Jordan,' Jess said.

The bunched fists opened and found their way to the top of Jordan's head. 'Jesus. Jesus. What about Troy?'

'He wasn't there. He's fine.'

He didn't break down exactly, but tears came. The real thing. Running down his cheeks and into his mouth, which had opened and stayed open as all the muscles around his lips quivered. His eyes stared but saw nothing in the room. His hands fell away after a moment, to flutter like injured birds in his lap. And all the while, his head moved from side to side slowly. Whether as a mark of denial or as if he was trying to find something to lock onto, to anchor him in this nightmare, it was difficult to say.

The solicitor, from a local firm and well known to Warlow, shook his head too. 'I don't think we should continue with this interview for now. My client is clearly upset.'

'Agreed,' Warlow said. They'd waited days for this interview, but they could wait a little longer.

'Can I see my gran?' Jordan's blurted words came out sounding like they came from a shocked and bereaved child, not the wiry nineteen-year-old that Warlow had captured at the railway station just a few hours ago.

'We can't do that, Jordan. There are no facilities for visitors here.'

'You're going to be charged on suspicion of murder, Jordan,' Jess said. 'But we'll be back to talk to you tomorrow. We're sorry.'

'Bastards,' Jordan whispered, but the word sounded as hollow as a wooden drum.

———

BACK AT HEADQUARTERS, in a room they used for visitors and therefore not as austere or claustrophobic as the custody suite in Ammanford, Catrin and Gil sat with Ronnie Probert's fed-up-looking brother and sister.

'Thanks for coming in. Again,' Catrin said and let a smile flicker over her lips. 'At the moment, all of Mr Probert's belongings are considered evidence. They will all be released in time. For now, they remain part of this investigation. But we discovered some papers which might interest us and you.'

Gaynor Richmond looked intrigued. Terry Probert sat expressionless.

Catrin addressed the brother. 'Mr Probert, we interviewed your son, Ralph. Has he discussed the content of that interview with you?'

'He has.'

Gil nodded. That would not have been a simple conversation to have. 'Then we don't need to discuss it here.'

'I've told Gaynor. She knows all about Ralph. All about the money.'

Gil glanced at Catrin. To hear your son admit to having been bailed out by his uncle more than once over the years, while continuing to call him a skinflint, must have been difficult.

Terry continued, 'Ralph has had his problems… still has his problems.'

Catrin moved on. 'We found a box in the attic. The box contained envelopes addressed to the two of you. But it also had some toys and two mocked-up death certificates. Do the names Jac and Betty mean anything to you, Mr Probert? I've already spoken to Mrs Richmond and they don't to her.'

Terry looked perplexed.

Catrin had considered what she was going to say to these two people and about how to couch it all. She'd concluded that there was no point sugar-coating it. 'Jac and Betty are the names Sian and Ronnie Probert gave to the children Sian lost in the second trimester of two pregnancies on two separate occasions. We've learned that they were not the only pregnancies that ended abruptly, but these were the two that went the furthest. In law, if a baby dies in the womb after twenty-four weeks, a death certificate is required. These babies were lost before that date on both occasions. However, it appears Ronnie and Sian wanted to mark the passing in their own way.'

Gaynor's hand went to stifle the cry that emerged from

her lips. Tears sprang to her eyes. Next to her, Terry let out a groan.

'My God. They never said,' he whispered, staring at the copies of the certificates Catrin had given them.

'From what I understand,' Catrin went on, 'Sian Probert wanted to keep these tragic circumstances private. I'm no psychologist, but it could explain her apparent coldness regarding your own children.'

Gaynor was crying openly now. 'I knew something was wrong. I knew it. But Sian, she was so closed-off when it came to kids.'

'Perhaps we now know why,' Gil said.

Catrin took out two envelopes from the folder. 'These are also what I found in that box. Two envelopes addressed to you two. You are under no obligation to open them, and, in all honesty, we doubt it has anything to do with the burglary or what happened. But I discussed it with DCI Warlow, and he agreed that out of courtesy we would let you open these letters in our presence.' She handed over the envelopes.

'That's Ronnie's writing,' Gaynor said.

Terry opened his first. He read it in silence and took his glasses off twice to wipe his eyes and the tears that spotted the lenses.

Gaynor opened hers, read it and, lips shaking with an unidentified emotion, handed it back to Catrin for her to read. There were two sheets. The first a compliment slip with Ronnie Probert's name and address and a hand-written sentence:

A little something for the grandchildren.
Sian would've wanted it, even if she never said.

Terry nodded. 'Mine is the same.'

'You have two grandchildren each, correct?' Gil asked.

Nods from each.

The other documents were from the Independent Financial Advisor, William Clement Associates. Statements of Ronnie Probert's Self Invested Personal Pension. Gaynor handed hers back to Catrin and Gil, confusion wrinkling her brow.

At the base of the letters, in an area marked 'Nominated beneficiary', were four names.

'Are those the names of your grandchildren?' Gil asked.

Gaynor nodded.

Terry kept staring at the number on the bottom of the letter. 'Is this really worth half a million?'

'It is.'

'When was this written?'

Gil read the date. 'Six months ago.'

Catrin sat back. 'Around the time Ronnie was diagnosed with leukaemia.'

For the second time that morning, Gaynor Richmond tried to stifle a sob and failed.

'I suspect there'll be caveats. They may not access the money until they're eighteen,' Catrin said. 'And by then this pot will be even bigger.'

'Even split four ways, that'll pay for uni and a deposit on a house,' Gil said.

'It's a good way to transfer money, a SIPP,' Terry said. This was his area of expertise, after all.

'I'll get these letters copied. We need to hang on to the originals for now.' Catrin took Terry's letter and put it with Gaynor's.

Brother and sister both nodded.

Gil and Catrin left them to it, shaken and emotionally bruised.

'Ronnie was putting his house in order,' Gil said. 'When was he going to give them those letters you reckon?'

'Is there ever a right moment? But it's one in the eye for Ralph Probert and the niece, Gaynor's daughter, Ruth. And she can't complain either, though she probably will. I found paperwork that showed Ronnie paid for half her wedding. Ten thousand pounds at least.'

'Had she forgotten that?'

'Probably didn't think it was enough. This way, the money bypasses them and goes straight to their kids.'

'Nice one, Ronnie. But all that bad blood.' Gil shook his head. 'Ronnie Probert sounds like he was salt of the earth.'

'Shame that earth was barren, though.'

Gil wondered if he should add to that comment and, wisely, decided that he'd better not, given Catrin's current situation. 'The Wolf is going to ask if there's enough to consider a motive here.'

'For killing Ronnie so that their grandchildren inherited?' Catrin mulled the idea over. 'Hardly instant gratification. And hardly an answer to "where's the effing money," is it? And from their reactions, I suspect they had no idea.'

'Agreed. I think we can strike the Probert siblings off the suspect list. That needle is swinging right back towards Jordan Nicholas.'

CHAPTER THIRTY-FIVE

GERAINT LANE LOOKED at his watch. He'd been sitting in his car for hours, still parked in the place he'd been driven to by the man who forced him, at gunpoint, to drive here. Forced him to give him his phone. Forced him to get into the boot.

Memory of the first hour with the man sitting in the car, scrolling through the phone he'd taken, tutting in disgust at what he'd found there made Lane cringe and squeeze his eyes shut at the memory and the shame of it. He remembered the instructions he'd been given, too.

Now he needed to follow those instructions and get two new phones.

One a cheapy, with a new number. The other to replace the one he'd, "lost". The one whose contents had been pored over by his "mugger". Lane backed up all phone data onto his computer at home. He didn't trust the cloud, preferred to keep his digital footprint as small as he could.

Being a journalist meant bending rules. Getting sensitive information could backfire.

But that wasn't the only thing on Lane's phone that

would detonate his world. There were other things, images he'd downloaded in weak moments. The man who'd waved a gun at him found all of those. He'd called Lane names. Names he dared not think about even though deep in his heart he was certain they applied to him. Lane's lame excuse that it had all been research fell on deaf ears. The man warned him that if he didn't cooperate, the images would find their way to his partner and onto the internet with good old Geraint's name firmly attached to them.

Lane didn't recognise the bloke at first. Not with the beard and losing weight. But then the penny dropped. The way he was dressed marked him as a cyclist. The cyclist that rode past Lane at the community hall. Yet, that wasn't where Lane recognised him from. Roger Hunt had made the front page of every newspaper just a few weeks ago. When that recognition dawned, Hunt saw it and smiled.

Lane almost voided his bladder on seeing that smile.

'So, let me tell you how this is going to go, Geraint,' Hunt had said. 'You and I are going to be friends. And, as a friend, I'll not send copies of all these disgusting bloody files I've found on your phone to your colleagues, who, like the piranhas they are, would strip the flesh from your professional bones in five seconds flat once they saw how much of a sick pervert you are. And you with a partner at home, too? God forbid the ex ever found out, eh?'

'Please,' Lane pleaded.

'It's okay,' Hunt had said. 'We'll keep it our little secret. But you know people. You have contacts. I'm looking for someone, and I think you're just the man to help me find him.'

'Who?'

'John Napier. Solicitor and arsehole. Not so easy for me to be out sniffing at the moment. So, you'll do the sniffing for me, or I press the send button.'

'You tried to kill Napier.'

'I did. And I would have if that shit of a police officer hadn't stuck his nose in.'

'Warlow?'

'That's him. But that's fine. There might be time for him after Napier.'

'I can't do anything, I can't…'

'You're supposed to be an investigative journalist, Geraint. Do some investigating. Or end up in prison, because some of the models in these images appear to be very much under the age of consent.'

'Oh, Christ.'

Hunt had looked at him with the gun raised in his hand. 'He's not here. Never is when you need him. So, let's go over it one more time. Two phones. One a pay-as-you-go. That'll be for me and you only. Get a different one to replace your phone. I'll keep the original. The one with all your personal details and personal… indulgences on it. Buy the phones separately. Online for the replacement, a newsagent for the pay-per-use. Buy some extra SIM cards, too, somewhere else. Once you get everything, send the pay-as-you-go number to yourself on your old number. I'll pick that up on your original phone. After that, you can stop your old phone from being used by its IMEI number. I've written all this down for you in your handy little note-book tucked under the sun visor. Understood?'

Lane had nodded. He'd said nothing of this to the big sergeant. Of course, he hadn't.

He'd just about stopped shaking now. It was a mess. The whole thing. But even now he began wondering if there was an angle here he could use.

Perhaps.

At some point, he'd be in a unique position to tell Hunt's story. There might even be a book in it. So long as he got the phone back. Lane sat up, sucked in air, and pressed the Renault's ignition. He'd get rid of everything on his hard drive at home. He'd used VPNs for the sites he'd visited. Still, there were those downloads. Things he could not resist.

'Shit, shit, shit.' He thumped the steering wheel with his open palm. Now he needed to stay focused and positive. Needed to get the phone sorted. Hunt had given him two days for that.

'In the meantime, be normal,' Hunt had said. 'Continue being the in your face, pervy little twat that you are. Shouldn't be difficult for you, eh, Geraint?'

Hard to believe all that had happened only yesterday. He'd frozen in the boot overnight, wondering if anyone would ever find him. But they had. He'd survived.

A blackmail victim, but alive.

A minute later, Lane reversed the car out of the space and drove off towards Llanelli.

———

GIL HAD the Human Tissue For Transplant box open and tea made by the time Warlow and Jess got back from Ammanford. Catrin ran through the meeting with Ronnie Probert's siblings.

'They were shocked by the mock death certificates, sir. That was plain to see.'

'But more shocked by Ronnie's generosity towards the grandchildren,' Gil added.

'Is there a will?' Jess asked.

'With the solicitor,' Catrin said.

'Probert's brother and sister are the only living relatives?'

'As far as we know, sir.'

'Families can be trouble,' Warlow said.

'Confirmation that the blood on the crowbar and

hammer is human and matches Ronnie Probert's blood type has come from Povey,' Gil announced. 'DNA to follow.'

Warlow watched Catrin post this new information on the Job Centre.

'The phone records for both Linda Nicholas and Jordan Nicholas came through, too,' Gil said.

'And?' Jess asked.

'On the night of, both were silent during the time of the burglary.'

'That's no surprise, is it?' Jess said. 'Surely, Jordan had the sense to switch his phone off while he robbed someone?'

'The records show communication between Jordan and his mother over the last few days, though. She was telling him to stay away.'

'What about Ralph Probert?' Jess asked.

Gil shook his head. 'No evidence to suggest he left his house on the night either.'

Warlow glanced at his watch. 'Buchannan says to hang onto the scaffolders until we speak to Jordan Nicholas. It's knocking on five. Jess and I will go straight to Ammanford tomorrow morning for a proper crack at Jordan.'

Rhys perked up at this. 'Should I go up there, too, sir?'

'No, there's enough to do here. Run a check on other recent lead roof thefts in the last six months. If it is our scaffolders, they might as well be hung for a sheep as a lamb. Let's see how busy they've been.'

'I'll start that now.' Rhys moved his chair back to his desk.

'It can wait.'

'I don't mind, sir.''

Warlow caught Jess's glance. Rhys's enthusiasm was something never to be underestimated. But this didn't seem quite right.

'We'll catch up tomorrow lunchtime after we've interviewed Jordan,' Warlow said as he got up from his seat and walked to the SIO room to check through the team's emails. One from Drinkwater caught his eye. A TV producer wanted to do a fly-on-the-wall reconstruction of the case. Drinkwater had volunteered the total cooperation of the BCU, with the added rider, aimed squarely at Warlow, that what might be a big plus would be to close the case as quickly as possible.

Drinkwater couldn't help himself. Warlow grimaced and scrolled through the list of uncharitable names that rolled through his brain. But what he wanted to do more than anything was make a phone call. Ten minutes later, he stuck his head out of the office door. Rhys was still at his desk, as was Jess.

'Rhys, a word?'

The DC's head popped up over his monitor, meerkat style, before he stood and loped into the office.

'Have a seat.' Warlow sat back while Rhys made himself as comfortable as he could.

Warlow saw it then. The thing that had bothered him since Rhys had sauntered up the corridor that afternoon. The DC was an open book, and his expression now was one of almost comical over-attentiveness. Difficult as it might have seemed in someone so normally keen, it struck Warlow that, even for Rhys, this was trying a bit too hard.

'I've just come off the phone with Gina,' Warlow said.

'Oh?'

Of all the responses Rhys could have given which might have reassured Warlow and told him he was wasting his time here, 'Oh,' was not it. Rhys, the normal Rhys, would have instantly demanded reassurance that all was well with his partner. This Rhys, this "glass way-more-than-half-full Rhys", hadn't blinked an eyelid.

'She's worried about you.'

'Me, sir?' Rhys laughed at this preposterous suggestion. It came out tinny and odd.

'Yes, you. And so am I.'

'No need, sir. Everything is fine.'

'Really? We live in an age of medical miracles. And though sliding a catheter into someone's heart may be routine, it's still heart surgery. So, "fine" might be stretching it a bit.'

'I've told you, sir, all is well. He's good.'

'Glad to hear it. But Gina said that you'd barely mentioned your dad to her in the last forty-eight hours. You've busied yourself with doing laundry, cleaning the car – in the dark, I heard – tidying the bookshelves, doing anything but sit down and talk it through.'

'What is there to talk through, sir?' Rhys wiped the palms of his hands on his thighs, ruffling the material of his trousers.

Warlow waited, seeing Rhys's almost smile come and go on his face.

'Some people cope with this job by compartmentalising,' Warlow said. 'It's one way to deal with it. I know because I've tried it and still use it to an extent. But I also learned that the best way to deal with being scared is to talk about it.'

'Scared, sir? I'm not—'

'A coward? No, we all know you're not that. But there's a difference between being scared for yourself and scared for others. It hurts like hell. Because there's nothing you can do about someone else's pain.'

Rhys tried to keep his expression neutral. But the fall came quickly. He gave a shudder and tears sprung to his eyes, his corneas instantly swimming behind a lake of fluid until he blinked, and the lacrimation spilled over in little rivulets that he let run untouched. The words that finally ruptured the dam came out in broken whispers. 'He's never been ill, not seriously, I mean. Not him, nor my mother. They've always been there for me. I don't know what… if he…'

Warlow had a box of tissues on his desk. He pushed it slowly across. 'There's nothing wrong with caring about your parents, Rhys. No shame in that. Now, the last time I looked, I was in charge here. And these are my orders. Go home, order a takeaway, tell Gina how brilliant the cardiac unit at Morriston is, tell her your dad will be home soon, fighting fit, and then tell her that all you've been able to do for the last two days is think the worst. Believe me, she'll understand. Maybe she won't have any words that will make you feel better, no words that will answer your imponderables, but she'll have a hand to hold, and in situations like this, not being alone in the darkness is the best medicine.'

Rhys sniffed and blew his nose. 'What do you do, sir?'

Warlow cracked a smile. This was the real Rhys. No harm intended, just lacking the odd filter, and saying it like it is. The DCI took no offence, and he had an answer ready. 'I have a paw to hold.'

Rhys sniffed again, but this time it ended in a little laugh before he blew his nose. 'See you in the morning then, sir… And thank you.'

'Lunchtime,' Warlow corrected him. 'In the morning, I am Ammanford bound to talk to a murderer, remember? And if Gina offers to put on any Leonard Cohen, you have my permission to walk out. There's a time and a place.'

CHAPTER THIRTY-SIX

In the morning, Warlow and Jess drove directly to Ammanford from Nevern. Molly stood on the doorstep with a silly grin to wave them off.

'Have a good day at work, you two.'

'Did anyone ever tell you your daughter can be quite irritating,' Warlow said.

'She's always known which buttons to press with me. She's learning yours day by day.'

Of course, this time, they shared a car. Stupid not to.

Jess got them a couple of Coaltown coffees from the convenient roastery across the road from the station when they pitched up at eight-thirty. The solicitor turned up spot-on at nine. And so, some sixteen hours after they started it, DCI Warlow and DI Allanby once again went through the PACE motions and began the interview.

Warlow kicked off. 'When you worked on Ronald Probert's property as a scaffolder, did you meet him?'

Jordan looked better this morning, though his puffy face suggested a troubled night. Being a belligerent oik, Jordan might opt for the no comment routine. But Warlow lived in hope. And the death of his mother had softened his hard exterior a little, judging from the red rims around his eyes.

'He made us tea now and again,' Jordan muttered. 'Always up for a chat.'

'So, he might recognise you if he saw you after that date?'

Jordan shrugged. 'Doubt it. He was a big cheese. Who the fuck am I?'

Warlow fended off the challenge. 'When you put scaffolding up, you get a chance to look into people's houses. See things close up which very few people other than the residents ever see.'

'There's no time, man. Scaffolding is all go.'

'But you would have seen into the kitchen, the living room, the bedrooms, right?'

'Probably.'

'So, you had an idea of the layout of the house?' Jess threw in the question.

Jordan glanced at the solicitor, who nodded. 'No comment.'

Warlow understood how this would go. The solicitor would have advised him to be cooperative, but to avoid answering questions relating to the Probert attack.

'Ronnie Probert's property is a big house. He had a nice car. A well-off man.'

'Nice house, yeah.'

'We have witness statements from more than one source indicating you were impressed. More than impressed.' Warlow glanced down at his notes. 'You said, "I bet he's loaded. I bet there's a load of cash in there somewhere."'

'I don't remember saying that,' Nicholas said.

'You said it in the pub the weekend after you'd worked on the house. You repeated it to your fellow workers at Castell Scaffolding. You said it to your brother Troy.'

Jordan looked down. 'What if I did? It is a flashy house.'

'A flashy house it took Ronnie Probert a lifetime to build,' Jess said.

'I never went back to the house after we did the scaffolding. I wasn't there when it was taken down. They didn't need me for that.'

'How did you get to work when you helped at Castell Scaffolding?'

'Bike.'

'You know your way around all those quiet lanes, then?' Warlow asked. 'It isn't easy, is it?'

'I don't have a car. We never had a car. Buses are shit.'

'You use a bike to get about?'

'Like I said.'

Jess slid a series of photographs across, showing the hole in the bathroom wall under the Respatex panel and the room containing the tool bag. 'Recognise these, Jordan?'

He nodded. 'I didn't make that hole, right? The twats who lived there tried to put a new shower in and ballsed it all up. Water coming in after they left, man. When the council took down the pipework, we got cracks in the wall and plaster kept falling off.'

'But you made the hole bigger and fitted the panel, correct?'

'To tidy it up, yeah. Otherwise, there'd be a big hole there when my mother took a ba—' Mention of his mother froze the words and a flicker of what might have been pain flashed across.

The temptation to sympathise again struck Warlow, but they needed answers. 'What about the tool bag?'

'Barry had an old bag at Castell. He gave it to me. The tools are stuff I've picked up over the last couple of years.'

For "picked up" Warlow read purloined from sites and

garden sheds, probably. He shifted the photos so that the hammer and crowbar, separated from the rest of the bag's contents, appeared, laid out on a plain, light-blue plastic sheet. 'Are these yours?'

'Might be. Hard to say for definite.'

'They were in the bag.'

Jordan shrugged.

'Can you tell us how they came to have blood on them, Jordan?' Jess asked.

He frowned. 'I don't know, do I? Maybe I cut myself. Scaffolding is rough work, man.'

'What if we told you that the blood isn't yours? Wrong type.'

The solicitor leaned in to advise. But Jordan had a temper. No comment didn't cut the mustard. He shook his head and pulled away from the solicitor's whisper.

'This is bullshit. I told you; I didn't rob Ronnie Probert. Yeah, alright, I could see he had stuff there. Stuff he probably wouldn't miss. But I didn't rob him.'

'You make it sound as if you're not a violent man, Jordan,' Jess said. 'But that's not what your record shows. Assault, affray, drunk and disorderly. Abusive behaviour.'

Jordan sighed. 'No comment.'

'That wasn't a question.' Jess smiled. 'Only a statement of fact, for the record.'

Warlow doubled down on the tools. 'As of this moment, we have confirmation from you that the bag is yours. These tools were found in that bag. And the tools have blood that is likely Ronald Probert's on them. Mr Probert told us he was attacked with tools just like these before he died. You understand where this is going, Jordan?'

Jordan sat forward, irritation boiling over. 'And I'm telling you, I never went anywhere near Probert's place.'

'We've checked your routes. We know where you

stashed your bike at the edge of the racecourse. We know there are tracks across to the bike path. We know that once you're on the bike path, it's a direct run to Ronnie Probert's house. Half an hour on a bike. What we have is a lot of evidence that the tools we found were used in that attack. Your tools. It looks bad, Jordan.'

Jordan squeezed his eyes shut in frustration. 'I wasn't there, and I didn't hit him with a fucking crowbar, man. Jesus.'

'So where were you?' Jess said.

This was what they'd been waiting for. If Jordan now admitted to being on a church roof in Pontardawe, they'd go back to the scaffolders.

'Come on, Jordan,' Warlow urged. 'Where were you at two o'clock in the morning of Tuesday, the 24th of January?'

'Jesus. I was at home. I was online playing GRC.'

Not what Warlow had expected.

'GRC?' Jess asked.

'Ghost Reign Crusade. It's a computer game,' Warlow explained.

'Was someone with you?' Jess asked.

Jordan folded his arms, dropped his chin in his default sullen pose. 'No.'

'That doesn't help much, Jordan.'

'I can't help that, can I? Troy fucked off to his girl-friend's place 'cos he had lectures the next day. When he wasn't there, I'd sneak into his cosy fucking den and play his games. He doesn't know that, man. I didn't want him to know that.'

Warlow resisted the urge to look at Jess. She would have registered the same incredulity at the fact that Jordan was more worried about upsetting his little brother than being charged with murder. Naïve or stupid? Warlow suspected a hefty dollop of both.

'If there was no one there—'

'I was logged on, man. You got to log on to play the game. It saves your game time. I was on there 'til gone three. I remember that because I was so knackered the next day.'

Jess showed him photographs of the scaffolder's van taken the night of the attack. Jordan stared at it in puzzlement. He denied ever having been in it or driving it.

At 9.45, Warlow's phone buzzed. He read the text message, glanced at Jess and suggested they take a half-hour break.

Warlow walked along a corridor and halted when he was far enough away from the interview room and the corridor was empty.

'What do you think?' he asked in a low voice.

'Not what I was expecting.'

'He wasn't in that van in Pontardawe. That question flummoxed him.'

'Agreed. He had no idea what we were talking about.'

'That lets the scaffolders off the hook.' Warlow nodded. 'Give Gil a ring. We'll charge them with the lead theft and let them go.'

'So, what now?'

'While you chat with Gil, I'll ring our resident expert on computer games, DC Rhys Harries.'

'Is that who the text was from?'

'No. That was the desk sergeant here at Ammanford. We have a visitor downstairs who wants to see whoever's in charge.'

'Let me guess, Jordan's grandmother.'

'Right first time.'

CHAPTER THIRTY-SEVEN

RHYS HAD BEEN on the phone with his dad, who was sitting up in bed in Morriston Hospital drinking tea. They'd talked about how his groin ached from where they'd threaded the wire in. How his mother was going to call in to Marks & Spencer on the way down for some sandwiches, and did Rhys want her to get anything? About how the man opposite him was related to his dad's best friend from school.

Nothing new in that. Wales was a small country. But Rhys had enjoyed the conversation for its normality. A nothing-to-see-here conversation. Almost as good as the telly-off heart-to-heart he'd had with Gina the night before. Rhys had opined, after that conversation, how Warlow must be a druid, or some kind of mind-reading wizard. Until Gina had come up with the more likely explanation that he had a doctorate from the university of life.

Rhys had liked that.

So, when his phone buzzed and Warlow's name came up, he wasn't at all surprised. If anything, he wondered why Warlow bothered with a phone at all and didn't just go straight to telepathy.

'Just thinking about you, sir,' Rhys said.

'How is your dad?'

'Very good, sir. Asking my mother for M&S sandwiches.'

'A man with taste, then.'

'How is it going with Jordan, sir?'

'Are you able to speak?'

Rhys looked around the Incident Room and decided on the stairwell of conversation. 'I will be in thirty seconds, sir.'

'Good. My question is about computer games.'

'Fire away, sir. I don't play as much as I used to, but I know a man who does. Steff, my drone-owning mate, is a big gamer.'

'Ghost Reign Crusade. Jordan Nicholas claims he was playing the game the night of Probert's attack. He was using his brother's kit. Any way we could check that?'

'Totally, sir. Ghost Reign requires you online to play. Because of in-game purchasing, and that you might play against someone else or as a team, you have to log on as a player. It measures the time you're online. There'd be a digital trail.'

'Excellent. I'm about to talk to Jordan Nicholas's grandmother. But what I want you and Catrin to do is to get over to her house and get hold of Troy's Xbox.'

'It's a PS5, sir.'

'A what?'

'A PlayStation—'

'Rhetorical question. Get over to the magistrate's court and get a warrant for seizure now. You can call in to the grandmother's house on your way back with a bit of luck. Take Catrin with you. I've texted her.'

Rhys hurried back to the Incident Room to find Catrin

walking out with his coat in her hand. 'You drive. I'll ring the court. See if we can slip in between cases.'

'Hang on, I need to get something from my desk,' Rhys said.

'Chop, chop.'

Rhys waved a hand. 'Two minutes. DCI's orders.'

———

WARLOW BORROWED a room on the ground floor to speak with Sylvia Reeves. The desk sergeant had suggested sending her packing, but Warlow and Jess had agreed to a quick chat.

The cup of tea on the coffee table had already been drunk when Warlow and Jess walked into the room, and an unsmiling Sylvia looked up at them from an armless chair.

'They say I can't see him,' she said. 'Please say I can.'

Warlow shook his head. 'Jordan is in custody, Mrs Reeves. He is not allowed any visitors.'

'Does he know about his mother?'

'He does.'

Sylvia sniffed and dabbed at her eyes. She wore a long shapeless black dress over black leggings. 'How is he?'

'As well as expected,' Jess said.

Sylvia let her head drop, and her voice took on a lilting rasp. 'He's not a bad boy. He hasn't had a chance. Not with his mother like she was and his father a complete waster.'

When neither officer spoke, Sylvia raised her head. 'I can tell what you lot think when you look at us. At me and at Jordan and Linda.' She turned away and exhaled. 'How could I let this happen? I didn't want it to happen. I didn't want any of it to happen. Linda was such a lovely kid. If you saw her when she was fourteen…' Sylvia shook her head. 'There was a bloke, an eighteen-year-old, who used to hang about on the gate of his house as the kids walked to school. I didn't realise he was a drug dealer then. If I had known, I'd have killed him. He had a car. He had money. It was him who got her hooked. By the time she was sixteen, she was taking heroin. She left school. Left home. She'd only come back to steal from me. I didn't want any of that.'

'No. You didn't,' Warlow said. 'You're not to blame for any of it. How is Troy?'

'Troy is tough. He's had to be. He hasn't talked about his mother, and that isn't good. But he's growing up, and I don't want to argue with him anymore.'

'It isn't easy,' Jess said.

'How would you know?'

'I have an eighteen-year-old at home. You can't stop them growing up.'

'Jordan isn't all bad. Troy isn't either, but they're different. And Troy knows what he wants. Since he met Lola, at least.'

'Is that why you fell out?'

'We fell out over lots of things. Too much time playing those games, him wanting his child allowance for himself. She eggs him on because she gets it from her parents. They don't see me as much of a parent, and I'm not his mother, but they're scared of upsetting Lola, so they give in to her all the time. Now Troy wants his money to spend on himself. Or his games. All me, me, me with this generation. I don't know where he thinks the food on the table comes from. My pension, I expect.' She stopped, took a breath. 'What's going to happen to Jordan?'

'It's likely he'll be charged, Sylvia.'

She let her head fall again, no words this time, just the slow miserable sobs Warlow had heard before.

'We're going to borrow Troy's games console, Sylvia. Is he at college today?'

'No. His mother just died, for God's sake. Lola has come over to keep him company.'

'Okay. We'll have a warrant for search and seizure, but it won't be necessary, I'm sure. How did you get up here?'

'A friend brought me. She's next door, in Lidl.'

'You've got a lift back, then?'

Sylvia nodded. The last thing she said to them as they left the room was, 'Jordan isn't a bad boy. Remember that.'

But Warlow didn't turn back into the station. Outside, the wind had picked up with a couple of degrees of wind-chill on top of a maximum of five. Though yesterday's greyness had blown off and the winter sun beckoned outside.

'Fancy another coffee?' Warlow asked.

'Why not?'

They fetched coats and crossed a busy A474. Jess found a seat at Coaltown while Warlow ordered a couple of flat whites. 'No point rushing this. I've asked Uniforms to tell the solicitor we're checking evidence and that it might be a while before we can get back to it.'

Jess arched her back and breathed in. 'This is very civilised, isn't it? This place has won awards.'

'I love the aroma,' Warlow conceded.

The espresso bar, where they were sitting, opened onto the roastery, and the aroma of burnt beans was every-where. Their seat nestled in the corner, right next to the roaster itself, under the open, exposed ceiling of this indus-trial unit.

'Factory chic,' Jess said.

'They're planning a TV special on Probert on the weekend. Him as the sporting legend. It'll be a big thing.'

'Drinkwater must be having kittens. As it were,' Jess muttered.

But Warlow only half heard. They were close to closing

this case, and he didn't like the whole thing hinging on them finding contradictory evidence on a games console.

'I know what you're thinking,' Jess said. 'He could be playing us. For time and just because he can.'

Warlow nodded. 'What if we find he was playing games online that night, though? Where does that leave us?'

'Not the scaffolders. What about Ralph Probert? He's the one with the weakest alibi. He claims to have been at his parents' house that night. But what if he left the house?'

Warlow rubbed his chin. A sure sign that he was unsettled. 'We ought to knock on some doors, then. See if there's anyone with a nice CCTV camera in the vicinity.'

'Do you want me to speak to Gil. Get him to chat to the neighbourhood team?'

'Why not?'

'The only other person we haven't looked at closely is the niece. Gaynor Richmond's daughter. Maybe I'll mention her to Gil, too. I don't think we ever got a statement from her about the night of the burglary.'

Jess got up and grabbed her coat to make the call outside. Warlow sat and inhaled the smell of coffee, hoping that the burnt Guatemalan beans infusing the air might give him a bit of inspiration.

CHAPTER THIRTY-EIGHT

THE CLERK at Llanelli magistrates let Rhys sneak in between some traffic violations and a custody case. The chair listened to his explanation, but Rhys sold it the moment he mentioned Ronnie Probert. In the twenty minutes it took to get from Llanelli to Kidwelly and Sylvia Reeves's flat, Rhys explained to Catrin all about Ghost Reign Crusade.

She listened without speaking as he outlined the game's third-person multiplayer perspective and how it was all about combat and exploration, traveling over wastelands and lush kingdoms, collecting spells and powerful weapons to encounter the Wraith Lords on the ultimate quest to find and return the seed of wisdom to its homeland.

'And you play this?' Catrin asked when he'd finished.

'A bit. I'm not into it. It's a time suck. I prefer simpler stuff. A bit of Mario Kart with Gina now and again, or Wii Sports. But my mate Steff's into it. It's lore dense. And it has a couple of Welsh guys as the voices. It's cool. How about you, sarge?'

'Never been my thing, games. I'd rather watch a film.

Craig likes the fishing games, though. And anything that he can pretend to drive, of course.' Catrin had been to Sylvia's address before and so, after parking up, it was she who rang the bell. Nothing happened. She rang again.

'Oh, hang on,' Rhys said beside her.

'What?'

He had a forced, rictus grin of apology on his face. 'Just remembered. Didn't DCI Warlow say that Sylvia Reeves was up in Ammanford with him?'

'Did he? So, what, there's no one home?'

'I—' But Rhys was saved further embarrassment when the door opened to reveal a pale, dark-haired girl dressed in baggy jeans and an overlarge sweatshirt.

'Lola,' Rhys said. 'Remember me? DC Harries.'

'What do you want?'

'Is Troy's grandmother here?'

'No. Only me and Troy.'

'Can you get Troy for us, please?' Catrin said. She held up her warrant card.

'He's busy. He's online.'

'It's important.'

Lola didn't close the door but shut it so that only an inch remained open. It took five minutes for a sullen-looking Troy to come to the door with red-rimmed eyes.

Might be red from being upset about his mum, Catrin thought. Or, more likely, from staring at a computer screen for hours on end.

'What do you want? My gran's not here.' Troy's tone matched his expression.

'It's you we need to speak to.' Catrin held up the warrant. 'As part of our investigation, we're going to borrow your console, the uh…'

'PS5,' Rhys said.

'Is this a prank?' Troy's mouth formed a slash of a

smile. He looked over Catrin's shoulder as if expecting someone else to be there.

'No prank, Troy. We'll need to borrow it for a few days. Get our tech people to look at it.'

'Wha… a couple of days?' Abject horror replaced the uncertainty on Troy's face. 'Why?'

'We can't tell you that, Troy.'

Troy laughed. 'Then you can't have it.' He threw the door shut. It got as far as Rhys's enormous foot.

'We have a warrant—'

Catrin got no further. Troy turned and ran towards an open door in the flat, his voice rising in panic. 'No, no, wait. You can't, you can't, you can't take my PS5, you can't. End of.'

Catrin looked at Rhys. 'It's just a game, isn't it?'

Rhys shrugged and hurried after Troy.

———

JESS CAME BACK in after chatting with Gil. 'Bit of luck. He's over in Carway checking on what's left of Jordan Nicholas's belongings after the Fire Investigator gave the all-clear. He'll pop up to Terry Probert's himself afterwards since he's out and about.'

Warlow nodded.

Jess stood at the table and inhaled deeply, head up, eyes shut. 'Mmm, I love this smell. You can get diffusers that put this stuff out. It's addictive.' When she opened her eyes, Warlow was staring back at her with a look of wide-eyed horror on his face.

'What?' she asked.

'That's it. That's what we've missed,' Warlow croaked.

'You've gone off into one of your fugues, Evan.'

'Addiction,' Warlow said, and only then did his eyes

refocus on Jess. 'It's all over this case like a pernicious bloody rash. Ralph Probert and his gambling. Linda Nicholas and the drugs and booze. We've been so hung up on those that we missed one.'

'One what?'

'Another addict.'

Jess sat down. 'I'm listening.'

'Someone who needs money for a habit. Who can't get it any other way and who will throw Jordan under a bus to get it.'

Still, Jess floundered, one eyebrow higher than the other.

'Who knew about the empty house? Who else had access to Jordan's tools?' Warlow hissed.

'The scaffolders? But what about the church roo—' She cut herself off. 'Oh my God. Troy Nicholas,' Jess hissed out the name as the penny dropped.

Warlow stood up, his phone out, already speed dialling Catrin as adrenaline surged through him. Suddenly, all the shaky mental scaffolding supporting the case against Jordan Nicholas in his head tumbled away, leaving only one greasy pole upright at the centre.

Troy, who'd fallen out with his grandmother over money.

Who listened to his brother's tales about Probert's cash.

Who could access his brother's crowbar and hammer for a bit of burglary.

In his ear, the phone rang, but no one picked up. He tried Rhys.

And then another thought struck him. A sickening thought that made him catch his breath.

Linda Nicholas had known.

In her drunken state, she'd even told them, slurring out the words.

'*You don't know the half.*'

Warlow didn't want to contemplate it. In a normal world, such harrowing thoughts as the ones he was having had no place in a civilised society. Should have disappeared with the banning of the rack, and hanging, and all the Machiavellian plots of centuries past. But this… this was straight out of the Borgias playbook, or a Dickensian labyrinth of avarice and injustice. However, the world he moved in resonated with the worst that human nature could throw up. And much as everyone liked to pretend that by airbrushing offensive words out of books, or not posting hateful thoughts over social media, the world would somehow become a better place, they needed to walk in his shoes for a few weeks to see the truth of it.

What if Linda hadn't smoked in bed the night she died?

What if she'd passed out and someone else set the fire? Someone who didn't want her sober enough to contemplate the truth and share it with others.

The phone kept ringing. Either Catrin and Rhys were out of the signal, or they were busy.

On a whim, Warlow rang Gil. He was in Carway, just four miles away from Kidwelly. Perhaps there was such a thing as luck.

Gil picked up on the second ring.

'Where are you?' Warlow barked out the question.

'Just leaving Carway—'

Warlow cut in. 'Put your foot down and get over to Kidwelly. I'll explain as you drive.'

———

Rhys was right behind Troy. He felt his phone buzz in his pocket. Ignored it. 'Calm down, Troy. We only need to borrow it.'

Lola was stooped over a bag in the corner while Troy stood in front of a monitor, the image frozen on an exotic scene in a fantasy castle as a man with a serpent's head wielded a glowing sword with a green handle.

'Troy, please move out of the way,' Catrin said from behind Rhys.

'No. Fucking. Way,' Troy bellowed. 'This is my life. Don't you understand that?'

Rhys took a step forward. Troy let out a scream of rage.

Lola stood up abruptly. Something glinted in her right hand. Rhys heard Catrin yell and felt her push him. Something flew past his head and hit the wall behind. He glanced back and saw a silver star-shaped blade stuck in the wall. He had time to think that it could have been his head if he hadn't been shoved out of the way as the second star flew through the air. It hit his chest. A solid thump as it struck the Kevlar of his stab vest and bounced off.

Lola tossed something to Troy. Something long and black with a serrated edge and lurid-green handle.

'Get fucking back,' Troy screamed and brandished a huge knife that looked eerily like the one on the screen.

But Catrin was already moving towards Lola. She reached for the girl's raised arm and yanked it down. They fell off balance onto the floor. Troy turned, the knife raised. Rhys launched himself. He wasn't close enough for an arm-around tackle, but close enough to reach a leg and push. Troy stumbled back against the table holding the monitor. Rhys had hold of a leg, but Troy kicked out and caught Rhys's shoulder and his grip gave.

The boy reached down and grabbed the white oblong unit next to the monitor, yanked it up, causing cables to fly off and, knife in one hand, the console in the other, he kicked out again at Rhys's flailing hand and ran out of the room.

Rhys scrambled up.

Catrin was holding Lola's arm, a multi-bladed star still in her fingers. Rhys twisted the wrist. Lola shouted with pain, but then he had her arm up behind her back. He turned her face down onto the floor. Catrin had her handcuffs out.

'Get after him,' she ordered.

Rhys turned and sprinted out of the flat in pursuit.

———

GIL DROVE into Water Street in Kidwelly towards Sylvia Reeves's address. He'd never been here before, although he had visited the castle twice with his daughters when they were kids. Few castles were as well preserved and as easily accessible. In an era so dependent on metalled roads, the strategic importance of rivers as a mode of transport had long been forgotten. And the River Gwendraeth was no exception. But the castle at Kidwelly had been altered and added to over four centuries since its first iteration as military strategy changed. Empty since the 17th century, in the modern era, re-enactments and medieval fairs drew tourists to a town steeped in history.

But even Gil was not prepared for the sight he came across as he drove up the street.

Ahead of him, a thin, hooded figure, brandishing what looked like a black sword, was being pursued by a large man in a shirt and a black vest. The figure took an abrupt right turn down a side street. Gil leaned forward to peer through the windscreen at his pursuer.

No, it couldn't be. Surely, that wasn't… 'Rhys?' Gil muttered.

He pushed down on the accelerator until he was parallel with the DC and wound the window down.

'What's going—'

'Troy,' Rhys yelled. 'He has a knife.'

Gil accelerated and turned into the unnamed side street the boy had ducked into. Thirty metres ahead, he spotted a play area with some swings on the left, and two people with dogs coming through a gated path where the road curved right.

Troy, sword in hand, hesitated at the path entrance, now blocked by the dogs, glanced behind at Gil's approach, turned, and ran around the curve of the road.

Gil followed, realising quickly that this was an access road with the backs of houses on one side and a grassy bank that led to an open space and the southern walls of the castle beyond. Troy veered left, attempted the bank, but it proved too steep, and he slipped back down, barely regaining his balance. Gil took the opportunity. He floored the accelerator, overtook Troy and screeched to a halt, slewing the car to the left at a wider section of the road with yellow cross hatchings, blocking Troy's progress, and leapt out.

Troy, out of breath from running, an activity he was clearly not used to, waved the wicked knife at Gil. 'Get out of my way.'

'And then what, Troy? Where are you going to go? The castle?' Gil dropped his eyes to the console Troy cradled under one arm. 'Nowhere to plug that thing in there, right?'

'Shut up.'

'This isn't a game anymore.'

'I mean it. Get away from me.'

The space between the bank and the road was now filled by Gil's car. He walked around the boot to face the boy, who stood with the knife, all fourteen inches of it, pointing at Gil's face.

'That's a hell of a knife you've got there, Troy,' Gil said. The blade was impressive. Zombie knives often were, though Gil didn't pretend to be an expert. All he wanted to do here was give Rhys a little time to arrive. 'What's that on the blade? A word, is it?'

'Severer,' Troy said, with just the right amount of emphasis on the sibilant s.

'Any good against vampires? There's one I'd love to try it on.'

'What are you talking about?'

'I'm talking about you knowing the difference between games and real life, Troy.'

A sickly smile spread over Troy's mouth. When he spoke, it was as a snarl. 'You know nothing.' He waved the knife a little higher. 'We hate you meddling bastards.'

'Who's you, Troy?'

'All of you. Fucking teachers, police, old arseholes who have no idea what the metaverse is. Meddlers who won't leave us alone. You who aren't us. This *is* my life.'

'Sadly, I think you might even believe that to be true.'

'Shut up.'

'Give me the knife, Troy,' Gil said.

'Where do you want it? Neck or gut?'

'Now would be a good time,' Gil said.

Troy frowned and then smiled a sickly smile. 'You want me to do you?'

'Honest answer? I wasn't talking to you.'

Rhys came down the bank at speed, his telescopic baton open. It came down on Troy's upper arm, the one holding the knife, with a crack. The boy stumbled, both knife and console spilling from his grasp to clatter onto the lane. Rhys was on him in a second, the sudden pain from Rhys's twisting hands forcing Troy up onto his toes.

'Let go of me, that hurts.'

Gil walked forward and grabbed the knife, using a tissue between his hand and the handle.

Rhys marched Troy, who was almost bent double now,

over to Gil's car and put him face down over the bonnet, none too gently. Troy twisted his furious face towards the sergeant.

'You're all goin' to die, you bastards.'

'True,' Gil said. 'But not today, sunshine, not today.'

CHAPTER THIRTY-NINE

THERE WAS room in the custody suite at Ammanford now they'd charged and released the scaffolders for the lead theft. They still had Jordan in custody, though Warlow was inclined to let him go to Sylvia Reeve's house. She needed the company as much as he did. Troy and Lola were under arrest and would be questioned, but Warlow let them marinate in their own juices overnight.

In Troy's room at his grandmother's house, they found a plastic see-through wallet with a popper fastener and two hundred and thirty pounds inside it stuffed in Troy's backpack. On a label stuck on that wallet, in a hand very much like Ronnie Probert's to Warlow's eye, were the words, Gardening Money. Later, they would trace Troy to a post office near the college in Gorseinon, where he'd put cash into a prepaid card account for him to use online.

Because they were both under 18, Lola and Troy would not be tried as adults, adding a layer of bureaucracy into the mix, and early chats with the CPS suggested their defence team would undoubtedly look at a psychiatric assessment for mitigation. Game addiction had been officially recognised as a mental health condition in 2019.

Warlow relayed this to the team through gritted teeth as they sat at Vespers that afternoon. Gil took a call from the techs a minute in.

'Well?' Warlow asked.

'Minimal damage to the console during the altercation. It's up and running. They'll have more information once they've looked at different players, but they've just confirmed multiple purchases for loot boxes had been made. At least eight hundred pounds worth over the last month.'

Warlow turned to his DC. 'Rhys, what can you tell us about loot boxes?'

'In-game purchases, sir. Often, it's a way of buying game currency. Coins you can spend in the game for new weapons, skills, shields, whatever. Depends on the game. In soccer simulations, you can buy players. Sometimes, it's a gamble. You buy a loot box, and it's potluck what's inside.'

'What the hell has he spent eight hundred quid on?' Gil asked.

Rhys shrugged. 'You might get these same rewards as you progress through the game, anyway. But buying them speeds up your progress. And the more loot boxes you buy, the more you might get as freebies.'

'Why Troy wanted money from his grandmother,' Catrin said.

'And from Ronnie Probert,' Jess said.

'He robbed and killed a man just to play a stupid game?' Catrin's incredulity spoke for all of them in the room.

'I still don't understand why he tried to run away with the console, though,' Jess said. 'I mean, what the hell was he going to do with it?'

Warlow sighed. 'It would be a mistake to attempt any logic here. But I doubt he took it because it had information incriminating him and exonerating Jordan. He stole it because his life was in that box. Take away an addict's drug, and they're facing cold turkey. Troy couldn't cope with that.'

'We still need to put him on Probert's property, sir,' Rhys said.

Jess nodded. 'We've fingerprinted the cash wallet, and I spoke to Povey earlier. The mask under the oil drum had blood stains. My money is on it being Ronnie Probert's.'

'You think Troy stashed the mask there to incriminate Jordan?' Rhys asked.

Jess shrugged. 'With a bit of luck, the inside of the mask will have Troy's DNA all over it.'

'Or Lola's, ma'am,' Catrin said.

Warlow grimaced. 'I presume we have a warrant for her house?'

'We're on it, sir. Her parents are in shock.'

'What about the knife?' Jess asked.

'It's a reproduction of one used in the game by the lead character,' Rhys explained. 'Totally illegal. Something else Troy spent his money on.' After a beat, Rhys added, 'Do you think he killed his mother, too, sir?'

'Unless he confesses to that, we'll never know.'

'I was close to him when he had that knife. He looked more than capable, the vicious little bastard,' Gil said. 'That reminds me, anyone heard any more from Geraint Lane?'

Rhys shook his head. 'Gone silent, sarge.'

'That worries me. The man's a snake. I prefer it when I can hear his tail rattling. When I can't, it's worse because I know he's still under that rock.'

'Drinkwater must be pleased, Evan,' Jess said.

'Over the moon. He's got the fly-on-the-wall lot coming in for a recce tomorrow. On that note, I've volunteered Catrin as the face of the team that broke the case.'

'Me, sir?' Catrin said, shocked.

'Yes. Obviously, I struggled with that decision between you and Gil. But when the focus group saw the photos of the two of you, they came down firmly on one side of that fence.'

'None taken,' Gil muttered, feigning umbrage.

'And opposite you will be the fresh face of DC Harries.'

A stunned Rhys blinked his surprise. 'Does that mean—'

'You'll have to comb your hair, yes,' Warlow said. 'The most the rest of us will have to do is appear in some background shots. But the crew will interview you for the narrative.'

'But you're the boss, sir,' Catrin objected.

'And that's why you'll be in front of the camera. DI Allanby and I both agree it'll be good for both of your CVs,' he added. That was all true, and there was no need to mention that Jess would not appear in any of the shots as her profile for now needed to be kept microscopic. 'That'll all kick off in a couple of weeks. Ample time to get the rest of it sorted.'

Eyebrows shot up. Though they had the attackers in custody, the hard work of gathering evidence and not leaving anything to chance was about to begin.

———

A FEW DAYS LATER, on the Saturday afternoon of Ronnie Probert's funeral, Warlow and Gil attended the crematorium at Llanelli. There'd been not a snowball's of getting inside the building, and so, both men stood in the gloomy afternoon with the crowd, listening to the proceedings through speakers. On the service pamphlet was a photograph of Ronnie, in British Lions' kit, about to touch down for That Try. Beneath it, a quote.

"There are some who bring a light so great to the world, that even after they have gone, the light remains."

—*Anonymous*

In a few weeks, The Cardiff Club would hold a memorial afternoon. It would be televised, but both Warlow and Gil had felt the need to show their respects at the actual service. Of course, there was a eulogy from one of Probert's many fellow players, some almost as famous as he had been. And what stuck in Warlow's mind were words delivered by one of these ageing stars, whose life had been influenced hugely by the advocacy of coaches and parents. He quoted from a book, *Rugby, Body and Soul*, by one of the game's most original thinkers, Bill Samuel, whose unselfish approach was summed up in one paragraph.

'We all have our basic principles or moral codes. Mine was acquired at home and in the community, where we were taught that the best service was given by unseen hands.'

Unseen hands.

'We could all do with a bit more of that,' Gil murmured.

And said hands had revealed a pair of trainers during the search of Lola's house. Trainers spattered with microscopic traces of Ronnie Probert's blood. There'd been no sign of a second mask. But now that didn't matter. Ronnie Probert had not been hallucinating when he thought he'd seen more than one thief.

———

IT HAD BEEN Warlow's idea when the weather changed and the clouds thinned, that afterwards, with dusk approaching, both men head east in separate cars to the cycle path. He and Cadi went to Horeb, Gil further north to access the trail at Cynheidre. Full dark was descending onto the still evening as man and dog walked along the empty track. The red light appeared at almost the same spot as Warlow had seen it previously. The difference, this time, was that he was not alone.

Warlow called to Cadi. She'd sensed something, too. She stood, nose up, staring toward that eerily waving signal.

'*Beth y'w e? Ble ma fe?*'

The what and where questions were all the dog needed. She set off at a sprint.

Warlow speed-dialled Gil and said, 'Bombs away,' before jogging after the dog. The access gate to the Llanelli and Mynydd Mawr Railway heritage site was open when Warlow got there. Lights, one red, one white, bobbed at the farthest end, away from the rolling stock that sat dark and brooding like huge sleeping beasts right next to the path.

'Gil?' Warlow called out.

'Here.' The shout didn't sound urgent or troubled.

Warlow took his time to step over rails and around the huge carriages and cabs. The renovators and volunteers who owned the stock and the buildings had erected big sheds, but Gil's shout and his torch were further north than these buildings. As Warlow rounded the last of the trains, he saw a sliver of light spilling onto the floor. When he got to it, he realised it was emerging through the open door of a small shed. Inside sat Gil and a bewhiskered man currently fondling the neck and ears of a delighted Cadi.

'Your dog is fasht,' Patrick McMartin said.

'She is when she wants to bed,' Warlow agreed.

'Pat, this is Evan,' Gil said.

Patrick extended a calloused hand, which poked through the many layers of suit and coat he was wearing.

'You're our Signalman, Pat?' Warlow asked.

'Yeah, should have told you earlier, but, I dunno, shlipped my mind.'

'Nothing like a bit of intrigue to keep the locals guessing,' Gil said. 'Cup of tea, Evan?'

Warlow took in the little Primus and the kettle and some enamel mugs that had brown rings around the inside. A bit like the rings of a cut tree, and likely just as old. But he nodded a yes, anyway.

'How often do you come down here, Pat?' Warlow asked, pulling up a wooden crate as a chair.

'Three times a week. The man I visit, my friend Keith, this was his job. A shignalman. He asked me to make sure no train gets into trouble. I make sure, like. And I'll keep doin' it sho long as he's ashking.' Pat's s's slid and his r's rolled like the stock on the rails once had.

There might have been a glance worthy of exchanging after that, but neither Gil nor Warlow felt it appropriate. Keith would be none the wiser if Pat stayed at home in the warm every night. But Pat would know.

And that was a mark of the man. Instead of judging, both officers simply listened in silent respect as if this was the most natural thing in the world to do.

'Do you volunteer here, Pat?' Gil asked.

'Me, no. I'm not a big fan of trains meself. But Keith had a key to the lock on this little shed, so when I'm down here, I grab a cuppa and wave a few lights to the imaginary trains.'

The cuppa turned out to be mahogany in colour and hot as hell. Gil told Pat to make sure he stayed warm, and at half six, sergeant and DCI bade him goodbye.

'So, that's our shignalman, then,' Warlow said, affecting Pat's accent.

'Nice thing to do. Nothing like loyalty, is there?'

'Agreed,' Warlow said, sealing an unspoken agreement

that nothing more would be said about this to anyone. 'Home to a warm supper?'

'Shepherd's pie. You're welcome to join us.'

'No, Molly is cooking this evening.'

'Of course, I forgot you have houseguests. But Molly…'

'No, she's getting good. Plus, her mother is supervising as it is a new dish.'

'Nice to have live-in chefs. Could become a habit you get used to.' Gil's smile glistened in the torchlight.

'Nah. They're on the lookout for something permanent. But they're both safe at Ffau'r Blaidd for now.'

'There is that.'

'*Nos da.*'

At the entrance gate to the Cab yard back at the path, Gil and Warlow parted ways.

THE DCI TURNED with Cadi at his side and set off into the darkness with another enigma resolved. He was looking forward to a glass of red and a little company this evening. From behind him, he heard Gil whistling the tune of *What a Wonderful World*.

Warlow shook his head, smiled, and hurried on towards his car and the lights of home.

ACKNOWLEDGMENTS

As with all writing endeavours, the existence of this novel depends upon me, the author, and a small army of 'others' who turn an idea into a reality. My wife, Eleri, who gives me the space to indulge my imagination and picks out my stupid mistakes. Others who help with making the book what it is like Sian Phillips, Tim Barber and of course, proofers and ARC readers. Thank you all for your help. Special mention goes to Ela the dog who drags me away from the writing cave and the computer for walks, rain or shine. Actually, she's a bit of a princess so the rain is a no-no. Good dog!

But my biggest thanks goes to you, lovely reader, for being there and actually reading this. It's great to have you along and I do appreciate you spending your time in joining me on this roller-coaster ride with Evan and the rest of the team.

CAN YOU HELP?

With that in mind, and if you enjoyed it, I do have a favour to ask. Could you spare a moment to **leave a review or a rating**? A few words will do, but it's really the only way to help others like you discover the books. Probably the best way to help authors you like. Just visit the book's page on Amazon and leave a few words, or a rating, if you have the time. Tidy!

Visit my website and join up to the Rhys Dylan VIP Reader's Club and get a FREE novella, *The Wolf Hunts Alone,* by visiting the website at: **rhysdylan.com**

The Wolf Hunts Alone.

One man and his dog... will track you down.

DCI Evan Warlow is at a crossroads in his life. Living alone, contending with the bad hand fate has dealt him, he finds solace in simple things like walking his neighbour's dog.

But even that is not as safe as it was. Dogs are going missing from a country park. And not only one, now three have disappeared. When he takes it upon himself to root out the cause of the lost animals, Warlow faces ridicule and a thuggish enemy.

But are these simply dog thefts? Or is there a more sinister malevolence at work? One with its sights on bigger, two legged prey.

A FREE BOOK FOR YOU

Only one thing is for certain; Warlow will not rest until he finds out.

———

By joining the club, you will also be the first to hear about new releases via the few but fun emails I'll send you. This includes a no spam promise from me, and you can unsubscribe at any time.

AUTHOR'S NOTE

Inevitably, with books set in west Wales, where, some would argue, beats the heart of the national game, a story involving sport, and by definition since we are in Wales, rugby, had to happen. And of course I grew up and watched those glory years in the 70's unfold like a fairy story. I played myself in school and at university and what an inspiration those icons were to a scrawny back like me. I also stood on the open terraces of Cardiff Arms Park, merry from the train ride up from the West, merrier from visiting the Cardiff pubs crammed full of supporters. If you've never been to a Cardiff rugby international, you need to put it on your list. But of course, eras come to an end. And with them so the stars fade. But, as per the title, one hopes a little of their light remains to shine upon us.

Rugby is still a huge part of the culture here. But under their magic capes, all these superstars have the same foibles and troubles as the rest of us mere mortals. And Warlow has to deal with those aspects of humanity, no matter who the victim or perpetrator is. Those of you who've read *The Wolf Hunts Alone* will know exactly what I mean. So once again, thank you for sparing your precious time on this

Warlow tale. With a lot more to come, I'm looking forward to giving you more glimpses of the incredible corner of Britain, and that it'll give you the urge to visit and enjoy a cup of tea and some bara brith.

Not everyone here is a murderer. Not everyone… Cue tense music!

All the best, and see you all soon, Rhys.

And do not forget that for those of you who are interested, there is a glossary on the website to help with those pesky pronunciations.

READY FOR MORE?

DCI Evan Warlow and the team are back in…

A MATTER OF EVIDENCE

In the desolate landscapes of the Bannau Brycheiniog army training grounds, DCI Warlow and his seasoned investigators find themselves ensnared in a deadly game of shadows. A man, recently released from prison after a 20-year wrongful conviction, is discovered dead, igniting a storm of doubt and suspicion.

As long-buried secrets claw their way to the surface, the line between truth and deception blurs. With everyone a potential suspect, they must tread carefully and confront the crimes of old as well as the present.

As the stakes escalate, can they decipher the puzzle of the past before the present claims another victim?

OUT April 2024

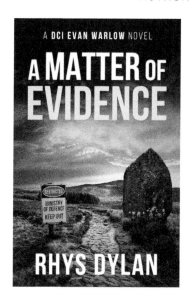

Printed in Great Britain
by Amazon